Under Contract

THE GEG SERIES
BOOK #1

JACQUELYN AYRES

Dedication

For my "Julie Posse" (my version of the GEGS, in no particular order): Jennifer McCloskey, Holly Dirato, Nicole Gibson, Amanda LaVita, Bernadette Titterington, and Lorin Falana.

I love you.

You have inspired so many of my gut-busting laughs, epic, and heart-warming memories.

I cherish you.

No matter where life takes us or how many kids we produce that gobble up all of our time, I know you are just a phone call away (with screaming-child background music…ahh).

I Thank you.

Not for just believing in me, but, for reeling me back in whenever I feel lost.

Okay—bye!

(Go read the book now!)

Chapter One

RETRIEVING A COMPACT out of my small clutch purse, I finally bring my eyes up for one last look in the mirror. I told myself—convinced myself, really—that I was just popping into the bathroom to check my appearance a final time. As I stare into my green eyes (my first qualification for this job), I realize I'm in here to have a conference call with my sanity. Clearly it went bankrupt and closed up shop, like most of the country, because there's no answer. My sanity is gone ... replaced by desperation and a mother's instinctive need to provide for her children.

I lay my palms on the cool marble countertop and take in a few cleansing yoga breaths like my friend Ava always recommends. Apparently, I freak out too much—so she says.

"Okay, Charley ... put your big-girl pants on. You can do this." Sometimes you need to just act bravely so you convince yourself you are. Of course, I have to push away the thought of my big-girl pants being pulled off later. I sweep a few wisps of hair off my temple. Thank

God Ava was able to do my hair. *Must look sophisticated, yet approachable.* One of many qualifications needed for this job. Ava had parted my long brown hair to the left, then crowned the sides with tight French braids 'til every strand was pulled to the back. There, she created a mass production of neat pin curls at the top of my neck. It looks great for the office or a night out on the town. "Sophisticated, yet approachable." *Good job, Ava!*

I step back for one more glance to make sure everything is in place. I'm wearing a black silk draped dress by alice + olivia. I never would've randomly spent this much on a designer dress, but luckily my Aunt Clara has more money than sense. She loves her some Saks Fifth Avenue! However, Aunt Clara shops blindly for people. I don't know about my cousins, but my sisters and I always end up with a store credit of anywhere from three hundred to fifteen hundred dollars, depending on the occasion for the gift.

The last big "occasion" was my husband leaving me six months ago with three kids and no pot to piss in. Said he was "tired of society and government." He didn't want this—any of it. He was going to live off the land. I've since learned that in Europe, they call this "going on a walkabout." To this day, I have no idea about where he's been walking. *Asshole!*

Aunt Clara, out of the goodness of her heart, sent me an Armani silk jumpsuit for my hardship; only cost her $1,700. Problem solved! I finally had something special to wear to all my "special" appointments—you know, WIC, fuel assistance, food stamps, and other programs that assist the needy. What would I possibly do with $1,700 in my pocket? Pay the mortgage? More money than sense, that one!

Punctuality is a must! Shit! I look at my phone—phew! Two minutes to spare. One more deep breath before I walk out of the bathroom and head to the bar in the Ames Hotel. Funny—until a few days ago, I never even knew this hotel existed. Then again, I don't usually have a reason to stay overnight in Boston's financial district. "Please don't be old and bald ... or creepy ... or ... eck ..." I chant to myself. "Please have kind eyes and a kind heart." I lower the bar. Small steps.

As instructed, I head over to the table in the far left corner and take a seat. So much for "punctuality"—where the hell is he?

Mitch

"SCOTCH ON THE rocks and a glass of your best Merlot," I say, looking up from my phone. The bartender nods and goes about my order. I slide my phone into the inside pocket of my jacket and glance impatiently at my watch. She'd better be punctual! Biggest pet peeve—one minute late and I'm out of here! I grab my scotch before the bartender can place it down, swirl it around, and take a good swig.

"Waiting on a girl?" he asks.

"Aren't we all?" I smirk.

"Pretty much." He laughs. "Well this one must be special ... you seem nervous."

"It's complicated."

"When isn't it, dude?" He shakes his head, wiping the bar down.

"True." I smile, partly because he has no idea about my type of complicated.

"Damn," he says as he glances over my shoulder. I look up at him. His mouth hangs open, his eyes wide and wild-looking, seeping with desire that only another guy would catch. I follow his eyes and my breath hitches. *Holy shit ... please be Charlotte*, I think as I watch her make her way through the lounge. I feel the corners of my lips curve up with satisfaction when she seats herself exactly where I was hoping she would.

"That, my friend, would be my complication." I turn back to him.

"I will gladly release you, sir, from such a burden. It's all part of the great customer service I like to give around here." He takes on a serious tone.

"Thank you, eh, Jim ... I appreciate your thoughtfulness. But, alas, this is a burden I must carry alone. Try not to feel sorry for me." I lift my glass to him and nod before heading over to her.

"I can't—I'm too busy feeling sorry for myself," he mutters.

"Charlotte?" I ask softly. She turns her head and looks up at me.

"Mitch?" She smiles.

"Mitchell." I correct her.

She nods. "Mitchell. Hi."

"Merlot?" I place her wine in front of her before taking my seat.

"Oh ... thank you." She picks it up to take a sip.

"Very punctual—that's good," I say as I take in the sight of her. I was very specific in my ad about the type of woman I wanted to "employ." So far, she's a vision more perfect than my imagination could conjure up.

"I try to be. I'm not always successful, I must admit." I watch as her smile hits her eyes with ease as she speaks. "Mitch? Everything all right?" She leans her head to the side.

"Yes. Why?" I sit up straighter and take another sip of my scotch.

"You were just staring at me ... for a while." She breaks eye contact and plays with the charm on the stem of her glass.

"Sorry. You're just ... you're a very beautiful woman." I swirl the cubes around and take my last swig.

"Um, thank you," she says hesitantly as she plays with a napkin. I place my hand on top of hers to stop the fidgeting. Her eyes fly up quickly to meet mine. Shit—did she just feel that, too? No. What am I thinking? She's a professional. Then again, I'm not quite sure why I felt a flutter of electricity—this isn't my first time around, either.

"Please call me Mitchell, Charlotte." I pull my hand away.

"Isn't that what I called you?"

"You called me Mitch a moment ago; only close friends and family call me that."

I sigh, half expecting her to roll her eyes at me.

"Well, I'm a little less formal. You can call me Charley." She smiles. There's something playful about her smile, as if she's teasing me.

"Charlotte is such a beautiful name. Why do you go by Charley?" I sit back, studying her again.

"Oh, that's my dad's doing." She takes another sip of her wine and leans back in her chair. "I'm the youngest of five girls. My dad, like most men, really wanted a son. My mom told him she was done. No more after me. So he asked if he could name me Charlotte. Of course, she didn't know it was so he could call me Charley. But it stuck. Everyone calls me Charley."

She takes another sip.

"Did he ever get over not having a son?"

"Oh yeah. Turns out, he named me perfectly. I was quite the tomboy, and his constant sidekick." She shakes her head, laughing at herself.

4

"Is he still alive?" I set down my empty glass.

"Oh yeah. Healthy as a horse, that guy! I think he'll outlive me!" I watch her face light up as she talks about him. I wonder if "dear old Dad's" health would be as good if he knew what his precious sidekick did for a living.

"The waitress is right over there. Do you want me to wave her down for another drink?" she asks just before opening her purse. "Excuse me," she says, then quickly texts. "Sorry." She puts the phone back.

"Turn it off."

She looks up. "Sorry?"

"No phone when you're with me," I say calmly.

"Okay, well, I, uh ... put it on vibrate. I will not turn it off, but I can assure you that we won't be interrupted again unless there's an emergency. I only answered to let my friend know that I arrived safely." She seems perturbed. "Why are you smiling like that?" Now she's just plain irritated. I think my smug smile just got a little bigger.

"Finish your wine, Charlotte. I want to go upstairs and go over my contract with you." I push her glass forward.

"Contract? What sort of contract?" Her eyes go wide. I can't help but laugh.

"Don't worry; it's not that sort of contract." I open my eyes wide enough to match hers, and she laughs again.

"I don't have to call you 'sir'?" she asks playfully.

"Hmm ... nope. No." I shake my head.

"Do I need a safeword?"

"Nope." Jesus, she's cute. She's perfect. Just what I wanted. I hope she'll agree to my terms.

"Any chains, whips, floggers, canes, or paddles involved?" She pushes back on a finger for each thing she rattles off.

"Jesus—I may need a safeword!" I give her a playfully horrified look. She laughs again and I think it's the loveliest sound I've heard in a long time. Charlotte takes the last sip of her wine. I stand up and hold my hand out to her. She smiles and takes my offer. I pull her to me. Her nervousness catches me a little off guard. Is she always like this with clients, or is it me? I tilt my head as I lean in and sweep her lips with a kiss. *Mmm ... soft.* "Let's go." I nudge her nose with mine.

Charlotte

MITCH HITS THE button for the ninth floor as I try to collect my wits about me. *Mitchell* ... that's going to be hard for me. He looks like a Mitch, but not a Mitchell, if that makes any sense.

He's a handsome man. Not drop-dead gorgeous, but definitely handsome. I'd peg him to be in his early forties and just under six feet tall. He has dark, dirty-blond hair. His eyes are hazel, and kind-looking. His smile hits them, and like magic, I can see him as a little boy. I have to keep reminding myself that this isn't a regular first date. Though if I were my friend Julie, the end result would be a regular first date. *And*, he's taking me upstairs to sign a contract, amongst other things. What did his ad say? *"If upon initial interview I feel you are right for the position, you will fill out all necessary paperwork and begin immediately. Length of employment, as well as salary, will be discussed at that time."* So, I'm guaranteed a phone call after our first "date." Definitely a step up from Julie's regular first dates. That, coupled with the fact that I instinctively like him, makes me feel a smidge better.

"What's going on in there?" he asks, pulling me out of my thoughts as his index finger softly taps my right temple.

"I was trying to find that out myself, but ..." I trail off.

"But what?" Smiling eyes. *Not a regular date, Charley—stop it!*

"I was rudely interrupted by someone knocking and asking me 'What's going on in there?' before I could even find out." I state in a matter-of-fact tone.

"Rudely, huh?" He bites back his smile.

"Hmm ... yes. Probably not the last rude thing you will do to me tonight." I sigh playfully and watch as the numbers light up in the elevator. It stops, but it's only the seventh floor.

"You think I'm going to do rude things to you tonight?"

His voice is full of mirth. I open my mouth to say something, but the door opening distracts me. Mitch yanks my hand, pulling me to the back of the elevator as two older couples get on and the door closes.

"Frank! This is going up!" One lady hits her husband's arm as her irritation pierces his eardrums, I'm sure.

He shrugs. "So what?"

"Charlotte," Mitch says, nipping at my right ear, "you didn't answer my question."

"That's because Frank got on the wrong elevator," I whisper, holding an accusatory hand out in the direction of poor Frank.

Mitch raises an eyebrow. "Charlotte."

"Charley," I correct him. He places his hands on my hips.

"*Charlotte*," he insists, squeezing my hips and pulling me back against him aggressively. I gasp—*Christ, I'm such a girl!* Frank's wife shoots me a look—*Christ, she's such a bitch!*

"Do you think I'm going to do rude things to you?" he asks again in a whisper.

"Well, I guess it depends," I say.

"Depends on what?" He crooks his neck to look at me. I gaze up at him.

"If our definition of what's rude is the same." I smirk.

"Christ ... I think I'm going to enjoy the hell out of finding out!" he says at his regular volume. Everyone turns to look at us. Luckily, we don't have to endure their stares. "Excuse us, please." Mitch leads the way through the older couples, holding my hand. "Good luck, Frank!" he says loudly as we head down the hall. We hear Frank's friend laughing.

"Mitch!" I smack his arm. "He's going to get holy hell for that!" I say with exasperation. Mitch ignores me and opens the door to the room. No sooner do I step in than he slams the door shut and pushes me against it.

"This is the last time I'm telling you—Mitchell!" he says through his teeth with a mixture of anger and irritation.

"Oh, honey, you must've had a little too much to drink. I'm Charlotte." I place my hand on my chest. "You're Mitchell." I move my hand to his chest. Mitch looks down and shakes his head, then backs away from me.

"Forget it. This isn't going to work. I'll pay you for tonight, but you can leave."

He pulls out his wallet. I'm trying to decide which action offends me more: his dismissal, or the reaching for the wallet? Of course, getting pissed about either and walking (storming, really) out of here is not going to put food in front of my kids and a roof over their heads. And

... I like him. Yeah, he seems to have some quirks—we all do. But I like him. I feel okay with him. okay with what I'm going to do with him. *Was* going to do. Unless I rectify this situation.

"Whoa ... wait." I reach out and touch his arm. "I'm sorry." I take a step or two closer. He stares down at me intently. "You made me nervous. I joke when I get nervous. I can't help it." He tosses his wallet on the table, then puts his hands on my hips and pulls me toward him.

"I made you nervous?" he asks before planting a light kiss on my nose.

"Well, yeah. You slammed me up against the door and yelled in my face." I pull my head back as he advances. "Third rude thing you've done to me in the hour I've known you, by the way."

"Third?" he questions with a smile.

"Yes."

"When was the second time?"

He leans in to kiss me.

"You made me gasp in the elevator ... in front of other people." I pull my head back again.

"The horror!" His eyes widen. "Well," he starts before he touches my cheek, "I can do better than that." He leans down and kisses me. My knees weaken as I part my lips, allowing him to deepen the kiss. *Holy shit—this guy can kiss!* I hear a slow waltz playing in my head. Our mouths remain in perfect hold while our tongues dance skillfully as if this was their millionth waltz, not their first.

Mitch pulls away abruptly. He stares down into my eyes again, his left thumb strumming across my bottom lip.

"What?" I ask, feeling self-conscious.

"You're different," he finally says after a few more moments of awkward silence.

"What do you mean?"

He shakes his head. "Nothing. Come. Let's look at the contract." He leads me over to the sofa, which has a bajillion pillows on it. It looks nice, but you have to pull off half of them just to sit. I scan the room while Mitch gets the contract out of his briefcase. *Must remember to call him Mitchell!* God forbid! What's up with that, anyway?

The Ames is quite the contemporary hotel. Not too overbearing, though—there's more softness to it than a sterile feel. The walls are gray. There's a beautiful, white, decoratively engraved fireplace. I'm not sure if it's real, though. The room is very calming, with gray, white, and deep purplish tones. I'd love to curl up on the chaise lounge over in the corner and read a good book.

"Charlotte ... here." He hands me a manila envelope. I turn it over and open it up. The first paper I see is a non-disclosure agreement. I look up at him. "This is to protect both of us, really." He leans in until we're almost cheek-to-cheek as he looks on with me. "Basically, this states that you can tell people about us. However, you cannot tell anyone about our business arrangement, or our real one." I can't help my confusion or the fact that it's all over my face. "You'll understand in a minute. Do you have any questions about what you can or can't say?" he asks, preparing to hand me the pen. I read it over. "C'mon, Charlotte." Mitch sighs impatiently. "I just explained it to you. Sign so we can move on."

"Excuse me." I look over at him. 'Do you have a lot of contracts handed to you at work that you have to make decisions on?"

"Sometimes several a day. Why?"

"Do you read them over, or do you just go by whatever your associates tell you?"

I look back down at the paper.

"I read them over. That's different. It's business," he says. I jerk my head back up and give him "The Look," the one that says, "what the hell do you think *this* is?" "Yeah, okay, but you haven't even gotten to the contract yet." He points for emphasis.

"Pen." I hold out my hand. He gives it to me and I quickly sign. I hand the NDA back to him and move on to the contract.

It's only a page long. I don't know what I was expecting, but I find this odd. Instead of questioning it, I decide to read.

Holy shit! I jump up out of my seat and walk over to the fireplace to keep reading. Most people need to sit when they receive life-altering information—not me! I need to feel the ground beneath my feet.

"Charlotte?" Mitch walks up behind me.

"Shh." I wave my hand and continue to read. I feel his arms slip around my waist. His lips fall to the back of my neck, gradually working their way to the side.

"Baby, it'll be so good, I promise," he murmurs between kisses.

Wait! Did Mr. Formal just call me *baby*?

"So I can't have any other clients?" I ask.

"No. I'm your only client, and as you can see," he says, pointing to the retainer fee of $25,000, "you're well compensated for it."

I turn to him. "And this is a monthly fee?"

"Yes. Did you read it all?" He flicks the paper.

"Yes ... but ... I'm not quite sure what to make of it. Am I right in that you're contracting me to be your girlfriend?" I wince, unsure.

"You are very right. Come. Let's sit down and I'll explain this in my words—not my lawyer's." He grabs my hand and leads me back to the couch. I sit and cross one leg over the other. Leaning my elbow on the back of the sofa, I rest my head against my hand.

"Okay?" he asks. I nod. "The reason I'm doing this is because I'm the owner and CEO of Colton Technologies. Unless you're big into cars and technology for their parts, you probably haven't heard of us," he says.

"Actually, I have."

"You have?" He appears taken aback. "Did you Google or Wiki me?"

"Not you, your company. I had no idea you were the owner. I was helping my dad do research for his stock portfolio. You have a very impressive company, Mr. Colton." I smile.

"Yes, I think so." A look of pride flashes across his face. "Then you know that we serve more than a hundred countries. I'm always traveling, leaving no time for the whole courting process. I take a girl out on a date, then I don't see her for two months. It doesn't go over too well. And if she does stick it out, it's usually for my money. If it's not about money and she actually likes me, she nags me about never being there. So ..." He takes a deep breath. "I've decided enough is enough. I know what I want and if I have to pay to get it ... so be it." He slaps his knee.

"But Mitchell, you're a good-looking guy and you seem nice to be around—" I start, but he cuts me off.

"Charlotte, I want to know every inch of your body. I will tonight. There's no waiting, there's no wondering, and there's no bullshit. I don't have time for that stuff. I let you know when I'm in town and I expect your focus to be on me. It's simple, Charlotte. You've got it made. Even if I'm a complete asshole—you still have it made." His argument *is* compelling.

I glance back down to the paper. "This says something about a house."

"I have a house in Andover. You will live there as long as we're under agreement." His left hand rests on my outer right thigh and he squeezes. "You get a house, twenty-five thousand a month plus double the going rate for each night we spend together, and health insurance."

"Uh ... health insurance?" I ask.

"Yes." He laughs a little. "I can't just give you a personal check each month for you to deposit in your bank. It'll raise red flags with the IRS. You'll be on my company's payroll, hence the medical benefits."

"Do you offer a 401(k) plan, and how much do you match?" I ask seriously, as one would during contract negotiations.

"You're quite the smartass, aren't you?" He grins and squeezes my thigh again.

"Well, your ad did say you wanted an educated woman." I shrug. He laughs lightly and rolls his eyes at me.

"Do you have any other questions?" he asks as he plays with the back of my hair. I feel him slowly pulling a pin out.

"What are you doing?" I instinctively reach back.

"Is your hair long?" He pulls another pin.

"Yes. Stop." I lean forward.

"Please try to leave your hair down for me, and never cut it shorter than just below your shoulders."

"Mitchell! It took Ava almost two hours to do my hair." I try to push his hand away.

"I want it down," he states calmly. "Who's Ava?" he asks as he continues with the destruction of her masterpiece.

"One of my best friends," I reply in defeat.

"The one who texted you earlier?" he asks. I nod.

"Does she know what you are doing here ... the nature of your business?" He taps my leg. "Turn," he commands.

"No. She knows I'm here for a date, but she doesn't know what kind." I uncross my legs and turn away, giving him full access to my hair. I can't help but smile at how careful he's being not to pull it. It's kind of sweet.

"Charlotte."

"Yes?"

"As soon as I'm done here, I'm going to bring you into the bedroom, whether you sign the contract or not. If you have any questions, now's the time to ask." His voice is soft, yet assertive. I feel like there are little gymnasts in my stomach, flying around a bar, getting ready to do a triple mound—or whatever the hell it is gymnasts do!

"Right!" I finally find my voice. "I have my own home. I won't need to live in yours."

"I want you to live there. It's part of the condition." He stops pulling pins out.

"I can't. I won't. But I am willing to compromise."

"Compromise how?" I can tell he's working hard at not becoming irritated—his voice is calm, but the words are obviously coming through clenched teeth.

"When you call me, I'll make sure I am at your house for when you arrive and stay with you the entire time."

I wait for him to shoot my offer down. Instead, he returns to pulling pins out.

"I'll deal with that for now, but it's not off the table. We will revisit this subject later." He tugs on my loose hair for emphasis. I decide it's best to carry on with my other questions.

"You mentioned you will be paying me double the going rate each day we spend together."

"Yes."

"Why?" It seems excessive. I mean, I'm sure I can make it on twenty-five thousand a month. Christ ... is he related to my Aunt Clara?

"I've learned that loyalty comes with a big price tag. You sign that contract, Charlotte, and you become mine. I don't want another man's hands on you, whether he's a client or not. I'm willing to pay you a lot of money to guarantee that you comply." He runs his fingers through my hair, combing out the curls he's released.

"Have you done this before? If so, how long do you usually stay with the same woman?" I try to hide the sadness I feel for him.

"Just once, and it didn't work out well. Apparently, I didn't pay her enough to keep her loyal. To be quite honest, I realized she wasn't really for me." He sighs, then continues on with my hair.

"How so?" I turn my head to look at him.

"I wasn't picky enough, wasn't clear about my expectations. But I chalk it up as a learning experience. By the way, I will be having my people randomly check in on you to make sure you comply." He stops again, I think to wait for my reaction to this information.

"From what I've read, your expectations are for me to be your girl-friend in *every* way—not just sex." I move along in my questioning, noting that he has almost all of the pins out.

"Yes. I want a companion, too. It's not just about sex. Although I should warn you, I have quite the salacious appetite. I'm sure, given your line of work, that won't be a problem for you." *Huh?* Oh, right. I almost forgot, I'm supposed to be a high priced whore—only I'm not, and now, thanks to Mitch, I won't be. Well, I'll be high-priced, but not a whore. I can't very well be a whore if I'm sleeping with only one man. Right? These moral conflicts, I fear, will be the death of me.

"I'm sure I'll be able to keep up with you." I smile.

"Does that mean you'll sign?" he asks, grabbing my chin and turning my head to face him again.

"How long is the contract for, and will there be others around the world?" The last of my questions—for now.

"Indefinitely, as long as we are both happy and content with it. And no, you will be the only one. It's only fair of me to bestow the same courtesy I expect from you. Besides, like I said, my free time is limited." He pulls out the last pin. "Beautiful," he whispers before undoing the braids at the top.

"Can I have the pen?" I hold my hand out.

"I need to see your physical and blood results first." He hands me my purse. "You did bring them, right?"

"Yes, yes, of course." I sit straight up. I didn't even realize I was leaning against him. I open my purse and hand him the papers.

I remember Dr. Timmins's look of confusion when I asked to be tested for every STD known to man. I was prepared for that, considering the man has known me most of my life. I told him I wanted peace of mind, what with Josh's odd behavior during the last year of our marriage. Like a lightbulb flashing on, he got it.

"Here's mine." He hands me the paper. "Are you on birth control?"

"Yes." I nod and scan the paper.

"And you're good about taking it properly?"

"Yes." Geez ... this is actually starting to sound like a business deal. I feel my stomach turn. "I get the shot."

"Oh, okay. Good." He nods. Taking the contract from me, he quickly scratches out the bit about my living arrangements and revises it to say what we agreed upon. He initials it and hands it back to me. "Before you sign, I feel the need to remind you again that you will be at my beck and call. I also want to make it clear that it will never be more than this. I will never want more. I will never give more. I'm not trying to sound like a cocky or arrogant bastard, but if you find you feel something for me and want more—our contract will be through. I don't do the marriage thing, I don't do the kid thing, and I certainly won't do the falling-in-love thing. Sorry, I just want to make myself clear." He holds the pen back from me.

I smirk playfully and grab the pen. "Cocky bastard," I murmur loud enough for him to hear me.

"Smartass!" he murmurs back, grabbing the pen and paper from me so he can sign as well.

"Now what?" I widen my eyes and bite back my smile.

"Now," he says, standing and grabbing my hand to pull me up with him, "I finally get to peel you out of this dress." He grasps my lips with his and unzips my dress at the same time.

"Don't you want to know my favorite color?" I pull away and tease.

"No." He yanks me back.

"Flower? School I went to? Names of my sisters? My philosophy on life?" I keep my hands on his shoulders, holding him at arm's length to continue my teasing.

He takes in a deep breath. "There's only one thing I want to know right now." He pulls my hands away and holds them behind my back.

"What's that?"

"What you sound like when you come." He pulls me aggressively to him, not allowing an inch between us. His mouth lingers over mine, his eyes telling me to knock it the fuck off. My only response to his behavior is my erratic breathing.

"Well," I say before I kiss him, "good luck with that." Good luck indeed! I can't remember the last time I came naturally.

"Good luck? You don't think I'll be able to make you come?" He arches his brows.

"Probably not, but since you're paying me so well, I'll make sure to fake in a believable manner," I say thoughtfully.

"I don't want you to fake anything!" he snaps. *Except our relationship.* A slow smile crosses his lips, and his temper seems to abate. "So ... a challenge?"

"Quite." I sigh with a mixture of knowledge and disappointment.

"Hmm ..." A flicker of amusement hits his eyes. "Have a little faith, baby." He nudges my nose with his before planting a quick, sweet kiss on my lips. Bringing my hands back around to my front, he continues to lead me toward the bedroom.

"What happened to the formality you insisted on, Mr. Colton? That's twice you've called me 'baby.'" I tug on his hand.

"You've signed the contract ... you're officially my baby." He tugs back, forcing me onward at a quicker pace.

"You called me 'baby' before I signed," I remind him.

"Yes, but I knew you would capitulate to the terms quickly, given the position you are in," he says as he enters the bedroom.

"And what kind of position do you think I'm in?"

I yank my hands away swiftly. Honestly, what an offensive thing to say!

"Charlotte," he says, pulling me to him, "I don't know exactly what position you are in outside of this room." His fingers push my hair behind my ears. "But ... in this room ... I can think of several positions you will find yourself in tonight, *baby*." He licks his lips before claiming mine again. Holy shit! He certainly doesn't fall short on saying the hottest things. Effortlessly, I may add.

Slowly, my lips part enough to allow his tongue entrance. A small moan escapes my throat as his tongue explores my mouth skillfully. I feel him slip my dress off of my shoulders.

Crap, this is it—the moment Charlotte McKendrick, aka "Pollyanna," turns into a dirty whore! *No, no! You are not dirty! Stop it, Charley! And one John certainly doesn't make you a whore.* Christ—did I just call him a "John"? I've been watching way too much *Law & Order: SVU!*

"Very rude, Charlotte," Mitch says as he kisses down my neck.

"What?" I refocus.

"Exactly. This is your one and only warning. I'm paying you way too much for you to get lost in your thoughts." His eyes find mine and he waits for my nod of understanding.

"Sorry." I frown as I reach up to the top of his dress shirt and undo the top button, then continue to the next. Mitch watches my every move, like unbuttoning his shirt is the most fascinating thing he's ever seen.

"Stop," I finally say.

"Stop?" He chucks my chin so I'm looking up at him. "Charlotte ... is this part of your 'act'? The innocence ... the reluctance?" He seems unsure. I'm almost certain I already suck at my new "job"—and not the kind of sucking that it involves.

"Do you want me to stop?" I play into his idea.

"No ... actually, I'm finding it to be quite the turn-on." His grin is laced with surprise. Aha! I don't suck at my job! Well, metaphorically speaking. "I almost feel as if I'm about to take away your virginity." He chuckles a little.

"Oh." I laugh. "Well, I can assure you, that's not the case." I don't know why, but I feel even calmer with him than before. There's just something about him. Maybe it's the whole knight-in-shining-armor thing. I'm relieved and beyond grateful. He and his little contract will be saving me from God knows what kind of trauma I may have endured. I slip my hands inside his unbuttoned shirt and slide them up to his shoulders, slowly pushing it off them. I step out of my dress and toe it to the side. Mitch reaches his hand around the back of my neck, bringing my hair around to sit on my shoulder. He leans down. His lips trail kisses down and into the curve of my neck.

"Set the scene for me, baby. I want to play along." His voice is soft and sexy. It sends my little gymnasts back into action.

"It's a simple scene, really." I lift the hem of his undershirt. He takes a step back, letting me pull it up over his head. I toss it on top of my dress. He's fit. I can tell he works out, when he can. There are no ridiculous muscles to outline with my tongue like I've read in so many of my favorite romance novels. He's just a regular guy. I like that— makes him even more appealing, for some reason. I place my hands on his strong shoulders. "I'm your girlfriend and this is the first time I'm letting you have all of me. I'm nervous. While this isn't my first time, it's my first time with you. I want to be perfect for you. I want to do everything right. I want to be even more than you've imagined." I bring my eyes up to find his.

His kind eyes. I begged for kind eyes before I met him, but I'm not sure I knew exactly what I was asking for, or if it really existed. Now I know. They are laced with warmth, generosity, and concern, held in place by small lines in the corners that show off many years of laughter and playfulness. At the moment, I am most certain that I can trust this man. The irony is, of course, not lost on me. I'm putting my trust in a man who pays for sex—not the usual sort I put my confidence in.

"Jesus, Charlotte," he says as his hand cups my left cheek, "I feel like you're staring into my soul."

"I am," I say, almost in a whisper. Leaning up on my toes, I brush my lips against his, noting the slight change in the tempo of his breathing. His hand wraps around the small of my back, pulling me close to him as he attacks my lips. I play at the belt of his suit pants and whip it off. Mitch unhooks my bra. Cool air hits my lips. I open my eyes, watching him watch me. I quickly glance to my shoulder. As Mitch slides my bra straps off my shoulders and down my arms, his eyes focus on mine. Sad to say, but I think this is the most erotic moment of my life. My bra falls to the floor.

"You okay, baby?" He traces the slight prominence of my clavicle bone with his index finger. I almost think he's asking for real, but then I remember—he's playing along.

"Mmhmm."

"I'll stop if you need me to." He leans down near my ear. "Not really," he whispers, and I can't help but laugh a little. He straightens up, his smile extending to his eyes. I reach up with my hand and lightly touch the laugh lines at the corner of his eye.

"What are you doing?"

"Admiring the evidence of joy in your life. No matter how great or small—it's all right here." I strum my fingers over the tiny lines. "I find that very attractive." My smile is small, maybe a little timid-looking. I can only hope my expression isn't completely revealing my sudden shyness or concern over my inexperience.

"I find your thoughts overwhelming," he says, grabbing my hand. He kisses the tip of each finger. I give him a quizzical look and he shakes his head dismissively. "Enough stalling, baby." He begins backing me up toward the bed.

"You started it."

I arch a brow and pop the button on his pants.

"Yeah, well—I'm gonna finish it, too." With that, he turns me around swiftly so I'm facing the bed. *Holy hell!* His breath hits my neck, hot and full of promise. His hands fall to my sides. Slowly they push forward to my stomach and travel up.

"Ah!" I gasp from the bolt of electricity surging to my groin. Mitch rolls and tugs my nipples with skill and precision. I lean my head back against his chest. Hooking my arm around his neck, I bring his mouth down to mine. After a beat, his hands quickly slide down to my panties. His fingers hook under the elastic. He pulls away from mouth and whips my panties down to the floor. *Good God!* After an affectionate nip at my bum, he comes back up to a standing position and slowly turns me back around, then pulls the duvet back.

"Lie down." He nods toward the bed. I hear him unzip his pants while I sit and gracefully (I hope!) crawl back onto the bed.

Laying my head back, I take to yoga breathing once again, only I don't exhale with Lion's Breath. *Shit ... I'm not exhaling at all! Breathe, Charley. Breathe.* My lungs finally give in to the pressure, and the feeling of Mitch's teeth lightly biting at the inside of my leg. He pulls my legs apart—wide. I feel so overwhelmed at the exposure, the vulnerability. I gasp again as he tenderly bites and licks at the apex of my groin. My hips rise, encouraging him. Mitch's finger traces ever so slowly over my cleft. I think I hear him whispering something, but I'm not certain. The pounding of my heart is deafening. Just when I think I can't handle any more of the tantalizing torture of his hesitation, his tongue glides over, tasting me. A moan escapes from my throat.

"Damn it, Charlotte!" he snaps. I can barely hear him over the pounding in my ears. *Damn it, Charlotte? What's that about?* Did I do something ... oh. Oh. My. God.

"Ugh ... Mitch ... please," I beg. He holds me open, his mouth violently attacking my vulnerability. The swirling, the biting, the plunging—it's more than I can bear. I'm in sensory overload, and his hand holds my pelvis down, forcing me to endure it all with no relief in sight. "Please ... oh please, Mitch," I cry out. I feel—I know—I'm on the verge of some sort of breakthrough here. Mitch slows his hunger to a savoring pace. I feel a finger circling my entrance, as if plotting its plan of attack. He slips two fingers in at the pace of a Sunday drive. They meticulously massage the upper front wall of my vagina, sending my body on a leisurely hike to Heaven. A delicious tightening occurs deep inside, traveling up to the pit of my stomach. I squeeze my eyes shut as my body celebrates the joyous occasion of my first orgasm not supplied by a battery-operated object. A rocket shoots off a burst of purple. Another burst, now of white ... blue ... green ...

"Ugh ... oh ... Mitch ... Mitch ..." I don't even recognize my voice, and the rockets are coming so quick, one explosion after another.

"That's it, baby. Let me hear you." His encouragement works me through the last of my quakes. My body stills after I give him the last of my whimpers. I stare at the ceiling, trying to steady my breathing. I feel tears rolling from the corners of my eyes. I quickly wipe them away while Mitch begins his climb up my body. My breast rises to greet his mouth, and I plunge one hand into his hair and grasp his chin with the other. Lifting my neck, I pull his mouth away from my nipple and attack his lips. He finishes his climb, allowing me to rest my head down, his tongue exploring my mouth. Ripping his lips from mine, he gazes into my eyes, strumming his thumb against my bottom lip purposefully. Mitch shifts just barely, never losing eye contact. I raise my hips for him, and at this moment I realize I have never wanted someone this bad in my life. My neck involuntarily bends back as I feel myself stretch around him.

"Charlotte," he gasps. A small sob flies from my mouth and hangs over us like a secret that never meant to be discovered. "Charlotte ... baby, look at me," he whispers. My neck relaxes and my eyes find his. They look confused. "Charlotte?"

"Shh." I lean up and kiss him. It turns from soft and reluctant to urgent, even desperate. Mitch rolls his hips again—skillfully, I may add. Within moments, we are in perfect rhythm. I relish in the feeling of my body finally accommodating his with ease. I swiftly turn my head away. My eyes go wide in disbelief as the newly familiar feeling creeps up on me once again.

"Look at me," he commands. It's meant to sound assertive, but it translates almost to a plea. I comply—eyes still wide, ready to be transported someplace incredible. "You're mine." His right hand palms my face and I feel like I'm hanging by a thread. "Say it!" he demands.

"I'm yours ... I'm ... oh ..." I'm gone, wild beneath him.

"That's it, baby. Tell me. Show me you're mine," he says, egging me on. I comply in every way. Sound. Touch. I'm his ... contract or no contract. I tighten myself around him, my final proclamation. The sound that escapes his throat brings me to my knees. "Char—goddamn." His nose scrunches up and his lips form an "O" shape. The tip of his tongue slides over the top of his teeth and pushes against them as if its life depended on it. "Ugh," he grunts one last time, then falls to my chest, panting. Mitch lifts his head.

"I'm sorry," I say quickly.

"About?"

"I called you Mitch." I wince.

"Christ, Charlotte, that's the furthest from my mind right now," he says with a hint of irritation. I don't know what to say, so I say nothing. He shakes his head slightly and takes in a deep breath. "Right now I just want to bask in our post-coital glow."

"But?" I ask, showcasing my nervousness.

"*But* ... we are going to have a *very* in-depth conversation tomorrow morning." He grabs my chin and rocks my head side to side gently for emphasis. I reply by swallowing hard—it's all I've got. He dips down and sweeps my lips lightly before pulling out. I cringe from the sudden emptiness I feel. Mitch rolls onto his back and pulls me with him. His fingers glide up and down my spine, then into my hair and back down again. The strumming of his fingers, the effects of two amazing orgasms, the stress and worry about what was to come of tonight, and the fact that I was up at four this morning with a feverish Brooklynn—I find myself in a soporific state that I can't fight anymore.

Chapter Two

Mitch

MY EYES FLY open in a panic and I glance around the room trying to place it. Ugh ... I hate when this happens. And it does—too often, thanks to all my traveling. Boston ... I'm in Boston. *Charlotte!* I turn my head to the right to find her resting with her back to me. She's sleeping so peacefully. I fight the urge to touch her.

What the hell was that last night?! No way has she done this before! I've had my fair share of professional ladies. Charlotte did not display one single characteristic in common with them. Well, her playfulness, but I could tell that was genuine, not forced. She signed at twenty-five thousand a month, no argument. Didn't ask me how much I thought "double the going rate" was, or even mention her fee. No, I'm most certain she's never done this before, especially considering she was so snug. Christ, was she snug!

Forget Charlotte. What the hell was up with *me*? I went down on her—I never do that with someone I'm paying! I made love to her—I don't do that with ... anyone. I have casual sex. I fuck hard. I never make love—not my thing—not usually—not ever!

I bring my hands to my face and try to rub away my confusion. I've got to look at her file again. Kyle said she checked out all right. I just skimmed over it, having full confidence in Kyle's abilities. Of course, he didn't know the real reason for her background check. I climb out of bed, slip my boxers on, and head to the living room. I grab a bottle of water and take a quick sip before I retrieve her file from my briefcase.

Charlotte Rose McKendrick ... thirty-three ... BA in English ... spouse: Joshua Thomas McKendrick ... Hampstead, NH.

"Spouse?!" How did I miss that? I look again. My eyes drop further down the page for the detailed biography Kyle always gives.

Her husband abandoned her? And her three kids. Kids ... *shit!* Brogan, Bennett, and Brooklynn. I'm sensing a theme here. Her divorce is almost finalized—good. House in foreclosure. Recently laid off from a doctor's office. Son Bennett has special needs. What kind of special needs? Hmm ... it doesn't say.

I close the file. I don't need to know any more ... not now. This is enough to know my suspicions were correct. I'm her first client. I sit on the couch, lean forward, and rest my head in my hands. Shit ... now what? This can't possibly work. She's *that* type ... not this type. She's the girl who falls in love, gets married, has a few kids, and lives out the rest of her life in domestic bliss (well, I'm sure that was her plan). She'll want more. I'll have to start all over with a less-than-perfect version of—her. Christ. She's exactly what I want. Somehow, her situation makes her even closer to perfection for me. First, she's probably too busy to bother being disloyal. Will she be too busy for me, though? Secondly, she doesn't have to pretend to know how to be a girlfriend. She was a wife for almost ten years! If I'm honest with myself, a wife figure is what I really want. One without all of the bullshit and strings attached. Ugh, God ... what the hell am I thinking? I'm not thinking! No, I can't do this with her—she'll want more. I won't give her that. I'll give her a month's salary and walk away.

"Hey."

My eyes shoot up at the sound of her voice. She's leaning against the doorframe of the bedroom in nothing but my dress shirt. Her long, wavy hair is pulled to one side. *Damn, she is a vision.*

"Hey," I say with a slight smile. "Go back to bed. I'll be there in a minute."

She nods. "Okay. Can I grab a water?"

"Here ... have mine." I hold it up. She walks over and takes it from me, then brings it to her lips. I match her smile—that sexy little smile—before she takes a sip.

"Sit back." She pushes at my shoulder. I rest my back against the cushions. She turns and pulls at my shirt to make sure it covers her bum before sitting across my lap and stretching her legs out on the couch.

"Yes, Charlotte, we must remain modest at all times," I tease her. She rewards me with her girlish giggle, then leans against my chest and tucks her head into the curve of my neck.

"Why are you up in the middle of the night, Mr. Colton?" She raises her head to look at me. Her fingers play with my lips. "Very rude of you, sir, leaving me all by my lonesome."

I touch her cheek. "Your eyes are beautiful."

"You're changing the subject." Her eyebrow arches. I shrug and look down at her legs, then rest my hand on her thigh and gradually let it slide up.

"Just thinking. That's all."

"Well, that's just the sort of thing that will get you into trouble." She rests her head back in the crook of my neck.

"Really? Thinking?" I humor her.

"Yes. Thinking can get in the way of doing. Sometimes you need to just do things without thinking, because they need to get done. Think about it!" She holds her hand out for emphasis, then quickly acts like she's holding a drumstick and sounds off a couple of beats that would come after a one-liner. I can't help but chuckle at her. *Damn it, she's cute!*

"So, I should do and not think about it?" I lay my head back.

"Yes."

I eye her. "Like sign a contract that pays me far less than what I'm worth?"

"Mitch ... did you not ask for an educated woman?" She lifts her head.

"Mitchell." I give her "The Look." "And yes, I did."

"That's right. It's only acceptable for me to call you Mitch when I'm coming ... right?" Her smile hits her eyes. *Damn it!* "Moving along ..." She winks. "Since I pride myself on being quite the erudite woman, I am not going to play dumb. I certainly don't believe you are lacking in the intelligence department, either. In saying that, I *am* new to this 'scene.'" She actually makes air quotation marks. "But that doesn't mean I haven't done my homework. I know there are women out there who charge two hundred and fifty thousand dollars for just a weekend. I know what I'm worth, Mitchell. I don't need a dollar sign attached to a ridiculous number for me to believe it. I'm not an avaricious person, either. I have priorities that require only the basic necessities, and most of those necessities cannot be provided by money.

"However, the things that do require money are costly. It's difficult for me to maintain a regular job right now that will meet both my financial situation and the schedule I require. My lack of negotiations is purely for my benefit, not yours. I do need the money. I feel it's a sufficient amount for your requirements, plus you're offering me the ability to stay off the radar, which is by far one of the most important requirements I have. Not that I've ever had trouble with the law. I haven't, and I'd like to keep it that way."

I almost can't believe my ears when she finally quiets that lovely mouth of hers. Good God! Did she just say all of that in one breath?

"Mitchell ..."

"What?"

"Say something." She looks down.

"Sorry. I'm overwhelmed by your veracity. You are quite the rare breed, aren't you?" I chuck her chin.

"Yeah ... I'm pretty much a bullshit-free zone. I don't take it, I don't give it, and quite frankly I want nothing to do with it. If I smell bullshit—I call it and leave the room." I can tell I have a goofy grin on my face as she rambles on. "Sorry."

"For?"

"Nattering on."

"I'm quite fond of your nattering." I curl my index finger under her chin and hold it with my thumb. Leaning in, I grasp her lips with mine. "So," I breathe, letting my mouth hover over hers. My hand moves down her neck and into my shirt. Slowly, my fingers trace around her nipple. I listen to the tempo of her breathing change. "How do you like the new career you've had all of six hours?"

"Oh, well, I'm not all that new at this. I've been doing it longer than six hours, Mitchell." She pulls away. I feel a spark of jealousy at this. My fingers still.

I look away from her. "How long?"

"Just about ... seven hours," she says after some thought.

"Ugh—Charlotte!" I say in irritation. "I can already tell you're going to drive me crazy."

"Crazy in a good way? *And* ... it's Charley," she taps my nose with her index finger.

"Well, that remains to be seen ... *Charlotte*." I grab her hand gently.

"Charley," she says, getting off my lap only to turn around and straddle me.

"Charlotte," I say very slowly while leaning my head back to look at her. What an idiot her husband was.

"Mitch," she says softly, placing her finger over my lips when I part them to correct her. She leans down near my ear. "Touch me, Mitch ... please."

I close my eyes, fighting back whatever she's stirring in me. She straightens back up and stares into my eyes as she unbuttons my dress shirt.

Placing my hands on her hips, I gently squeeze them. "I thought I was the boss here." I smirk at her and lick my lips. The curve of her breast becomes visible from her seductively slow unbuttoning.

"Don't you think staff morale would go up if you allowed them to take charge of a few things?" She matches my smirk with her playful banter.

"Baby." I shift and her eyes go wide. "As you can see—er, feel—the morale of my staff has been up since you sat on my lap." I push against her and listen to her gasp.

"We should probably debrief the staff immediately, then take advantage of the raise in morale." I find myself eager to play along with her flirting again. I almost hate how fucking cute I think she is.

"Why should we debrief?" I raise my eyebrows as the tips of my thumbs slowly meet each other in the middle of her stomach. From there, my hands begin their patient crawl up her torso.

"Because there's a touchy situation that may have a very sticky end result." Now she's the one licking her lips as my thumbs circle around her nipples at a pace I'm sure may kill her.

"Oh, I think we'll be drowning in the effects of the touchy situation." My hand travels back down her body and searches between her legs. I swirl a finger around her entrance a few times before plunging it in. "I see you agree with me." I brace her with my arm as she arches back from the intrusion. Pulling her closer to me, I taste the skin at the base of her neck. I nip gently, avoiding the urge to savor it. I don't want to leave marks on her, and yet I want to somehow brand her. Anyone that looks at her—dares to think of touching her—should know that she is *mine* and move on without another thought of her.

"Mitch ... Mitch, please," she's breathless. Wanting. She embraces my face with her soft, sweet hands. Their coolness calms me in a way I haven't felt in a long time.

"I need you, Mitch."

She needs me ...

"I want you."

She wants me ...

"Baby ... please."

Baby ...

I stare into her jade-colored eyes. They show me her words are pure and true. My head says to run ... run fast, or she'll destroy you. Except, no other part of me is listening to my head as I toss her onto the couch. I will brand her. I will make it so she will not want another man's hands on her body. No other lips will do. My hands, my kiss will be all she thinks about—craves—when she is not near me. My fingers and mouth comply with the plan as they worship her body, like she's an exotic goddess. I believe she is, actually.

I GLANCE AT the clock on the wall as it ticks to the exact minute I began my worshipping, two hours ago. Charlotte is cradled in my arms, softly crying. Every few minutes, she stops long enough to kiss my neck and shoulder. I am almost certain it is her way of telling me, without words, that no man has ever adored her the way I just did.

"The sun will be up soon, baby." I glide my hand up the length of her body. "We should get back to bed." Charlotte lifts her head to look at me. Her eyes pierce mine and I swear, if I let her stare long enough, she could uncover every last secret I have. "What?" I touch her cheek lightly.

"Nothing," she murmurs, shaking her head.

"Don't lie to me." I strum her bottom lip with my thumb. "What's on your mind?"

"I'm not lying. Not exactly. I'm not quite sure what to think. I don't want to say any more. You know I ramble. I don't want to say anything that may scare you off." She offers me a half smile before she lays her head back down.

"Charlotte," I say, trying to mask my building frustration. "You can't say all of that and not explain what you mean."

"Mitch, there's nothing to explain. Nothing that I can really articulate well enough to form an explanation." She leans on her hand and runs her fingers over the stubble on my chin.

"Charlotte ... why do you think it would scare me off?" I grab her hand and allow my voice to show my impatience.

She gives it back to me with an exasperated sigh. "Okay—here it goes." She pauses, closing her eyes momentarily. Seems a bit dramatic to me, really. I almost laugh.

"C'mon!" I slap her ass playfully when she takes too long.

"Ow—sorry."

"There's more where that came from if you don't spill it." I bite at her pouty lip and rub where I just smacked.

"Ha ... well, I was going go to say, before you rudely interrupted me—fourth rude thing, by the way." She taps my chin with her index finger.

"I'm going to show you 'rude' in a minute if you don't get to it—just so you're clear on my definition." I give her my sternest look, and she replies with that sexy little smile, a hint of sass on her lips. I bring my hand down again on her ... harder than I intended. Charlotte jumps up from my arms.

"Whoa ... wait ... wait." I pull her to me. "Sorry, baby. Sorry. I didn't mean to do it that hard." I laugh nervously as I try to hold her to me. "Baby." I kiss her shoulder. "Look at me, please." I touch her chin lightly and turn her face to me. "I'm sorry ... honestly." I lean forward and nudge her lips with mine.

"Don't do it again," she says quietly.

"I promise, I won't."

"C'mon, let's go to bed," she says after a deep sigh and nod of her head.

"Wait, you didn't tell me what you were thinking." I stand up with her and help her back into my shirt. I don't know why she's bothering; it'll be back off in a minute.

"I've changed my mind."

"Oh ... that's not fair." I grab her hand and walk to the bedroom with her.

"No rewards for bad behavior, Mitch." She climbs onto the bed. I run a hand through my hair as I try to figure her out. I shouldn't have to figure anything out.

"Shirt off, Charlotte," I say before climbing in. She glances at me before taking it off, and then curls up on her side, facing away from me. "In my arms, Charlotte!" I snap. She turns to me and slowly slides halfway onto me, into my arms.

"Goodnight, Mitchell." She kisses me, then lays her head down. *Mitchell? Shit!*

"Charley," I whisper, cringing at the use her nickname. "Don't be like this, please. Not even an hour ago you were like butter—melting under my touch." I run my hands up and down her back. "I want this to work with you, Charley, but I'm not going to put up with this behavior."

"You fucking hit me, Mitch! You want me to be all warm and fuzzy toward you now?" She lifts her head.

"I said I was sorry! What else do you want me to do?" I yell.

"Just give me a goddamn chance to calm down and get over it!" she yells back. I grab her face and kiss her hard. Christ, she's fucking hot as hell when she's mad! She tries to pull away. I turn her and pin her down on the bed.

"Get off of me!" she says through clenched teeth and tries to break free from my hold. I tighten my grasp on her and knee her legs open wider. She bucks her hips and pushes off the bed with her right foot, flipping me onto my back. *Damn, she's strong!* She holds my arms down and whips her hair over onto her shoulder. I sit up quickly with enough force to knock her on her back and pin her once more. I attack her lips, biting at them—savoring them. Placing both of her arms above her head, I use my free hand to pin them together. I free my trapped hand and grasp at her breast, then pull her nipple into my mouth and grind it gently with my teeth. She squirms and bucks, trying to break free. I bring my mouth up to her ear.

"Charlotte, Charlotte, Charlotte," I sigh. "The more you fight me, baby ... the harder I'm going to fuck that sweet, tight pussy of yours."

"Ah!" she gasps.

I bite at her earlobe. "Keep fighting me, baby ... I want to make your pussy so sore." I notice Charlotte go limp and start breathing erratically, so I lift my head to look down into her face. Her eyes are wide. "Is my choice of words offending you?" I grin playfully and continue to torture her nipple with my fingers.

"Well ... uh ... no, I just," a very flustered Charlotte starts, "you haven't talked to me like this all night." On a hunch, I choose to ignore her comment and shock her some more.

I keep my voice low. "Charlotte?"

"Yes?"

"Who does your pussy belong to, baby?" My hunch is right—her breathing is out of control.

"You."

"Say it, baby. Tell me who this belongs to." I bring my hand down and let my fingers trace her cleft. "Full sentence, please," I add.

"My pussy belongs to you, Mitch." Her voice shakes, the volume just above a whisper.

"Baby, baby, baby ... it's okay for a good girl to be a little bad," I say as soothingly as possible.

"I'm going to let go of your arms. I want you to touch me and see what you do to me." I release her hands and anticipate her touch. Slowly, her hand travels down between us. My breath hitches as she wraps her hand around to stroke me. "No. No, baby, don't." I pull her hand away. "Tell me what to do with my morale." I kiss her. "Say it the way you know I want to hear it." She takes in a deep breath. "Say it, baby ... tell me," I encourage her, desperately trying not to come undone at the thought of her talking to me that way.

Charlotte grasps my face aggressively. "You take that morale of yours and fuck my pussy so hard I'm begging you to stop. When I do start begging ... fuck my pussy harder. You don't stop until you're convinced my pussy is the sorest it has ever been!" *Holy shit!* Did that just come out of her mouth? "Now, Mitch!" She heels me in the ass. "By the way, I'm very flexible—I suggest you take advantage of that," she says against my lips before kissing them.

After a moment of disbelief I fly into action, whipping her legs into the air wide and down on either side of her head. Shit—she wasn't kidding! I slam into her hard and relish in the sound that escapes her throat.

"Ready, baby?" I ask, breathless and anxious.

"Are you?" she counters, her tone mocking. I push her legs down hard and have at her as if my life depended on it. My efforts are rewarded by her whimperish moans. When she finally begs me to stop, I call on my reserves and pound into her harder. The good thing about fucking this hard is that just when you don't think you can keep up another minute with this stamina, the tightening and tingling occurs. It travels up into my shaft and the pit of my stomach. I erupt inside of her with such force I half expect it to pour out of her mouth. Releasing her legs, they fall to my side as I give my final pumps and crash on top of her. I lift my head to look at her. Her eyes are still closed and she's breathing deeply.

"Baby," I say, touching her face, "are you okay?"

"Mmhmm." She smirks. Taking reassurance from this, I pull out of her, enjoying the face she makes. My right hand runs from her breast, down her torso, and between her legs. Charlotte opens her eyes and stares into mine as I swirl my come around her pussy. I can tell she likes this by the way she softly moans and gyrates against my hand. I love how much she likes it.

"We're so good together, Charlotte." I kiss her.

"Let me taste how good we are together." She licks and nips at my mouth. I bring two fingers up and run them along her parted lips. She opens them, fully taking my fingers in and sucking our taste off of them. I close my eyes to squash the tightening in my stomach. Charlotte stops sucking. I open my eyes.

"Do we taste good?" I smile.

"Uh-huh ... c'mere." She pulls my face to hers. "Taste for yourself," she mutters and softly presses her lips to mine. I suck all of our taste off. Damn, she can kiss. I deepen the kiss and pull her close. We spend the next several minutes making out like a pair of teenagers. Christ, I feel twenty years younger with her.

"Mitch, I need to go to the bathroom, baby." She smiles against my lips.

"Go. I'll straighten this mess out." I eye our bed; everything is twisted.

Once the bed is tidy again, I rest my head back and wait for Charlotte. It's almost six. Thank God I don't have a meeting until the afternoon!

"Hey ... what are you thinking about?" She climbs in.

"The meeting I have at two." I kiss her head as she snuggles against me.

"Anything interesting?" She leans her head back to look at me.

"No, nothing as interesting as you." I smile. "Incidentally, Charlotte ... I'm very shocked at your vulgar language!" I try to look appalled. She smacks my chest, making me laugh.

"The Devil made me do it." She rolls her eyes.

"I thought you might have been possessed," I say after some thought.

"Well, you exorcised the shit out of that demon ... didn't you?" She bites back her smile.

"I hope not. That was hot as hell!" I kiss her again. "Get some sleep, baby."

"Sleep—now there's a concept!"

"Mm," I agree and kiss her hair again before we both drift off.

Chapter Three

Charlotte

I TAKE A deep breath and am fully awoken by the glorious aroma of coffee in the air. I reach my arms above my head and have a good stretch.

"Hey, sleepyhead." I open one eye, not sure of the voice I'm hearing. Oh, it's Mitch—mmm.

"Good morning." I smile and sit up, bringing the sheet with me. Mitch walks over to the bed and leans down for a kiss.

"I ordered brunch for us. You didn't bring a bag up last night. Do you have one in your car?"

"Uh, yeah, I do actually."

"Then give me your keys, the make, and where you're parked so I can have my assistant get it. You go jump in the shower." He hands me my purse.

"I'll get it," I offer, looking around for my dress.

"Baby, you need to shower and eat so we can get to the bank. My meeting is in two hours." He pushes my purse in front of me again.

"Did your meeting get pushed up? I thought it was at two." I pull my keys out and hand them to him.

"It *is* at two. It's noon, Charlotte. C'mon, get in the shower." He pats my leg.

"Noon? No. No, no ... it can't be noon!" I grab my phone and check it. Five texts, ten missed calls, and yes, you irresponsible asshole—it's noon! "Shit!" I yell and jump out of bed. "Shit! Shit! Shit!" I scramble for my things.

"Charlotte! What are you doing?" He grabs my arm.

"I have to go, Mitch! I was supposed to be home this morning—no later than ten! Ava's gonna kill me!" I look frantically at the phone. "Shit! She's gonna think I'm dead!" I pull up her texts. The last one says *"ARE YOU DEAD???!!!!"*—confirming my suspicions.

"You can't go. You signed a contract. Call her and tell her you're fine and that you'll see her tomorrow!" He points to the phone. I stare at him like he has five heads. Just as I'm about to ask him if he's a moron, I remember he doesn't know I have kids.

"Mitch, I can't do that. I have to go home. I'm sorry. I wish I could stay. I realize I signed a contract, but I had no idea that I would be spending another night with you. You didn't tell me how long you were in town for, or that you expected me to start right away with the whole 'beck and call' thing." I explain the best I can while dialing Ava's number.

"Charley?!" she screams.

"Yes, it's me. I'm so sorry, Ava. I overslept. I'm leaving now," I say as I frantically throw on my clothes.

"Your parents are with them, Charley. I couldn't stay," she says quickly.

"What? Oh no! Ava—ugh!" I pull at my hair.

"I tried calling you, damn it!"

"I had to keep my phone on vibrate." I look up and find Mitch gone.

"Well, I told them that you were at an interview in Boston. I didn't know what else to say," she explains with a sigh.

"No ... thank you, Ava. I'm sorry I scared you. I'll call you later." I rummage through my purse for a hair tie.

"You'd better—I want full details!" she says before we hang up. Quickly, I hit the number to my house.

"Charley-baby! How'd the interview go?" my dad asks, his tone cheerful. God, I hate lying to this man.

"So far, so good, Dad! They want me to stay and interview with another person and possibly create a few samples."

"Listen, sweetie, Mom and I have the kids—we're all fine. You concentrate on what you need to do! Don't worry about rushing home, baby doll. You just knock their socks off!" I can almost see him swinging his fist in his "Go get 'em, champ" way.

"Thanks, Daddy. I love you." I choke back my tears.

"I love you, Charley. You make me so proud," he says.

"Thanks, Daddy." I can barely keep it together. "Call you later."

"Okay, honey—good luck!"

"Thanks! Bye." I hang up and sit on the bed to sob. I don't deserve his pride. I take a deep breath and call CiCi.

"Hey, Charley, I was just thinking about you. My friend Reagan is selling this vitamin-powder-supplement thing at parties and she's doing great with it, so I told her that you may be interested." I don't think I have ever called CiCi and gotten a simple fucking "Hello, Charley."

"CiCi, thanks, but are you busy tonight?" I ask.

"Depends."

"I met a nice guy and I'd really like to go out with him again. Will you stay over tonight so I can?" I cross my fingers.

"All night? Are you sleeping with him?"

"Well, I'm not sure what time I'll be in, so it's best if you just stay over, and *please* do not tell anyone!" I beg.

"What do I get?" *Crap!*

"I will host a vitamin party thing for Reagan and consider the benefits of pushing the powder on unsuspected loyal friends who feel obligated to buy it from me just so it can sit on their shelves and collect dust! Do we have a deal?" Fingers still crossed.

"Deal!" she yells excitedly. Christ ... I thought I was the easy one here.

"Thanks, babe—call ya later!" I smile and hang up. Phew! With a deep breath I head out to the living room.

"Mitch ... I think I've worked things out," I say with a smile as I approach him at the table. He holds up a check. "What's this?" I take it.

"Payment for last night. I gave you the most I could as a gift so there would be no red flags." He sips his coffee and I spot the ripped-up contract on the table. I look down at the check and see it's written for $13,000.00.

"That's it? You're done with me?" I sit down in disbelief. "I just lied to my family and friends so I could spend tonight with you! My dad thinks I'm on a job interview and just went on about how proud he is of me!"

He looks up. "You're spending the night with me?"

"No ... not anymore." I shake my head and get up to leave, disappointed. Why did I think he would be different from any other selfish prick I've been with?

"Charlotte." He grabs my arm and spins me around in front of the door. "Don't go. If you've made it possible to stay with me ... then stay, baby." He brings his hand up and grazes my cheek with the back of it. I meet his eyes. "Stay ... tell me how I can ameliorate this situation."

I roll my eyes at Mr. Big Shot. "You can start by telling me what the hell *ameliorate* means, or at least spell it for me so I can look it up," I say. Mitch laughs a little.

"Sorry, I have a love of words that aren't said often. It's the nerd in me." His smile reaches his eyes, again showing me Mitch as a little boy. "I have faith in you, though. You're a smart woman. If I just reacted irrationally ... "

"Like a spoiled brat," I interject.

"Ooh ... ouch!" He winces. "Hold on while I pull your claws out of me." I give him a smirk that says, *your time is running out, buddy*. "If I want to ameliorate my behavior ..." He waits for me to get it.

"You want to correct it," I say.

"Yes!" He says with a little too much excitement. It makes me laugh.

"Christ ... you are a nerd, aren't you?"

"Shh ... don't let anyone know." His lips linger over mine for a beat before he finally collects them. "Now, get in the shower. I'll have your bag up here and our contract scotch-taped back together."

"Better make it duct tape in case your irrational impulsivity gets the best of you again!" I tap his cheek in a mock slap before heading to the bathroom.

"I'm gonna get some duct tape for that mouth of yours!" he calls after me. I continue on toward the bathroom without looking back as I raise a defiant middle finger. "You've got a fucking pair on you, don't you?!"

"And a spare set for backup, just in case!" I yell back, shut the door, and make sure to hit the lock. Of course, the lock is a push button. If he wants to come in, I'm sure this won't hold him back too long. Oh well ...

I put my purse down and take my dress off once again, then climb into the shower. The pelting hot water is like a small slice of Heaven. As much as I want to analyze Mitch Colton, I can't muster the energy to do so. I am bone-tired, muscle-tired, mind- and heart-tired. I resolve to just stand here mindlessly and turn into one big prune. After several minutes—I don't know, three, possibly ten—I pull my face out of the stream of water and reach for the shampoo. I feel a cool breeze and hands slide onto my hips.

Can someone die from having more sex than should be humanly possible? I may be the first case. I can see it now—my body displayed on a cold slab at a university somewhere, medical students probing me, trying to figure out the mystery of the woman who died from too much sex!

I lean my head on Mitch's shoulder and reach back with my arm, circling it around his neck. His lips find mine. The kiss is possessive, yet patient. Christ—I'm floored every time this man kisses me. Mitch turns my body toward him and slowly backs me up to the wall. His hands cup my face, his thumbs caress my cheeks, his eyes study me. He had me in some very precarious positions last night, yet nothing he did made me feel more exposed than this right now. Just when I feel I may cave from the pressure of his stare, Mitch dips down and claims my lips. His tongue encourages them to part so he can further the kiss. A cello plays in my head as his tongue meticulously caresses mine—powerful, yet soft. I'm butter. He's got me melting at his touch again. He sucks at my lower lip, pulling away reluctantly.

"Jesus, Charlotte, why can't I get enough of you?" He leans his forehead against mine.

"Mitch," I say, breathing his name before attacking his lips. He brings his hands down to my bum and hoists me up. I wrap my legs around him. He wastes no time filling me to capacity.

"Look at me," he commands, his voice low and sexy. I open my eyes and stare into his. Mitch rolls his hips, smirks at the sound I make, then rolls them again. It becomes a slow pattern of rolling ... listening ... rolling, until finally, he picks up a pace that makes me want to cry. Within minutes, we come undone together.

"You're going to kill me," I say after he lets me down. "Death by probing—it'll be on the six o'clock news."

Mitch chuckles. "I told you I have a salacious appetite. You said you could keep up." He chucks my chin.

"Yes, I believe I can. I just don't think my vagina agrees with me."

"Vagina?" He bites back a smile.

"Yes, well, that's what they'll call it."

"They? They who?" He moves a strand of wet hair off my face.

"The medical students who'll be examining me, trying to figure out how I died from sex!" Mitch throws his head back and laughs before he pulls me into a fierce hug. "Will you come to my funeral ... say a few words?" I carry on.

"Probably not, since I'll be in custody for murdering you with my dick. Same medical students will be testing it for superpowers."

"Oh, it definitely has superpowers." I smile and wrap my arms around his neck.

"You think so?" He kisses me.

"I know so." I widen my eyes.

"Yeah? Like what?"

I smile thoughtfully at him, then lean up to his ear. "It has the power to make me come at the speed of light."

"You're right, Charlotte. You are definitely going to die from too much sex today," he states before grabbing a handful of my hair and bringing my mouth to his.

"Mitch ... Mitch, you have a meeting at two." I try to push him off.

"Ugh!" he groans. "We have to get to the bank, too."

"C'mon, let's wash up, Superman." I smile and slap his butt. Mitch gives me a full-wattage smile that takes my breath away.

"BABY, C'MON!" MITCH pounds on the door of the bathroom.

"Coming ... geez." I open the door before throwing my damp hair up in a tie. "I still have to put makeup on."

"You don't need makeup, baby, you're gorgeous." He kisses my cheek. "Cheese Danish okay?" He hands it to me on a napkin. "We have to go."

"Yeah. Coffee?" I look to the table.

"Right here. Just cream?"

"Yes, thanks." I take a sip and slide into my flip-flops.

"Ready?"

"Yup. Why are we going to the bank?" I take a bite of the Danish, following him to the door.

"I decided not to put you on the books at work. We're going to do this a little differently." He opens the door.

"No 401(k) plan then?" I smirk.

"No ... smartass." He taps my butt and closes the door behind us. "Do you have something in your purse or car that shows your proof of residency?"

"Yes?" I say, feeling unsure. What's he up to?

"Good." He hits the button for the elevator.

"I wonder how Frank made out last night." I laugh a little, shaking my head. Poor bastard!

"Not as well as me, I'm sure."

When the door opens, he waves me forward.

"How long do you think your meeting will be?" I swig my coffee.

"Hopefully, no longer than an hour," he says, glancing at his watch.

"Oh, okay. So we can grab a late lunch and then I'll head out at four ..."

"Wait! *What?!*" His voice rises.

"I have to head home for a couple of hours, but I will come back." I try to remain calm—a hard feat when Mitch is pacing and cursing under his breath.

"Why didn't you tell me this before?"

"When, Mitch?"

"I don't know!" He throws his hand in the air. "In the shower!"

"Before or after you used your superpowers on me?" I smile. Mitch starts to smile in spite of himself, but quickly pushes it away.

"You lied to me!" He points at me, regaining his pissed-off attitude.

"I did not lie to you, Mitch!"

"You said you could stay."

"The *night*!" I emphasize. "Christ, how long is this elevator going to take?" I yell, looking at the numbers. "It's only a couple of hours." I lean up against the wall trying to compose myself.

"I want those hours with you, Charlotte." His voice is softer now. "I'm not going to see you for three months," he adds. Oh.

"Three months?"

Mitch clears his throat. "Yeah."

"Well, let me know which weekend and I'll fly to you," I offer.

"You can't fly to me for a weekend." He shakes his head.

"Why?" I touch his face.

"I'm going overseas. One weekend will give you enough time to fly there and back; that's all." He takes my hand and kisses my palm.

"Oh ..."

"Yeah ... oh. You can barely finagle two nights down in Boston."

"That's not fair, Mitch," I say as the elevator finally stops.

"C'mon." He nods to the lobby and grabs my hand.

I slip my shades on as we walk outside on this sunny May fifteenth. I tilt my head back to take in the warmth of the sun.

"What are you doing?" he asks me impatiently.

"Taking in the sunshine, *sunshine*," I say, smiling over to him. "Oh, Mitch, please don't behave so petulantly." I pull back on his hand.

"I'm not."

"You are." I squeeze.

"Maybe a little." He half smiles as he leads us to Congress Street. He opens the door for me at Charles Schwab. "You have your info?" he asks, placing a hand on my back to guide me.

"Yeah. You want me to open an account here with the check you gave me?" Lightbulb flickers on at half wattage.

"Yes and no. Rip that check up when we leave," he says quietly, before the bank manager almost trips over himself to get to Mitch.

"Mr. Colton!" His tone is a little too enthusiastic as he extends a hand.

"Good afternoon, Mr. Wilson," Mitch says. They shake.

"What can we do for you today, sir?" Wilson asks ... again, too eagerly. *How about not climbing so far up his ass there, Wilson, aye?*

"It's simple today, Wilson. My girlfriend and I want to open a joint account."

Girlfriend? Oh yeah ...

"Of course. Follow me, sir."

Of course? Has he done this before?

"Charlotte ... baby, c'mon." Mitch nudges me along and then bends down to my ear. "What's that look about, baby?"

"Have you done this before?" I whisper.

"No ... why?" He shoots me a quizzical look.

"Why did he say 'of course'?"

"I don't know. Why does he shove his nose so far up my ass every time I come in here that I end up walking out like John Wayne?"

I cover my mouth quickly before a burst of laughter erupts. "Sorry." I smile.

"It's okay ... I like making you laugh." He gives me a sheepish smile. I nudge his shoulder playfully with mine as we walk into Wilson's office. We each take a seat and I notice several awards lining the wall. Glad to see his overzealous brownnosing has paid off for him.

Wilson pulls up Mitch's account like he's on his favorites list. I'm briefly inspired to concoct a plan to see if he indeed keeps such a list, but nah ... I know it's there. A shortcut app on his desktop. Mitch shoots me a curious look. I shake my head at him and mouth "later."

Wilson asks only for my ID. I'm relieved. The only thing I had crammed in my wallet was a notice of disconnect from the electric company. That, I fear, may have embarrassed us both.

"Checking only?"

"Savings too, please. I see you guys offer a 401(k) plan as well?" I ask.

"Yes we do, Ms. McKendrick."

"Good. That opportunity was recently taken away from me." I look over at Mitch, who smiles and shakes his head.

"Do you have a check to deposit or will you be transferring from your other account, sir?" Wilson looks at Mitch.

"Transferring." Mitch nods. Wilson gives him a slip to fill out while having me sign my portion of the paperwork. Wilson's eyes bulge—painfully, I believe—when he looks at the slip. What's that about? Surely he's made deposits for twenty-five thousand dollars before. Wilson asks me to pick out my checks.

We're done in ten minutes, new debit card and starter checks in hand. Wilson walks us back to the door and opens it for us. I hold my hand above my eyes, searching down both sides of the street.

"Now what are you doing?"

"Looking for your horse, Mr. Wayne." I continue my search.

"Knock it off." He chuckles and yanks my hand to bring me along with him.

"So, did it hurt?" I ask.

"Did what hurt, Charlotte?"

I can tell he's trying to humor me.

"When you walked out the door and Wilson's head finally dislodged from your ass."

"Christ, it's awful, isn't it?" He shakes his head.

"Yeah ... a little bit," I agree, swinging his hand after a beat. "Now what, sir?"

"Stop." He gives me "The Look." "My meeting is in twenty minutes. We'll just head back and relax, sound good?"

"Sure. Do you have a laptop I can borrow?" I could set up my bill pay and get rid of some of those pesky creditors that call. Mitch is busy texting. When he finishes, he pockets his phone.

"You'll have a laptop in thirty minutes." He brings my hand to his lips before we reenter the hotel lobby.

"Do you want to order in or go out for lunch?" I ask as we enter the elevator. Mitch just stares at me. He pulls me close and pecks at my lips lightly. "Any food allergies or dislikes?" I ask between kisses.

"No." He kisses me again.

The elevator opens. "It's our floor, Mitch." He smiles slightly and leads me out. "Hey ... what's going on with you?" I ask as we head down the hall.

"I don't know. Sorry." He opens the door. I kick off my flip-flops and lead him over to the couch.

I sit on the end and slap my thigh. "Lie down and rest your head."

"Uh ..." He looks at his watch.

"Your meeting is in the conference room here, I presume?" I arch a brow.

"Yeah."

"You have ten minutes. Head here—now!" I point to my lap and order him sternly.

"All right." He smiles before lying on his back and placing his head in my lap.

"Close your eyes, baby." I say softly and run my fingers over his lids. He closes them and I, using the lightest touch possible, trace over every little line and curve of his face. My right hand gently combs through his hair over and over again.

"Mitch," I say, my voice just above a whisper. "Mitch, baby, wake up."

"Hmm? Huh?" He opens his eyes. "Shit!" He jumps up to a sitting position.

"Shh ... you're okay. You're not late." I rub his back.

"I fell asleep?" he asks, turning forward.

"Yes. I wish you didn't have that meeting. I hated to wake you." I kiss his shoulder. He doesn't say anything. After a moment, he rubs his face.

"I'll see you in an hour," he finally says as he gets up. He leans down and plants a kiss on my forehead.

I look up at him. "You okay?"

"Yeah. I'll be back soon." He gives me a quick peck on the lips, then leaves me alone to twiddle my thumbs.

What to do, what to do? Just as I turn on the TV, there's a knock at the door. I open it to find a man with a box.

"I was told to set this up for you, ma'am." He nods.

"Um ... okay." I let him in, but leave the door open for safety reasons. Of course.

After fifteen minutes or so, the tech leaves me to stare at the screen of a brand-new Mac laptop. *Yeah, I said "borrow," dude!* I hit the icon for the Internet and sign in to my new bank account. My balance pops up and I have to do a double take. What?! No, no ... Wilson put too many zeros! Shit! Well, Mitch can just transfer the money back. Yes ... stop flipping out, Charley.

"HEY," MITCH KISSES my head.

"Hi." I smile up at him, covering the receiver of my phone. "I'll be done in a minute." I point over to the table where the lunch I ordered awaits. "Yes ... the balance," I say to the guy on the phone, confirming that I want to pay off my entire Discover card bill. I give him the number to my debit, get the confirmation after a series of yeses and noes, and hang up the phone. It always amazes me how helpful people are when you have money to pay your bill. "How'd your meeting go?" I walk up to Mitch and wrap my arms around his shoulders from behind, planting a kiss on his cheek before pulling up my chair.

"Very well, thank you." He passes me a salad. "How's your new laptop?"

"Mitch, I asked to borrow one, not for you to buy me one," I complain. He just winks at me with the makings of a smile at his lips.

"So what were you doing when I got in—shopping?"

"No." I open my salad. "I was paying bills."

"You have all of this money at your fingertips and the first thing you do is pay bills?" He looks at me strangely.

"Well ... yeah," I say with some discomfort. *It's been a while since I've been able to pay bills.*

"Buy yourself something, baby." He taps my knee.

"I did."

"What?"

"A roof over my head." As soon as I say it, I wish I could hit rewind and delete. Why did I say that? I can't even muster the courage to look at Mitch.

"Who's your mortgage carried by, baby?" he asks after a few minutes of awkward silence.

"Speaking of banks." I look up, firmly enacting my amazing ability to change the subject. "Wilson had his head so far up your ass, I think he cut off some oxygen to his brain."

"What do you mean?"

"He put one too many zeros in for the transfer. You should go into our account and transfer the money back," I say, before forking a bite of salad too big for my mouth.

"You say he put too much in and you want me to take it out?" He looks at me like ... hmm. I don't know. This is a new look.

"Yes." I nod. He stares at me. "What?"

"Nothing. You're just ... you're a rare breed, Charlotte McKendrick." He looks mystified. I shrug. "So," he starts. "I need to head up to my house in Andover to check on a few things. You'll meet me and we'll stay there tonight."

"What about this place? You've already paid for tonight."

"So what?" he asks, continuing with his lunch. I just stare at him.

I sigh. "I should introduce you to my Aunt Clara."

"Why's that?" He takes a sip of his flavored water.

"She has more money than sense, too."

"Charlotte," Mitch says, and closes his eyes to compose himself ... I think. "Have I once put you down for not having any money?"

"No."

"Then don't put me down for having it!" he snaps.

"Uh ... sor ... sorry," I stammer, feeling like a complete idiot. He's right. That was rude of me.

"I'll give you the address before you leave. That was good, baby, thanks." He throws his container back into the bag.

"Oh, good—can't go wrong with a Cobb salad, it has a bit of everything. There are some huge soft oatmeal-raisin cookies in there." I point to the other bag.

"I'll wait for you." He props his elbow on the table and leans his head against his closed fist.

"Few more bites ... I'm getting full." I chew on another piece. "Mitch, don't do that," I plead.

"Don't do what—talk with my mouth full?"

I roll my eyes and swallow. "Don't just sit there and stare at me like you're trying to figure me out."

"I'd have to be a genius to figure you out in one night. Truth be told, I have a feeling I'll never really figure you out." He reaches forward and thumbs away the dressing at the corner of my mouth. I grab his hand and take his thumb between my lips. My tongue swirls around the tip before I suck purposefully at it. His breath hitches.

"Damn it, Charlotte," he says under his breath. I release his thumb and shoot him a mischievous smile. I take my last bite and start cleaning the table. I peek at the clock—thirty minutes. I come back to the table to stand next to Mitch and grab the bag with dessert. Mitch takes it out of my hand and tosses it. "My dessert isn't in that package," he says, pulling me to him by the waist of my jean capris. He pushes his chair back and moves me in front of him. "Do you know what I thought about the entire time I was in that meeting?" he asks, keeping a steady lock on my eyes. His fingers work at my button and zipper.

"What?" I can barely hear myself.

"I thought about," he says, pulling my capris and panties down, "these lovely legs wrapped around my neck. Then I thought about my face buried between them, my tongue tasting this sweet pussy of yours." A single finger traces my cleft.

"Jesus, Mitch," I gasp and feel myself turn about a hundred shades of red.

"Are you always going to gasp when I say that word, baby?" He smiles—proud of himself, I think.

"Well ... it's the middle of the day." *Wow ... really, Pollyanna?* Mitch laughs and shakes his head. "Don't laugh at me."

"I'm sorry. You're just so cute." He shakes my hips.

"Well, just don't call it the C-word. I hate that word." I sigh.

"Cunt?" He raises his brows.

"Yes. It's a turnoff—don't do it."

"I wouldn't. I don't like it either." He pats the table and I sit on it. "Besides," he says, nudging me to lean back on my elbows, "I couldn't call something so soft, that purrs every time I touch it, anything but a pussy." He opens my legs, sits, and places them over his shoulders. "You ready for your pussy to start purring, baby?" He yanks my hips down to him.

"I think it's already started, Mitch," I say truthfully.

"Jesus, Charlotte," he gasps, then dives in.

I've got one word with four syllables: *me—fucking—ow*!

Chapter Four

SLOWLY (AND BY that I mean fifty miles per hour) I merge onto I-93 North to head home. I should've left half an hour ago, but Mitch was all like, *Purr for me, baby*, and I was all like, *Purr, Mitch*, and so on and so forth.

"Ugh!" I groan and grab my cell to text Mitch.

Why didn't you remind me that it's Wednesday? I just rushed off frantically so I could be surrounded by all the other assholes trying to get home from Boston @ 4:30!

Don't text and drive, Charlotte!

Who's driving?! Certainly not me!

Well, come back here. I'll give you a ride. ;-p

It's your ride, sir, that has me delayed! I could've been in the middle of this party a whole half an hour ago!

It was a good ride, though ... so purrfect. Here, kitty kitty.

Oh, shut up you! I can't believe you branded her with the name

Kitty!
Actually, Kitty Wans'more is her full name.
Okay 007! BTW ... Kitty did wans'more.
Christ—morale is through the roof here!
Bypassed the ceiling, did he?
And the other five fucking floors!
This is Kitty Wans'more, reporting live from the Zakim Bridge ...
How are things in the belly of the beast? Any signs of movement,
Kitty?
I'm afraid not, Morale, and I hate to say it but it's a sad scene
down in the trenches. I'm surrounded by dissatisfied people who
all look zombish.
Zombish is not a word ...
It says right here, "Looks like a zombie but isn't really one ... just
looks that way."
Says right here where? (Eye roll)
In the McKendrick I-know-my-shit-so-shut-up dictionary.
Tell me to "shut up" one more time and you will find yourself across
my knees tonight!
SHUT
the front door! Guy on my left has a very satisfied smirk on his
face.
Why—is he looking at you? ☺
Aw ... but no. I am no match for what has brought on such a
satisfied smirk.
Shall I guess?
You'll never get it ...
I believe I did.
Blush Now guess—you only get 3 chances!
Is he slappin' Pappy?
X
Making nut butter?
XX and ... good God ... WHAT?
Taking a shake break? Slinging jelly? Doing the Roman Helmet
Rhumba? Punchin' the Munchkin? Hacking the hog?
XXX and ... you lied ...
About?

You have WAY too much time on your hands!
☺ **Blush**
Dirty boy! Would you like to know what has satisfied the man next to me so?
Did you flash him your tits? ☺ *WAIT—did you flash him your tits?* ☹
I tried, but like I said, what he has is far more interesting.
I give up! What is it?
He has retrieved something the size of Rhode Island out of his nose! It looks a bit suspect. He's been staring at it and playing with it for five minutes now! His satisfied smirk seems evil. It may very well be RI. You should call the President, just in case. If RI is missing—he's our guy!
You saw through the Booger Shield? Is that your superpower?
Holy crap! It must be! How else could I have seen him pick his nose through the clear window of his car? The Booger Shield must have gone up so no one could see!
But you did! Amazing!
And now, I must do something else.
What are you doing?
I've beeped my horn ...
And?
I've got his attention ...
And?
I've asked him to roll down his window.
No you didn't!
Yes ... shh ... I'm asking him ...
Asking him what?
Asking him what, Charlotte?!
Oh dear ... it couldn't be helped.
What?!
I had to do it ... I had to ask.
Charlotte, goddamn it! What?
I said, "Dude ..."
Ugh ... What?!
"You gonna eat that?" But in a tone that said "'Cause if you're not, I'm totally on it!"
Damn it ... you just made me laugh like a girl! What did he say?

He said ...
Ugh!
"Here ... I'm still full from yesterday's."
I can't stand you!
True story ...
My ass!
Yes ... you do have a nice "ending"! Traffic's moving, baby. Thanks for keeping me company! ☺
Flat leaver ... again!
Can we stop being 12 now?
You started it! ☺

I plug my phone into the car, hit the Pandora app, and put my cello station on. I need to analyze my new situation. That requires a station I won't sing along to. Minimal distractions ... only ... 2Cellos just came on with their version of "With or Without You." *Damn it!* I'm totally gonna belt that shit out—it would be illegal not too!

I look down at my speedometer as the slow crawl picks up pace. I can almost hear her scream, *That's it, baby ... that's it ... give me needle!* She climaxes at sixty-five miles per hour. I giggle at my thoughts. I'd like to blame Mitch for this side of me, but I've always been a closet whore—so to speak. I have a dirty mind with a clean mouth ... well, an acceptable mouth. I think Mitch has cracked my closet door open, though!

Good Lord, what that man has done to my body! I have never been touched like *that*! Sure, I have three kids—I've been touched—but that, that was worship status. His hands felt so incredible on my skin, like they were made to touch my body only. His words were so hypnotic; I was completely under his erotic spell. *"Baby."* His voice was so soft, matching the light touch of his fingertips. *"Your body knows it. Look at how it responds. It knows it belongs to me."*

His fingers slid down my neck to my breast, a barely there touch as he circled my nipple. It hardened so fast—painfully fast. He took it in his mouth, sucking long and hard before biting it. My hips wasted no time moving obsequiously. He had me right there, ready for the taking, but he didn't take me. He was patient and attentive to every inch of my skin. After half an hour or so, I was shivering. And not because I was cold. It was adrenaline ... the anticipation was killing me. I wanted him to fuck me like the dirty whore I was aspiring to be (well, not really, but you know what I'm getting at).

He flipped me onto my belly. I thought surely he'd make me get on my knees and bang the shit out of me, but no! His hands began to worship my backside. Oh, the way he bit my ass! Oh, the way his hands felt. Oh, the sexy way he told me he would have me there, too. I shamelessly pushed my ass hard into his hands. *"Oh, baby ... soon ... when you're ready to take me there."* Christ—damn him and his sexy voice! He had me so riled up; I wanted him inside me. I didn't care where. He could've tried to fuck my ear and I would've been all, *Hell yes, Mitch!*

"Oh ... God!" I yell out. Good Lord ... I just Kegeled my way to an orgasm on I-93 North exit 36. How the hell did he make Kitty purr for him without being remotely close to me? I pull over and grab my phone.

Kitty just purred for you at exit 36. Damn you and your sexy voice and seducing hands!

I get back on the highway. After a few minutes, my phone pings.

Tell Kitty when I see her, she is so FUCKED! And you think my voice is sexy? ☺
Don't text and drive!
Okay ☺

My phone rings. I answer.

"I said don't text and drive!" Mitch yells.

"Not so sexy now, are we?" I ask, a hint of smile in my voice.

"Kitty purred, baby?" Sexy voice ... damn him!

"Oh, did Kitty purr." *I'll give you sexy, bitch.*

"Why, baby?" Even sexier. *He's killing me.*

"Mitch ... stop." The ache in me is unbearable.

"Morale is down ... he misses Kitty. We need to have a staff meeting, stat."

"Hey, you haven't yelled at me for calling you *Mitch*." I have a way with impeccably timing what I mention.

"I'm picking my battles."

"Oh yeah? What battle are you picking next?" I smile as I switch lanes.

"I'm going to have a huge battle with Kitty tonight," he says.

"How come?" *Oh, the aching ...*

"She's getting out of line."

"You gonna put her in her place, baby?" My sexy, seductive voice beams in all its glory.

"Jesus, Charlotte ... I'm gonna fuck you so hard, you might split into two." There's urgency in his voice.

"Don't worry, baby—I have nine lives." I give him a smooch sound and hang up. After a beat, my phone rings. It's Mitch. I hit ignore and smile.

Within no time, I'm getting off exit three in New Hampshire. It's like every neuron in my body can sense that we're almost home. I feel calmer, clearer. Everything's back in its place, surrounded by an invisible safety net—my comfort zone. I pull up to my brick-red Colonial and smile as the kids wave to me from the window. I navigate around the bikes in the driveway and pull up to the garage. Turning off the car, I take a deep breath before grabbing my bag and heading in.

"There's my little girl!" Dad barks out his standard greeting for me.

"Hi, Daddy, how's the fort holding up?" I smile as I walk into his arms.

"Well, we've got 'Giggles' dancing to The Wiggles in the living room. No fever today. Brogan was a champ and got his homework done straight away. He's setting the table now. And Bennett is assisting Gramma in the kitchen. Charley ... his speech is improving every time I see him, I swear. It's because you're a great mom. I'm so proud of you." He kisses my cheek and hugs me a little harder. I suddenly feel the urge to cry. If he only knew what I've done, it would break his heart for sure.

"Thank you, Daddy. Lucky for them, I have wonderful parents who I still learn from every day." I take his arm as he leads me into the house from the mudroom. "Mmm ... Mom, smells good!" I kiss her on the cheek, then turn to Bennett. "Wutcha makin', bacon?" I ask and sign to him.

"I'm nont bacon! I'm Bennint!" He smiles up at me with his huge dimples.

"Ben—net," I say slowly.

"Ben—nint," he replies.

"Getting there, buddy!" I kiss him again.

Brogan walks into the kitchen. "Hey, Mom, can I sleep over Colby's house on Friday?"

"Hi to you too, pal!" I tap the bill of his cap. "Hats off in the house. Where are your glasses?"

"Uh," he says, taking his hat off. "They broke, like, into smithereens. I'm sorry, Mom." He looks down and my heart aches. At nine years old, he looks like he has the weight of the world on his shoulders. Too many nights this guy has snuck up on me when I was having a good cry. He rubs my back and tells me everything's going to be okay. What nine-year-old boy does that?

"It's okay Broge, we'll go tomorrow and get you a new pair." I pull him to me for a hug and kiss his messy, dirty-blond hair.

"But, Mom," he whispers, "how can we do that?"

"Well, I guess I'll make my announcement now," I say.

"You got the job!" Dad throws his hands up in the air.

"I did, and with an advancement, so go ahead, Happy, and give us a jig!" I laugh because Happy is already ten steps into the little jig he does when he hears great news, or just gets excited about something. Everybody's laughing at him as he twirls me around. God, I love my dad!

I started calling him "Happy" when I was around Brogan's age because he just always was! He's always laughing, singing, and dancing. Everybody loves to be around "Happy" Jack O'Brien—I swear most of my boyfriends loved hanging out with him more than me! He's an insightful man who's always ready with a good piece of advice, and he comes up with the best damn metaphors.

One day when I was feeling particularly pissy about things, I turned to his humming self as we raked leaves on this very lawn and said, *"Dad ... how the hell do you stay happy all of the time?"*

"Charley ... you okay, babydoll?"

"Yes, I just don't know how you do it—through the lemons and all!" I threw my arms up in defeat.

"Come, let's sit on the stoop and take a break." He gestured and I followed.

"Charley," he started after a moment of sitting. *"I want you to think of nice big pot of beef stew."* Dad loves him some beef stew! *"Let's*

talk about what we got in that stew. You got your carrots ... they help you to see. You got your onions ... they bring you to tears. You got your potatoes ... they give you comfort. You got your peas ... they give you sustenance. You've got your beef ... that's your strength. Salt and pepper ... your balance. All of these ingredients work together to bring a well-blended flavor to your broth. Only you have control over the flour to make that broth rich and hearty. You know what the key is to keeping your stew in a well-blended, hearty condition?" He shook a finger out at no one.

"What's the key, Dad?"

"To not let anyone come along and piss in your stew."

"Dad," I laughed. "Who would want to piss in a perfectly good stew?"

"The people who can't get their own stew right, honey." He patted my back.

"People really do that? Intentionally, I mean?"

"Honey ... the world is filled with wicked pissas." Dad was so straight-faced when he said that—until we started laughing our asses off, of course.

"Were you afraid you wouldn't get that in?"

"I was ... I was!" he gasped between his laughter.

"Dad, you want me to make you some beef stew now that you got your mouth watering?"

"Jesus, honey, would ya? Your mother's stew is okay, but nothing compares to yours," he whispered, even though Mom wasn't around that day.

"Anything for my dear old pops. I am a little concerned, though," I said.

"About what, honey?"

"Do you think someone's pissing in mom's stew?" I asked, and he swatted at my knee for teasing him.

"So tell us about the job," Mom says after rolling her eyes at Dad and chuckling—her usual reaction to his "Happy" jig. She grabs her mashed-potato casserole to bring to the dining room but almost drops it.

"Mom, are you okay?" I stare straight into her eyes as I hold the dish with her. She stares back too long before answering, which always gives her away.

"I'm fine. Just slipped." She shakes her head, then stops and looks down to her left, avoiding my eyes. Second sign that something's wrong.

"I'll take this, Mom." I gently pull it from her hands.

"I'm not an invalid, goddamn it," she says, then sighs.

"No, you're not, so stop standing there and grab the squash, will ya?" I tease her and grab the potatoes.

This, thankfully, lightens her mood. Mom only gets snippy when she has no control over situations, mainly when she's affected by her— no, she's in remission, it's not that! I eye Dad as I walk into the dining room. He glances away. Fuck, this is not good! This is sooner than last time. Dad brings the oven-roasted chicken legs in while I go to pull Brooklynn (a.k.a. Giggles) away from The Wiggles.

There she is, dancing and giggling to the music. She finally takes notice of me and gives me a face of pure delight, like I'm a puppy she's unwrapped at Christmas.

"Hi, honey!" I hold my arms out for her.

"I, on-nee!" She sort of repeats me and runs into my arms. She's the only one with my dark brown hair and green eyes.

"Ready to eat, mama?" I kiss her little chubby cheek and turn off the TV. Brooklynn gives the best little hugs and I'm smack-dab in the middle of one. Sometimes they make me sad because I know she's my last. I always thought I'd have a couple more. I always wanted a big family. It feels odd, though, that I am the only one out of us five girls that wanted to have a large family. Maybe it's because I'm the baby. Who knows?

Grace is immediately followed by awkward silence at the table. The O'Briens and the McKendricks don't normally *do* awkward silence. We're certainly not going to start tonight!

"So my new job," I start. Oh boy. I wonder if these two can still tell when I'm lying—not that I've had a huge history of it.

"Yes, tell us!" Mom looks happy to be focusing on someone other than herself.

"I've been hired by Colton Technologies. You know that company, Dad, you have stock with them?"

"Very profitable stock, thanks to my daughter." He winks.

"Well, they have a lot of large meetings that need to be catered, and they wanted someone with a flair for comfort food to be responsible for them. They are marketing this whole 'Welcome Home' campaign for their customers, so they want the food to reflect that." I'd like to say that I'm impressed with how quickly that flew out of my mouth, but truth be told, I just described the dream job scenario that I've secretly thought about for a year! I have a Bachelor's in Education, but cooking has always been my passion. I especially love comfort food—from everywhere!

And while I'm thinking about it—all hail Paula Deen, queen of all things buttery and delicious! Ahh ... if I didn't love my mama so much, I would totally fantasize about Paula being my mother. She'd knock on my door, and when I'd open it, her beautiful blue eyes would be glistening, her silver hair perfectly in place. And she'd say, "Baby girl ... I'm your long-lost mama, and I'm so sorry I had to give you up, baby. I was poor and wanted you to have a good life." I'd go right into her arms and cry that I always knew she was my mama. "Don't cry, Charley, I'm here now. We gonna fix ourselves a nice treat and catch up on things." Eh ... okay, so I've daydreamed about that a little. *Sorry, Mom.*

"That's amazing, Charlotte! What an opportunity! How did this all come about?" Uh ... um ... think, Charley!

"Oh, an acquaintance of mine had a little barbeque last week. I don't know if her husband is friends with him, or where the connection was, but ... Mitch Colton, the owner and CEO, was there. Somehow we got to talking, and when I told him what I do, he said they were looking for someone. I told him that I wasn't officially set up as a catering company, that I only catered friends' parties. That seemed to convince him I'd probably be the best candidate." Holy hell—I could totally be an undercover detective!

"See that, Charley?! He tried to piss in your stew, but he missed!" Dad slaps the table, and I know he's talking about Josh.

"He's a wicked missah," I say, and we both laugh.

"Oh, would you two stop speaking in code!" Mom snaps. We do this often.

"Be nice, Shannon, or we won't teach you our secret handshake." Dad wiggles a finger at her. She rolls her eyes.

"So, Mitch," Mom says. "Single?" She mouths the last part. I immediately feel myself blush as I nod.

"Well, from the look on your face, not for much longer." She smiles.

"Mom!"

"Oh, honey, your face lit up from the moment you mentioned his name." She winks. Huh? It did? I try to shrug it off and put more focus into eating my dinner.

Everyone's focus breaks when we hear a ruckus at the front door.

I look around. "Hey, where are the dogs?"

"With me, dipshit." CiCi sighs and comes in, my two Dobermans, Loxy and Vader, following behind her. They immediately attack me with their puppy kisses, although they are not so puppyish anymore.

"Nice to see you too, Ceese."

"That's some greeting, Carissa Catherine!" Mom snaps.

"What can I tell ya, Mom? Nothing but first-class behavior from me," she says playfully, giving our parents a kiss.

CiCi is older than me by eighteen months, and she's the sister I've been closest to my whole life. We've always traveled in the same circles, and while we don't always have similar interests, we like to compare notes. Funny thing is, our sister Caroline is her twin, and they love each other solely because they're supposed to. Other than that, they are polar opposites with completely no understanding of each other.

Dad taps her arm. "When did you get a nose ring?"

"Uh ... like a year ago, Dad." She rolls her eyes.

"I like it." He shrugs.

Her eyes light up. "You want one, Dad?"

"No, honey, I'm happy to live vicariously through you," he says with a chuckle.

"Sit down and eat." I nod to the empty chair. She grabs a plate and does so.

"How was work today, honey? Did you have to wrestle any of your clients?" Dad asks.

"Has Buddy been back?" Brogan laughs. My sister owns her own pet-grooming business and has had one too many battles with this irate little Chihuahua. Despite his name, he's nobody's pal. His owner knows it and pays CiCi double for her troubles.

"No! He's banned—that little fucker!" She forks a chicken thigh.

"CiCi!" I snap.

"Sorry," she says, except her tone is more like "whatever ... get over it" instead of remorseful. "Business is starting to pick up, actually. I can give you some hours, Charley."

"Mom got a new job today, Aunt CiCi!" Brogan interjects, so prideful it makes me love him just a tad bit more than a minute ago.

"Cee Cee," Brooklynn adds.

"Oh yeah? Where?" She smacks my arm. Mom and Dad happily fill her in. I'm grateful to not have to lie again.

"Mitch? Is that the guy you're going out with tonight?" As soon as she says it, she remembers and covers her mouth. *Too late, bitch—I've already unleashed my daggers.*

"Mom?" Brogan looks at me, unsure.

"Hold on, honey." I hold a finger up to him before I turn my eyes back onto CiCi and glare at her some more.

"Stop with the daggers already," she says quietly as she rubs her arm in a protective manner.

"It's not a date-date, honey. We're just hanging out as friends." *Yeah, friends!* I look around the table and see not one person who believes a shittin' thing coming out of my mouth. Even Brooklynn has an eyebrow arched up at me.

"Is he nice, Mom?"

"I think so." I tread lightly.

"Can we meet him?"

"Eventually." *Like when I need to break the contract.* "He's very busy. He flies all over the world, so we won't see much of him."

"So nothing will change here?"

"No, honey. You guys will always be the center of my universe, you know that." I smile. "Although," I add, "This job will need me at the drop of a dime. They are paying me a lot of money to be able to be there when they need me. So I will be hiring a nanny to help us out here."

"Charley, we'll help out," Mom pipes up.

"I know that, Mom," I say with a half smile, "but I may have to travel or stay in Boston overnight. I need someone here so when I have to leave, there's not a step out of place. I don't have to worry about other people's schedules this way. Besides, it'll be good to have someone, if anything, around here to get stuff done." I take my last bite. "And, Brogan, don't worry, I'll make sure we all like this person. Okay?" He just nods. This poor kid—too many changes in such a short time. I'm beyond grateful that I've managed to save our house from foreclosure. I think losing this house and moving would've been more than we could all bear.

"CHARLEY, HONEY, YOUR phone is ping-ponging!" Dad yells up the stairs as I finish tucking in the boys.

"Grandpa," Brogan says, chuckling at the "ping-ponging" comment. I laugh with him. "Have fun tonight, Mom." He hugs me.

"I will. Get to sleep now." I kiss his head, then turn around to find Bennett has already passed out. Loxy and Vader walk in and take their respective places, Loxy with Brogan and Vader with Bennett. I give them kisses, too—vicious sweethearts.

I close the door and head downstairs, but immediately pick up my pace when I hear my dad yelling. Dad *never* yells!

"Listen here, you disrespectful son of a bitch, don't you ever let me hear you talk or text, or however you kids communicate with each other, that way to my daughter again or I won't put you over my knees—I'll break your fucking knees with a baseball bat! I don't care who you are!" he yells into my cell phone.

"Daddy, who is that?" *Josh?*

"Charley, you don't need to be dating a prick like this!" he snaps, then continues on the phone. "She's a smart, beautiful girl, and a wonderful mother. You ought to consider yourself lucky to know her, and even luckier she's giving you the time of day! Do your parents know you talk to women like this?" he yells, then listens. "Well, I'm sorry about your mother, son," Dad cools off a little. "Were you close to her?" he sighs. I stare at him, baffled at his sudden mood change. "Well, how would you feel if someone had talked to her the way that you talked to my daughter?"

"Dad! Who are you talking to?" It's not Josh. *Oh, for the love of*

God ... please, no.

"It's Mitch, honey," he says, giving me an assertive nod to let me know he's handling the "situation." "Oh ... she did?" His eyes wrinkle at the corners. "Yes, yes she is. Yep ... everything! Uh-huh ... yes ... did she?" He laughs, and I can't believe it. Mitch is charming the pants off my father. Happy threatened busted kneecaps, and now he's warning Mitch not to take me fishing because I'll shame him. "I'm always up for fishing, Mitch! Sure ... sure! You want to talk to Charley now? Okay, son." *Son?* "And we have an understanding, right?" Dad gets all serious again. "She's been through a lot, Mitch. She deserves only someone with good intentions. Don't piss in her stew, Mitch! Here she is, son." He hands me the phone, but I stare at it as if I've never seen one before and have no idea as to what I'm supposed to do with it.

"Charlotte?" I hear him call out. I finally bring it to my ear.

"Uh ... hi." I'm barely audible. Dad gives me a nod of encouragement.

Mom walks in the living room with a very upset Brooklynn. "Charley, she won't go down for me."

"I'll take her, Mom." I grab her. "Sorry ... can you hold on?" I ask in the phone.

"Of course, baby," Mitch says, with not a hint of anger. *Huh?* I'm a little—okay, a lot—confused.

"Mama ... ow-wee," Brooklynn whimpers.

"Your toothies hurt, baby?" I ask her as we climb the stairs. She nods. "Let's get you some medicine." I kiss her cheek and walk into the bathroom. I give her some pain reliever and then bring her to her room. Satisfied that the "ow-wees" will be gone soon, she snuggles up to her lovey. "Night, mamas," I say softly and put on her Pooh Bear light show. I close the door behind me and head to my room.

"Hi," I sigh.

"Hi," he says, followed by a loud burst of silence from both of us. "So ..." he starts. *Oh God, here we go—here it is!* I sit on my bed, waiting to hear him tell me that it's over. I fight off the little ache in my chest. "I think your dad will let me take you to the prom now," he finishes, and my relief brings on a fit of giggles. That's not exactly what I was expecting him to say. At all. "Can you still come tonight?"

"Will you have me back before curfew?" I grab my overnight bag and put a few things in.

"Absolutely not."

"Okay. Well then, I'll be leaving here in about ten minutes." I throw in my new lingerie.

"Is your baby okay?"

I'm taken aback by the concern in his voice.

"Yeah, she's just teething." I stop packing. "Mitch?"

"Hmm?"

"I have kids."

"Is that a hidden talent of yours?"

"What—having kids? I suppose I'm good at it, I have three." I finish packing and crack a smile at the sound of Mitch's laughter.

"Stating the obvious—is that your hidden talent?" he clarifies.

"Oh, yeah ... that too!" I say.

"Hurry up and get here, baby. I'll text you the address."

"Okay. I'm heading out now." I whip my capris and T-shirt off to throw on a short sundress before flicking the light switch.

"Drive safe, baby. I'll leave the door unlocked for you." Sexy voice ... *mmm.*

"Okay. See you soon. Love you, bye!" I hang up. *Shit! Oh crap, oh crap!* My phone pings.

:-o!!

Stop it! It's habit! I love most people I talk to on the phone, so I always say that. No need to loosen your tie and pull at your collar to get more air!

It is a little warm in here, isn't it?

It's about to get real hot in forty minutes ...

Mmm ... ☺ Just don't shoot hearts out of your eyes at me.

How about out of Kitty?

I ♥ Kitty

More like ♥on

Get here five minutes ago, please!

I'm on it!

You will be!

Me♥w!

I head downstairs and find my parents getting ready to leave.

"Call me tomorrow. I want to hear about your date, honey." Mom hugs me. *Oh geez!*

"Sorry I got carried away, Charley. I just didn't like what he said." Dad says, then hugs me as well.

"That's all right, Daddy," I say.

We all head out together, leaving CiCi to hold down the fort and watch reality shows I've never heard of like it's her job.

Chapter Five

Mitch

LOVE YOU. I know it was accidental, but those two simple words suddenly sounded like the most amazing thing I'd ever heard, simply because they were powered by her voice.

Ugh! This is Gram getting in my head! We were knee-deep all of five minutes into our visit and she asked, *"What's her name?"*

"Charlotte," I said, then went back to what I was originally talking about, which was not Charlotte.

It creeps me out when she does that shit.

"What?" I finally asked her, after a few minutes of her huge smile.

"I'm not saying. It's too soon," she said.

She didn't say any more, partly because Maggie complained about us signing so fast to each other, which made it difficult for her to properly "eavesdrop." Which reminds me, I need to ask Gram what she was going to say. I'll stop by tomorrow before I leave.

Another half an hour. Thirty minutes 'til she's back in my arms. Christ—I haven't craved a woman like this in years. Just five hours, and I feel like it's been days ... weeks, even. This feeling is achingly familiar, and yet so foreign to me.

I'm just in a weird funk. We'll have three months apart—long enough for me to cool my jets. Tonight, though, I'm going to bathe in this ... in her. It's been too long. Too long since I've touched a woman the way I found myself touching her ... worshipping, really. Too long since there was someone I wanted to protect and provide for. Since a woman made me laugh so easily (shit ... I laughed like a teenage girl today!). Too long since I've felt ebullience.

Her honesty—cripples me.

Her green eyes—Kryptonite to my soul.

Her touch—ignites every fiber of my being.

Her mind—intrigues me.

Her heart—inspires me.

Fuck ... I'm doomed. I'm going to take the next three months to talk myself down and shake her out of my system, but I know what's going to happen. After three months, she'll walk into my arms and I'll want more. How the fuck did this happen? *How did I let this happen?* No, no ... I'm in a funk. Gram's got me going crazy—her and her sixth-sense shit!

She tells me all the time that I have it too, that's why I've done so well for myself. That it's that gut instinct I never hesitate to follow. She's right about that—I do what my gut tells me to. I never falter from it. My head usually follows suit; no internal battle.

Now here comes Charlotte, and I've got my gut and my head pulling my heart into two different directions! *Fuck. Fuck. Fuck and shit.* Sometimes, those are the only words one can use in a certain situation. And this is certainly a situation.

"Shit, baby, that must be a real humdinger! If your face looked any more perplexed, you'd turn into a shar-pei." I jump, and Charlotte smiles. I glance at my watch and back up to her. She's fifteen minutes early. I should be happy about this, but I feel like I'm about to boil over instead.

"Goddamn it, Charlotte! How fucking fast were you flying?" I get up as I scream at her.

"There was no traffic. I don't live that far away." She seems unsure as I close the gap between us.

"How fast?" I ask through my teeth and grab her upper arms.

"What is the matter with you?" She tries to pull away.

"What is the matter with me?!" I yell in her face and let go of her arms. I walk away, running my hands through my hair. "You said a couple of hours, Charlotte—it's been five!" *Stop, Mitch. Pull yourself together.* "You left your phone out in the open for anybody to see my texts, and I got my ass chewed out by your father like I was some punk kid down the street!" *Fuck it ... I'm gone!*

"Then you drive here like some crazy bitch in heat." At this, her eyebrows arch and she bites back her sexy little smile. *Damn her and that smile!* I have to look away. "With no regard for your safety." I turn my back to her, calming down as my chest tightens. "If anything ever happened to you, baby ... " I almost don't recognize my own voice, so I let it trail off.

I feel Charlotte's arms wrap around my waist from behind. One hand stays on my stomach. The other travels up my chest and rests over my heart. Her lips press against my back and my shirt fails to extinguish the warmth of her kiss. I slowly exhale through pursed lips and try to keep my heart from beating out of my chest.

"I did seventy, like I always do. It's rare for me to go above that, and it's only five miles over the speed limit. There was no traffic. I overestimated how long it would take just in case, so I wouldn't be late. I'm sorry I scared you." Another kiss. "I'm sorry my dad ripped you a new one, but after reading that text you sent me, I can say my reaction wouldn't have been any different than his," she says.

"I still want to throw you over my knees and spank the shit out of you—even more so now," I say truthfully.

"Traffic was a bitch today, as you know. I also have a family that needs me, Mitch, and I'm not set up to handle our arrangement yet. I will be when you come back, I promise. If it's any consolation, those five hours were the longest ever. I feel like I haven't seen you in days."

I inhale sharply at her words. Christ, her veracity kills me. I cover her hands with mine. She rests her cheek against my back and slowly tightens her squeeze on me. I feel as if I'm diving off a cliff with the most breathtaking view, only I don't know whether there will be beautiful, clear water greeting me at the bottom, or if I'll fall to my death.

"You hungry, baby? I brought stuff to make you something to eat, just in case." She lifts her head.

"You're going to feed me, baby?" I turn to her, embracing the calm she's managed to bring me once again. Finally, I take in the sight of her for the first time since she's made her presence known. "Damn it, Charlotte." I touch her face. "Why do you have to be so pretty?" I whisper before nudging her lips. I probably should have said "beautiful," but sometimes a simpler word like "pretty" seems like a bigger statement to me.

She has her wavy mane up in a mess of hotness, tendrils falling everywhere. She changed into a simple yellow Calico-printed sundress (damn it, Gram, for being the reason I know what a fucking Calico print is—Christ!) with spaghetti straps. I prefer her hair down, but Jesus, her neck is gorgeous. My hands glide down it. Her skin is so soft. They fall to her breast, my thumbs quickly greeted by her hardening nipples.

"You went out with no bra on? One swift wind and anyone could see this." I pinch hard.

"Ah," she gasps, then smiles. "I wore a sweater, baby. No one could see what's yours," she says. I nod, feeling a bit ridiculous now—and completely turned on by her words. She throws her hands around my neck. "So, you want to eat?" This time I raise an eyebrow. She giggles. "Food!" She shakes her head and I can't resist smiling. *So damn pretty!* "Don't worry, Mitch ... when I'm done feeding you, I'm going to fuck you ... being a bitch in heat and all."

"Charlotte," I gasp.

"What? It's not the middle of the day anymore, and you know what they say ..." She smirks, pulling away from me to head to my kitchen.

"What do they say, baby?" I love to humor her. She hasn't disappointed me yet.

"The freaks come out at night," she says, smiling back at me. I swat her ass playfully, making her yelp and laugh. *Doomed. I'm fucking doomed.*

"OKAY, ERICA, I'LL check my schedule now. See you in Tokyo on Tuesday. Have a good night." I sigh and hang up. Shit, if I'm staying an extra week in Japan, this is probably going to push Germany back, which will create a domino effect. Normally, I wouldn't care about extra time overseas, but I didn't have Charlotte to come home to before.

I head back to the kitchen and I'm hit with the wonderful aroma of bacon. Charlotte's cutting stuff up at the counter next to the stove, and she pauses to turn the bacon. I quietly put my phone down on the island before walking up behind her. She jumps a little when I grasp her hips and bury my face into her neck.

"It's almost done." She lowers the heat.

"Mmm ... between the smell of bacon and my woman," I say, inhaling her scent deeply at her neck, "I have to admit, I'm fighting off the urge to drag my knuckles on the floor like a caveman." *Did I just fucking say that out loud?*

She turns her head and looks up at me, laughing.

"Jesus, you're not going to clobber me over the head with something, are you?"

"I did, baby—a big ole bank account!" I smirk. Her smile fades and she gives me a slight nod before looking back to the bacon.

"Go sit while I put this together," she says quietly.

"Charlotte," I whisper near her ear and squeeze her hips.

"Please, Mitch ... go sit," she begs. Her body tenses.

"No," I stay as sternly as I can. "I shouldn't have said that. I'm sorry."

"It's okay, Mitch. You spoke the truth." She places the bacon on paper towels.

"Don't, Charlotte ... don't pull away from me." I close my eyes and rest my forehead against her messy bun.

"I have to toast your bread." She holds the bread in front of her and points over to the toaster.

"What are you making me?" I let go but stand near her with my back against the counter.

"Turkey club. Is that okay?" She eyes me for my approval.

"I'd eat anything you make, baby." I reach for her cheek with the back of my fingers. She flinches and jerks away. I wince from the crushing feeling in my chest and let my hand fall back down, then study her. In the short time we've known each other, this is the first time I'm aware of this wall she has. Here it is though, in all its glory—resurrected by my words.

I continue watching her as she puts my sandwich together and walks my plate over to the table. I grab a drink and take a seat.

"Do you want me to sit with you while you eat, or shall I go to your room and get ready for you, Mitchell?"

My head jerks up at her formality. She looks away from me.

"Why don't you take a little tour of the house and learn where everything is?" I try to keep my voice steady. She's overreacting, but I certainly don't want to add fuel to the fire. She stands, staring at me. "Go ahead, Charlotte," I say gently. She lets out a frustrated sigh. "What?"

"Take a bite of your sandwich." She points to it.

"I will. Go on your tour."

"I need to see you take your first bite." She rolls her eyes, but somehow I don't feel it's directed toward me.

"Why—is it poisoned?" I widen my eyes, teasing her and hoping to get a glimpse of her old self.

"No, you dumbass! I need to see that you like it!" Her impatience makes me chuckle a little. I think she's more frustrated with herself for needing to see me take the first bite than my procrastination.

"Did you just call me a dumbass?" I'm having a terrible time trying to keep the grin off of my face.

"It's a step up from what I called you in my head a few minutes ago." Her stolid expression makes me laugh out loud. I can't believe I'm taking this crap from her—and enjoying it! I stop laughing, curious about the look she's giving me.

"What does that look mean?"

She sits. "What look?"

"The one you just gave me when I was laughing." I pick up a triangle of the sandwich. Damn it, she even stuck each triangle with a toothpick to hold it together. Who does that at home? *Charlotte does ...*

She sits at the edge of her seat as I go in for my first bite. "This is riveting for you, isn't it?" I ask. She slumps back with frustration.

"Can you just take a bite?" She sighs, defeated. I bring the sandwich up to my mouth, but quickly pull it away and smile.

"Let's make a deal."

"I would, but I don't have a crazy costume and I already know what's behind door one." She smirks sarcastically.

"I'm interested in exploring door number two." I wink at her. She fidgets in her seat and turns a hundred shades of red.

"You're blushing. Do you not want me to touch you like that?" I ask.

Charlotte swallows hard, closing her eyes. "I'm yours to touch any way you choose," she finally says.

I would've rather received a sucker punch to the gut than sit here and watch another level of that wall she's building go up. I know it's my fault. I reminded her of what we are. I didn't mean to. I take in a deep breath after a moment of awkward silence.

"I won't touch you again until I'm invited to do so." I exhale forcefully. *There's that look again.* "What is that look, Charlotte?" I no longer hold back my impatience.

"You're enigmatic, and I'm not sure if I can handle that." She starts off strong but finishes weak.

"I think you handle me just fine. In fact, I think you handle me so well, it makes me uncomfortable." I glance down and shake my head. While I'm looking, I should probably check to see if my balls are still attached.

"Eat your sandwich, Mitch." She pushes the plate closer. I stare at her, shaking my head. "Ugh! You wanted to make a deal. I'll make a deal with you! If you will please eat, I'll give you a Get Out of Jail Free card!"

"Get-out-of-jail-free card?"

"Yes. You've mentioned spanking me several times. You know that's a deal breaker for me."

"Is it?" I smirk playfully.

"Yes. I don't like it."

"If it makes you feel any better, you're the only woman I've had a desire to spank," I offer.

"Why would it make me feel better to know I do everything wrong?" she asks.

"Baby—the glass is half full."

"Stop speaking in riddles, Mitch!"

"Don't be so pessimistic. It might just be because you do every-thing right." I wink again. She rolls her eyes. "So, if I eat this sandwich, I get a Get Out of Jail Free card?"

"Yes. I won't break up with you." She said *break up*, not *rip up the contract*. Is she feeling the same way I am? *Is she fighting it too?*

"Why is it so important to you that I eat this?" I lift the food.

She groans and takes a minute before a lightbulb apparently comes on. "Have you ever seen *The Wedding Singer*?"

"Yes. What does that have to do with this?"

"You know the little old lady who pays him in meatballs, and needs to see him eat them?"

"Yes." I look at her funny.

"I'm the little old meatball lady, Mitch! It brings me joy to see sat-isfaction on people's faces when they eat my food." Her animation is killing me. I feel like my Charlotte is back.

"Hi, baby." I smile at her.

"Yes, hi ... please eat," she begs.

"I missed you," I say, then take a bite. Her eyes widen—totally re-minding me of the meatball lady. I'd laugh, but I just got hit with a burst of flavor I was not expecting. My eyes roll back and Charlotte claps her hands with excitement. "What's in this?" I groan, then laugh at her.

"You like it?" Her smile is huge.

"Almost as much as I like you." I take another bite. "Charlotte?"

"Yes?" She plays with her hands.

"You misconstrued what I said before." I wait for her to look up. "I meant it playfully, and certainly not in the way you took it. I don't see you like that. If I did, I would've stuck to the original plan of payment. Today was a statement, in a way, that I want this all to be very real. I want to provide for you like I would if there were no contract."

"But there is a contract," she interjects.

"Yes, and you will adhere to it as planned." I feel my frustration building. Christ—I've almost laid out my cards without even knowing what's in my hand.

"Mitch, I will never give or ask for more. I have enough 'more' on my plate. I will follow the contract and be at your beck and call. I will lay my body down for you, but not my heart. Don't ever expect my heart—it's not for sale."

Her words choke the very breath out of my lungs.

"I'm going to finish this." I nod to the sandwich. "Go upstairs and get ready for me." She offers me a weak smile and heads up. As soon as I hear the door close upstairs, I practically knock my chair down, jumping to my feet. I think more clearly when I pace.

I know I need to stay calm. Cool heads will prevail! *Settle down, Mitch. Think.* There's nothing to think about—it's all right in front of me! I'm going with my gut; it's never steered me wrong before. I just need to go about this a little differently ... like being patient. She's been through a lot, like her dad said. Josh, that fucking idiot! Though I am grateful to him. If he weren't such an idiot, she wouldn't be in my arms now. I plan on keeping her there. I can't hit her with too many feelings; it causes a flight reaction in her. I'm not going to behave beyond the contract's requirements, which actually gives me plenty of room for interpretation. *No, Charlotte, I won't buy your heart, but I will earn it!* Game on, baby!

"Another humdinger?" I turn around to find Charlotte biting her smile back.

"You have no idea, baby." I grab my drink.

"So ... you don't like it?" She points to the sandwich.

"No, I do. I'm going to finish it right now." I smile and grab the last piece.

"Do you have any red wine?"

"I should." I head over to the corner cabinet. "Cab Sauv okay?" I look over my shoulder.

"Sure." She takes the bottle from me.

"Uh ... this one." I open the drawer next to the one she's digging in and hand her the corkscrew.

"Thanks." She takes it from me and tries to figure out how to use it.

"Here." I smile and stand behind her. "This goes on here ... and ..." *Christ, she smells lovely.* She looks up at me. I stare down into her beautiful eyes—Kryptonite.

"Mitch," she manages before rising on her toes for a kiss. I sweep her lips softly. "Do you want some?" she asks. It takes me a moment to register that she's talking about the wine.

"No, I'm good. Need to finish my sandwich or I won't get a free spank-Charley-good card." I kiss her nose.

"You're gonna spank me good?" She's trying to sound playful, but I can hear her nerves clear as a bell.

"Yes I am, but I am going to save it for a situation when you've behaved very badly." I palm her ass. "Jesus, baby ... I may have to *create* a situation." I squeeze and listen to her breathe erratically. "What do you have going on under here, by the way?" I try to lift her short, white silk robe.

"Stop it, you!" She smacks my hand away. "I thought you weren't going to touch me until you were invited to do so," she says, then turns back to the wine and tries to open it.

"It's gonna be like that now, baby?" I lower my voice near her ear.

"Mmhmm," she hums, then throws her hands palm-down on the counter, clearly frustrated.

"Need help?"

"Yes, please." She looks up at me. I trap her between the counter and me and slowly push up against her as I unscrew the cork.

"I see Morale is up," she murmurs, then gives me a dose of my own medicine as she pushes back against me.

"Invite me to touch you, baby." My lips almost touch her ear.

"No."

"Invite me." I push harder.

"No." She pours her wine.

"Baby, I may have to go back on what I said." I run my nose up her neck, inhaling her.

"Are you sniffing me?" She giggles.

"No! Please ... I wouldn't do that." I jerk my face back and chuckle. "Okay ... maybe a little."

"Mr. Colton." She turns to me with laughing eyes. I immediately go for the knot in her robe.

"Uh-uh ..." She taps my hand.

"I need to touch you, Charlotte." I close my eyes, almost begging.

"Okay, but if you go back on your word, you're going to miss out."

"Miss out on what?" I take her extended hand.

"Me touching the hell out of you." She walks backward, staring at me like I'm a big juicy steak. It makes me want to hand her a fork and knife so she can dig in. "Well?" She raises an eyebrow.

"I'd like you to touch the hell out of me, baby." *Damn, she's sexy.*

"Good." She sips her wine. "Me too." She walks forward again, holding my hand behind her. She climbs the stairs slowly, offering me a view to die for: white lace panties that end just above the curve of her cheeks. *If I just lean forward a little further, I can nip at the skin there.* I shake my head and try to find something else to look at. My gaze drops, taking in her gorgeous bare legs. Legs that were wrapped around my neck this afternoon while I greedily feasted on her pussy—her delicious pussy. I slap my head to force myself to focus.

She looks over her shoulder. "Everything okay back there?"

"Yep ... just trying not to drag my knuckles back here," I say truthfully, and am rewarded with her giggle. I am amazed at how easy things are with her, yet still so difficult.

We walk into my bedroom and I can already smell the essence of *her*.

"What?" she asks, setting her wine down and pulling her hair out of its tie. It tumbles down, and I fight the urge to dive my hands in.

"It smells like you in here," I start. She crooks her head sideways. "I like it."

"Good." She slides her hands up my chest and slowly unbuttons my shirt. I place my hands on her hips. "Uh ... no touching, Mr. Colton." She taps my hands. I squeeze before I let go. "Bad boy," she mumbles.

"I can be." I try to kiss her. She pulls her hands away and crosses her arms.

"Let me know when you're ready to behave."

"Sorry, baby. I'm ready." I try to hold back my smile.

Satisfied, Charlotte runs her hands up my chest again and pushes my shirt off my shoulders. She bites at my left shoulder while pulling my tank top out from my pants. I help her tug it over my head. Her mouth travels hot up my neck to my chin and then down my jawline. She nips below my ear and every muscle in my body twitches as I try to control myself.

"Mitch."

Damn her sexy voice.

"Yes." I clear my throat as her lips hover near my ear.

"You may kiss me only when I am kissing you. Under no circumstances will you touch me unless I tell you to. Do you understand?"

"Yes."

"I'm going to taste and touch every inch of your skin until I'm satisfied with the level of crazy I'm driving you, and then, Mitch ..." She takes a break to suck at my earlobe. "I'm going to take you in my mouth and then fuck you so hard you erupt like a volcano that's lain dormant for a thousand years. Would you like that, baby?" She starts at my belt.

"Jesus Christ, Charlotte ... Jesus Christ!" It's all I can say because I think I may be having an asthma attack. Christ, I might even come undone from her words.

"Mitch, before I get started, I need to show you what my thoughts are doing to me. What *you* do to me." She looks straight into my eyes as she guides my left hand onto her hip. "You can touch me this once. Stop when I tell you and don't do it again until I'm ready for you to take me." *God help me ... she's going to make me lose my mind tonight.* She takes my hand and brings it to the knot on her robe. "Undo my robe, Mitch." My heart is pounding so loud in my ears. I untie it and she pulls the robe off.

I can't even stand the sight of her in her lacy white babydoll. It's split open at her belly and I want to trace her navel with my tongue. Her nipples stretch against the material, eager to greet me. She takes my hand again and brings it to her stomach. Slowly, she slides it down. "Mitch, I want you to touch me. Touch what's yours, baby, and see what you do to me." *Oh, those jade eyes.* I turn my palm to rest against her belly. I watch her close her eyes, lick her upper lip, then bite her bottom one as my hand slowly slides under the band of her panties. It travels over her mound and slides underneath. My fingers push her open and I take in a sharp breath.

"Goddamn it, Charlotte." I can barely breathe as my fingers swirl around in her wetness.

"See what you do to me, how ready I am for you, how badly I want to stretch for you, baby?" I barely let her finish saying "baby" before I plunge my fingers deep inside of her. Her pelvis rocks with my thrusts and a few soft moans escape her throat. "Mitch ... oh, Mitch ... you have to stop now." She tries to pull away.

"No," I say sternly. "I want inside of you now, Charlotte." I start to nudge her back to the bed.

"Mitch." She looks straight into my eyes. "Please, stop."

"Ugh!" I groan, pulling my hand away.

"Good boy. My hip ... eh, my ass, I guess, too." She laughs, looking down at the hand that I've slid around her. She grabs it and leads me to the bed. I try to pull myself together as she undoes my pants and then whips them down. "Jesus, Mitch!" Her eyes widen at my erection.

"Yeah, I thought I'd knock a few walls down while I was up here." I look around.

"I think you could ... with no problem." Her eyes dance playfully at me and once again I'm captivated by her beauty. I never thought I'd meet another woman who would make me feel ... *everything*. Everything you feel when you've found someone who helps you naturally be yourself. There are no reservations, just acceptance.

"Lie down, Mitch," Charlotte says, pushing my chest lightly with a curious look on her face.

"Why are you looking at me like that, baby?" I ask as I climb back.

"Because you're deep in thought."

"I was, but now I'm back, focusing on my gorgeous girlfriend."

"You'd better be." She gives me a crooked smile as she climbs on top to straddle me. "No, Mitch." She smacks my hands away. I let out a frustrated groan. "Close your eyes, sweetie." She kisses me. *Mmm ... so soft.* I close my eyes and inhale deeply her lovely scent.

Charlotte takes my hands and places them just above my head. Her nipple skims over my lips. I nip gently.

"Mitchell—I don't know your middle name—Colton!" she yells. I can't help but laugh. *Carefree ... I forgot how nice this was.*

"I don't have a middle name, baby," I say, a huge grin stretched across my face.

"Mitchell Colton." Her breath hits my face. "The longer you behave badly, the longer it will take me to please you." She strums her fingers over my lips.

"That's not possible." I kiss them and open my eyes to look into hers. "You're here ... in my arms. Consider me pleased." I lean up and grasp her lips. She parts them and palms my face as I deepen the kiss. Christ! Her tongue is so soft and seductive.

"Mitch," she complains against my mouth when my hands find her ass.

"These panties are killing me. I want to bite you all along here." I run my fingers along the bottom where her cheeks pop out.

"Okay ... hands off," she says, too much amusement in her voice for me to take her seriously. She tries to grab my hands, but I get hers and swiftly roll her onto her back. She fights me as I raise her arms above her head.

"That's it, baby—fight me. Make me work for it." I pin both arms down with one hand and let the other slide up and under her babydoll. Her left nipple greets my fingers eagerly. My touch is gentle at first, but that quickly changes to accommodate her sensory needs. I'm already learning my baby's signals. When she arches her back, giving me more access, she wants me to be harsher. Her moans tell me I'm right. My mouth replaces my hand so I can pull at her panties.

"No!" She jerks her lower body in an attempt to push me off.

"You're not going to make this easy for me, are you?" I pin her legs down with mine. "Hope you're not attached to these." I rip her panties. "'Cause you're not anymore." I pull them off her. She stares at me in shock as I climb over her, still holding her in place. "First mistake you made was taking too long to seduce me. I'm an impatient man, baby." I kiss at her neck. "Second mistake was showing me how I affect you." I force her legs open and grind up against her.

"Third mistake?" she asks, trying to control her breathing. I shake my head. "I like when you take charge ... it turns me on." She pushes against my arms, making me tighten my grasp.

"For someone who doesn't like to get spanked, you sure don't know how to prevent it from happening." I bite at her lip.

"You're mad at me?"

"What? No, baby!" I look at her strangely. "I want to spank you be-cause you turn me on, not because I'm mad at you. That, and you have an ass that screams 'Spank me!'" I echo my voice and she laughs. "I'll never hurt you, Charlotte ... not with intention." I soften my gaze and collect her lips.

"You gonna make Kitty hurt, baby?" She raises her pelvis to me, enticing me.

"Does Kitty want to hurt, Charlotte?" I use my sexy (as she calls it) voice and nip at her earlobe.

"Baby, Kitty's been aching since I left this afternoon. Aching so deeply inside." *Damn her and her seductive tone.*

"Aching for what? Tell me." I release her arms as I trail kisses across her chest.

"A boost of Morale, baby." She pulls at my hair as I take her right nipple into my mouth. Just when I let my guard down, she flips me onto my back.

"Damn!" I sigh. She giggles and puts all of her weight into pinning my arms down. I watch as she moves her mouth down my chest. The lower she goes, the less of an advantage she has on me. As soon as she releases enough pressure, I fling her onto her back again and harshly enter her.

"Checkmate, baby," I groan as I bury myself deeper inside of her. "You okay?" I lightly graze her cheek as she finally exhales.

A smile forms at her lips. "Control freak."

"I heard a rumor that you like that." I nudge her nose with mine before kissing her.

"You heard correctly, Mr. Colton." She kisses me back.

"Perfect. Just ... perfect," I whisper as I trace the few lines on her face.

"Uh ... Mitch, Kitty would like to scratch your post now, if you know what I mean." She nudges me with her knee.

"This post?" I roll my hips.

"Yes," she gasps.

"This one?" I roll a little harsher and deeper.

"Oh God ... yes." Her fingers dig into my shoulders and her legs wrap around my back.

"Is this what my baby wants?" I thrust again. Quite frankly, I'm not sure who I'm torturing more here. "Because whatever my baby wants, she will always get. I'll give you the world, Charley." *There I go ... laying my cards down again, damn it!* In my defense, my dick is caught in a vice grip, telling me that Kitty definitely wans'more. It may be cutting off circulation to my other head.

"Mitch ... that's nice," Charlotte says. "But will you kindly shut up and fuck the hell out of me now?" Her voice is driven by sexual frustration, and just in case I didn't gather that on my own, she heels my ass.

"Baby," I say, grabbing her hands and pinning them above her head, "buckle up."

"Oh, thank Christ!" she says before I begin a course of relentless pounding. She orgasms almost instantly, which just drives me to a whole other level of crazy. I let go of her hands and quickly feel arms encircle me, holding me as we rock slowly together. Her body relaxes when she finishes her last quake. I raise her leg, and her calf casually falls onto my shoulder. I stare deeply into her eyes. *It's all there.* I can see it—my future. My gut finally has my head convinced and I feel my heart exploding.

"Mitch?" She reaches up to caress my face. I bring her leg back down to go around my waist. Slowly, I dip my head down and kiss her lips. My hand firmly finds a place on her hip, and I move at an agonizing, torturous pace. My eyes stay on hers as I make love to her, savoring every sound that escapes her throat.

Chapter Six

Charlotte

"MA'AM ... I said that's two hundred, forty-three ninety-six," the cashier sighs impatiently and pops her gum.

"Huh? Oh." My fog lifts. "Sorry." I shake my head and run my new bank card through.

"Have a nice day." She smirks. Christ—what a brat! Shouldn't she be in school? Brooklynn leans forward in the cart and rests her head against me.

"Can I get someone to help me out to my car?" I ask the bagger as I stare at my two overflowing carts. She waves over a young man who grabs my other cart.

"You know, Brooky ... I think I'll take a nap this morning, too," I say around a yawn as I back our fully-grocery-loaded Highlander out of the parking space. I turn the radio on, hardly believing it's after ten a.m. It's been almost four hours since I left the clutches of Mitch's arms. He was in such a deep sleep; I didn't want to wake him, so I left him a note. Besides, I'm a little ... hell, *a lot* more upset about not seeing him for three months. It'll be good for me, though. I'm falling hard and fast for him, against my better judgment. The things he said to me didn't help, either. I'm not quite sure what all of that was about. I almost feel as if he's developing the same feelings for me, but then I have to remind myself that he's paying me to be his girlfriend. He's just playing the part, making it seem real for himself—right?

I glance into the rearview mirror quickly. "Oh, Brooklynn." I sigh at the sight of her completely passed out. *Shit!* I hope she transfers well today—I desperately need her to nap! Although, the fact that I was up most of the night having amazing sex instead of dealing with a sick child (which would be my usual reason for being up all night) puts a little spring in my step. I pull up to the garage and cut the engine. First thing is first—Loxy and Vader need to be sent out back so they don't jump up on us while I carry her in.

Slowly, I unbuckle Brooky, having survived my vicious Dobermans. Their method of choice is always death by licking. My "Beware of Attack Dog" sign is a big joke that warrants an eye roll from me every time I see it.

My silent prayer seems to be working as I transfer Brooklynn to her crib. Okay ... forty-five bags of groceries and maybe a nap? I run out and grab the first batch of bags (which means if I add one more bag, my arms will pop of their sockets) and head back in. Just as I turn around from placing them on my floor, I gasp and jump at the sight of Mitch bringing in more bags.

"I'll get the rest. Put only the cold stuff away now!" he snaps and walks out. *He's angry?* I shake my head and immediately follow his orders, mainly because I need to do something. "This is all of it," he grumbles, plopping it on the floor. He starts rummaging through the bags, pulling out everything that needs to be refrigerated or frozen. His jawline is twitching and he hasn't put any effort into looking up at me.

"Mitch." I touch his arm. He flinches away. *Huh?* "You're mad at me—why?"

"Because you left before I could get my two-hundred fifty-thousand dollars' worth of pussy out of you!" he yells. Normally my mouth flies into action a lot quicker than my hands ... normally. I cradle my hand protectively. *Damn it—that hurt!*

"Baby, let me see." He reaches for my hand with no regard to his red, slightly swollen cheek.

"Don't touch me!" *Oh, and here come the waterworks! Goddamn it! Sometimes it sucks to be a girl!*

Mitch steps back and fishes something out of his back pocket. I forget my anger for a moment and realize he's wearing loose-fitting jeans and a white cotton T-shirt. He looks so "boy-next-door." I've never seen him dressed so casually. Not that I've spent a lot of time out of bed with him.

"Here." He passes me something shaped like a business card. "I was going to use this for its original purpose, but I'd like to trade it for being an asshole who says things he doesn't mean. I was mad and I went for your jugular. I'm sorry, Charlotte. Please forgive me." He shuffles his feet and won't maintain eye contact, which makes him seem ridiculously nervous for someone who's always confident and in control. Then again—he's flown off the handle a lot since I met him.

I finally pull my eyes away from his and look down. I don't know whether to laugh or cry. It's a fucking Get Out of Jail Free card from Monopoly.

"I sat out in the parking lot of the toy store 'til it opened at nine. I don't do shit like that, Charlotte! If you knew me well enough, you would know that it meant something. You don't know me well enough yet, and so you can only take me at my word. Trouble is, I've hurt you terribly with my words. Twice, now. All I can say is that I'm sorry. I haven't been myself the past few days—not that you would know that, either. Christ, baby—will you say something? Your nattering has rubbed off on me." He runs his hands through his hair and grasps it tightly while he exhales forcibly.

I don't say anything. Part of me wants to tell him to leave, and the other part wants my aggressive Mitch to take me up against the kitchen wall. I slip the Monopoly card into my purse (I could hand it back and spank the shit out of him!) and decide to put the groceries away. Groceries are a safe decision; they won't hurt my mind, heart, or body—although, that wall-banging thought is still enticing me. *Closet whore!* Mitch takes this as his cue to shut up and help me.

"You pack quite a wallop, Ms. McKendrick," he says after a few minutes and bumps my hip playfully.

"So do you, Mr. Colton," I say flatly, shooting my daggers at him. I'm not playing. He winces.

"Baby ... I ..." he starts, but I put my hand up, not wanting to hear another word. "Okay." He sighs and continues to help me.

"So ..." we both say in unison after five minutes of silence and the last grocery finding its home. "Go ahead," we both say, then laugh lightly.

"Ladies first," he says, and gestures to me.

"You sure about that?" I cock an eyebrow.

"Baby ... stop." He closes the gap between us and runs his hands up and down my upper arms. *Damn his sexy voice and seductive hands!*

"So," I say, trying to pull my wits about me. "You were coming here with the intent of spanking me?"

"Yes." He pushes my chin up to look me in the eyes.

"Why?" *Breathe, Charley ... breathe. Damn him and the way he looks at me!*

"You left me." He looks down. "You didn't wake me to say good-bye."

"Mitch, you were sleeping so soundly. I didn't want to wake you. I know for a fact that you've gotten less sleep than me these past few days." I crook my neck slightly to make his eyes find mine. "Besides, I left you a note. Did you not see it?"

Mitch scoffs at the mention of my note. *"Dear Mitch, Safe flight. See you in three months. Love, Charlotte."* He says every word verbatim, not that there were many. "What the fuck was that, Charlotte?" Uh-oh, jawline clenching—telling how little muscles in the cheek are. His face is so close to mine, I'm finding it hard to concentrate. "Answer me," he says through his teeth. The very teeth that nipped about every inch of skin on my body last night.

"I ... uh, I was in a hurry, Mitch. I ... didn't know what to say. I didn't wake you for two reasons. First, I couldn't be delayed in getting home to my kids." I pull away from him and head to the sink. "Second, I wouldn't have been able to leave knowing ..." I stop myself, and hopefully the forming tears.

"Knowing what, baby?" His hands slide onto my hips, causing a deep ache in my body. *What the hell is wrong with me? I'm just react-*

ing to a long dry spell. Or to having a long marriage with a man whose hands never felt *this* incredible on my body. A man who never made me feel the way Mitch makes me feel—in bed or out.

"Damn it, Mitch, why do your hands have to feel so good on me?" I lean my head back on his chest as said hands slide my short sundress up.

"Hmm, Charlotte," he breathes against my ear, "why must you wear these cute little sundresses?" His hands slide under the band of my panties and palm my ass. "Jesus, I still want to spank you." The gymnast in my stomach springs into her floor program, running into a roundoff and three front flips as I push my ass against his hands.

"You don't have a Get Out of Jail Free card anymore." I'm barely holding it together as his mouth travels down my neck.

"Make me a sandwich so I can earn it back." He nips at the skin just below my lobe.

"Uh-uh, mister ... it's not that easy." I laugh, but my breath hitches when his hands slide up my back and reach around to the front.

"No bra again, Charlotte. No sweater. You let people—other men—see what's mine."

I gasp as he tugs harshly at my nipples and follow it up with a whimpery moan. Christ, I'm like putty in his hands.

"It was warm out. Nobody saw." I turn my face and pull his mouth to mine. He tugs harder. "Oh, Mitch ... please." I'm in sensory overload. Morale is at an all-time high and pushing against Kitty's neighbor.

"Bow chicka wow wow!" CiCi pipes up. Mitch abruptly stops and jerks away from me. *Fuck!* "Charley ... you ever think about going into porn? That was hot! I can see it now—*Charley Does CEOs*! Should I get the camera?"

I scowl at her and glare daggers at her.

"Hi, Mitch, I'm CiCi. I'd shake your hand, but I'm offended by your pointing ... it's rude." She smirks. I look over at Mitch who suddenly matches her expression and stands up straighter. My eyes scan him to see what she's talking about. *Oh, good Lord!*

"I only point when I see something I like." He's grinning now. "Are all the O'Brien girls as hot as you two?"

"Don't get any ideas, dude."

"A man can dream, can't he?"

I stare at the two of them in disbelief while they continue their flirt fest! I glance down, somewhat confused as to how I'm actually feeling about this. I can see Mitch isn't losing any momentum in the morale department.

"That's all you'll do is dream, baby!" She blows him a kiss. He catches it and places it on his heart. "Keep him around a while, he'll do just fine with our lot." She smiles at me, then proceeds to let Loxy and Vader in.

"CiCi ... when did you move in here?" I ask sarcastically.

"I like it here. Nobody likes me at my house," she says, almost depressingly.

"Ceese ... you live by yourself!" I roll my eyes and Mitch chuckles.

"Yeah ... I'm a fucking bitch to deal with, so I come over here." She holds her hands out and gives me the "duh" look.

"To get away from yourself?" I laugh. Christ—she's an asshole!

"Yeah, and apparently for the live porn." She gives in to the dogs' licking. "Don't let me stop you two. Go back over to the sink and back into position. Mitch, you were just about to tell Charley you were gonna ram it up her ass, just the way she likes it."

"Good Lord!" I walk away.

"Is she on medication?" Mitch laughs lightly, following me.

"She would be if there any existed for her." I look at the clock. Goodbye, nap!

"You gonna be around for a while, CiCi?" I call out to her.

"I live here, don't I?" she calls back.

"No!" I answer.

"In that case, yeah, I'll be around for a while." She follows us into the living room.

"Will you grab Brooky when she wakes up? Mitch and I need a nap," I say as I yawn

"Up all night, aye?" She wiggles her eyebrows.

"Yeah, I was ramming it up her ass all night. You know how she likes it, Ceese." Mitch shakes his head with an exhausted look.

"I don't care how you give it to her, Mitch, I'm just glad you do!" She smiles. *I want to die.*

"Just don't 'yes' her to death like Josh did." *No ... now I want to die.*

"What do you mean?" he asks.

Oh, Christ!

84

CiCi shakes her body to prepare for the performance. "Yes, Charley ... yes ... yes ... oh, yeah ... yeah ... yes ... yes." She breaks. She's only revving the engine a little. "Yes! Yes ... yes, Charley ... yes ... yeah ... yeah ... yeah, you like? ... Yeah ... yes! Yes! Yes! Take it, Charley, Yes! Yessss ... ugh ... yes, baby ... yeah?"

I'm laughing because nobody impersonates Josh and I having sex like CiCi. Of course, she only knows how to do this so well because after I nonchalantly told her about it, she made sure to eavesdrop one night. She's a twisted bitch!

"Poor Charley. That was her sex life for ten years. Josh walked around like he gave it to her good, never once noticing that she just laid there doing nothing," she says sadly.

"That's not true, CiCi," I roll my eyes again   it's an affliction when I'm near her. "I did my grocery list, planned parties, all sorts of things. Once, I even filed my nails," I say proudly.

"Are you guys joking? Baby, that's how it was for you?" He touches my cheek, having finally calmed down from his laughing fit over CiCi's impersonation.

"Yeah," I say, suddenly feeling depressed by it all. "I'm heading up."

"Okay, let's go." He smiles. CiCi pulls him back and, because I'm as bad as her, I eavesdrop.

"He was a worthless, shit-for-brains asshole! He never thought of her. She was his trophy wife. Please, Mitch, be good to her. She needs someone who sees how amazing she is." My eyes fill up as I hear her choke on her words. Mitch says something, I think, but I can't hear him. I head into my room to collect myself. *Why did I stay with that asshole so long?*

CiCi's right. I was his trophy wife. Not sure why, though. I mean, I'm okay to look at, I just don't think I'm trophy-wife material. Half the time my hair's up in a messy bun and I'm wearing frumpy clothes, like I just got out of bed. Actually, Josh did complain about that. He always wanted me to dress "hot" whether it was for some sort of event or the town grocery store.

"This hot number is my wife." That's how he'd introduce me. Any reference to me after that was about how he couldn't keep his hands off of me. Never once did I hear him talk about what I did, or what my

interests were. It was the same thing at home. Everything was about him. Correction: Him and his law firm. He worked extra hard at making partner for eight years.

I love my children, but I don't know why or how I ended up having three with him. His disinterest in them was so obvious. I kept telling myself it was work. All he did was hurt us by not caring. Never went to anything for the boys. I think in the end, me ... the kids ... we were all a part of his image. He would pull us down from the shelf and dust us off when the need arose. The perfect family. The perfect family man. The perfect partner.

He even used Bennett's diagnosis to pull at their heartstrings. Asshole couldn't even remember the name correctly or what the hell it meant. Never once had he gone to a therapy session or a meeting at school. Yet, miraculously, this kid was his "pride and joy" to his co-workers. Prick—never even learned one damn sign so he could talk to his kid!

Ugh. I should've left long ago! I should've known as soon as he got passed up for partner he would leave! I should've been the one who left—not him! That's what burns the most.

"I don't think I will ever want to leave this room." Mitch sighs as he climbs in next to me and pulls me into a spooning position.

"Why's that?" I wipe away a tear.

"It's heavenly—bathed in my favorite scent." He inhales deeply through his nose.

"What scent?"

"Charlotte. Mmm ... love the way you smell." He sniffs me, making me giggle. *Josh never sniffed me.* I grab a tissue off the side table and blow my nose. "Baby? What's the matter?" He rolls me in his direction. "Charlotte?" He thumbs a tear away.

"Sorry. I was reflecting." That sounds better than admitting to my pity party for one.

"Did I do or say something to upset you?"

"No. My life before. My marriage." I take in a deep breath and play with the stubble on his chin. "You wanted loyal, Mitch? Well, you hit the jackpot. I stayed with that self-absorbed, narcissistic, pompous ass for ten years. That idiot left *me* in the end." I shake my tears away. Why am I even telling him this? I sound so pathetic.

"You have no idea how grateful I am that he was such a moron." His voice is as soft as the index finger tracing my quivering lip. "I wish I wasn't leaving tonight. I know I'm going to be gone for three months, but I'm asking you to please be patient with me and give me the chance to cherish you the way you should be cherished."

I look away from his gaze. "Damn you and your ability to say all the right things."

"Well, we both know that's not true." He kisses down my jawline. "When I'm mad, I say all the wrong things. When I'm not mad, I speak only the truth. When I'm near you, I say things that frighten the hell out of me." He leans his forehead against my temple.

"What do you mean, Mitch?"

"Just be patient ... please." He kisses my temple. Sure ... but he didn't answer my question.

I told him I was a bullshit-free zone (that may have been a load of bull right there!). It would be a lie if I didn't tell him how I'm feeling. "Mitch," I close my eyes and try to gain my strength.

"What, baby?" *Ohh—sexy voice!*

"I need to tell you something. It may make you want to rip up our contract for good." I swallow hard.

Mitch flies up onto his knees. "What is it?" Crap—he went straight to flaring nostrils.

"Not going to take this lying down, huh?" I try to lighten the mood.

"What is it, Charlotte? Tell me now!" He has to be the most temperamental man I've ever met. I actually like this, as much as I hate it about him. He's got fight and drive ... with me ... love that! I sit up and look at him with yearning eyes. His eyes soften slightly at this.

"I may be developing a crush on you," I finally admit in defeat and look down.

He grasps my face in his palms and yanks it back up. "You have a crush on me?"

"I'm afraid so."

"Well, that's too bad, because like I said yesterday—I can't fucking stand you!" And before I speak a word, his mouth slams hard on mine. Um ... so this answers ... nothing! But Jesus, can he kiss!

"Mitch ... Mitch, we can't," I whisper as he tugs at my panties.

"Why? The baby's asleep." He pulls my right strap down to uncover my breast and takes my nipple into his mouth. All I can think about is how hot his comment was ... so natural.

"She is, but CiCi isn't, and she's eavesdropping." I smack my head. That cockblocker!

"No! She wouldn't." He looks at me in disbelief.

"Uh ... you have met her, right?" My eyes widen.

He looks at the door then back at me with a wicked grin on his face.

"No ... no, Charlotte ... no!" he yells. "No ... oh God no. No! No! No! No, baby!"

I cover my mouth and go into stitches.

"Milk!" I yell.

"No ... no milk!"

"Cookies!"

"No ... what kind?"

"Oreos!"

"No! No, not Oreos!"

"Nutter Butters ... you want nut butter?"

"Oh God no, nut butter! Oh no!" he bellows out.

"Very funny, assholes!" CiCi yells from the other side of the door, then kicks it. Brooklynn cries.

"Good luck with that, Aunt CiCi!" I yell, breaking from my laughter.

"Nut butter?" Mitch is holding his stomach, still laughing. He finally stops and rubs his face. "We'll nap for two hours, and then I want to take you somewhere. What time do you have to be back for the boys?" He pulls his hands away from his face.

"Uh ... three-thirty. But we'd have to bring Brooklynn with us," I say, unsure of how he'll react.

"I know." He gives me a sheepish smile. "Take your dress off, baby. I want your bare skin next to mine."

I take it off as he sets my alarm, then spoon against him.

"Try not to give my ass a boost of Morale, please," I mumble.

Mitch chuckles. "Is that an invitation?"

"No ... it's a warning."

"A warning?"

"Yes. Kitty's not ready to share."

"Go to sleep, baby, or you won't be allowed to in a minute." It's almost a plea.

"Yes, sir." I yawn and snuggle closer to him.

"Are you trying to crush me?" he asks playfully.

"I'm totally crushing on you, damn it!"

"Crush all you want, baby. I'm happy to take it from you ... only you."

"Hmm ..." I sigh.

I'M NOT SURE what stirs me out of sleep first—the alarm or Mitch's caress. God, his hands feel incredible on my skin. His soothing touch glides up the back of my thigh ... over my bum ... my back ... my shoulder ... and down the length of my arm. His hand retraces its steps, and his lips lightly tickle various areas of my back. *I'm in heaven ...*

Heaven aside—I'm out-of-my-mind confused! I'm feeling things I've never felt before. *I'm a fraud.* He's paying me to act out feelings I think—*know*—I'm naturally having for him. But am I? Is it the attention? I've had more from him in three days than I got in ten years from Josh. I mean *real* attention, like the kind a man in love shows his woman. Well—in the movies, at least. It's an act, part of the deal. *Stay focused, Charley ... don't screw this up!* I think about what he said to me before I signed the contract.

"Before you sign, I feel the need to remind you again that you will be at my beck and call. I also want to make it clear that it will never be more than this. I will never want more. I will never give more. I'm not trying to sound like a cocky or arrogant bastard, but if you find you feel something for me and want more—our contract will be through. I don't do the marriage thing, I don't do the kid thing, and I certainly won't do the falling-in-love thing."

And yet—I have kids. He's taking my daughter and me somewhere. And I said I have a crush. He seemed happy about it. In fact, the only time he tried to run for the hills was when he didn't think I took his intentions seriously. I left this morning, which angered him. He followed me rather than dismissing me. His behavior toward me last night and this morning—well, confused doesn't seem like a big enough word to encapsulate *confused*!

"Baby," he says, nipping at my shoulder, "how long are you going to pretend to be sleeping?"

"Figured me out already, huh?" I smile with my eyes closed.

"Hmm ... like I said before, I don't know if I'll ever figure you out." He rolls me onto my back.

"I could easily say the same thing about you." I gently touch his cheek.

"Well, you're not alone. I can't figure myself out right now, either. What kind of wonderfully evil spell have you cast over me, Charlotte O'Brien?" He plays with my lips.

"O'Brien?" I shoot him a quizzical look.

"I hate that you have that bastard's name." The look on his face matches the disgust in his voice. If I've learned anything about Mitch these past few days, it's that he's impetuously temperamental. Which gives me an idea ...

"Antipathy," I say in my sexiest, most seductive voice before I lightly brush my lips across his.

His face softens. "Damn you and your sexy, manipulative brain." He nudges my lips back. "Say it again," he pleads with a slight growl.

"Antipathy," I whisper.

"That's a great word. Definitely—not—used—enough," he says between kisses. I try to squash the need to giggle, but fail when he asks me to repeat it. "You're laughing at me, Ms. O'Brien?" He tickles my sides.

"Stop!" I gasp. He complies and smiles down at me. "How can you be so sexy and be such a nerd at the same time?" I laugh.

"You have a thing for sexy nerds, O'Brien?"

"Is that what you're going to do now?" I ask.

"What?"

"Refer to me as *O'Brien* because you want to erase my marriage?"

"Yes. I would like it if you changed your name back. Actually, I want you to do that while I'm away. Have it switched before I'm home."

The tone in his delivery was fine. It's the absurdity in his demand that has me pissed off once again.

"Not happening, Mitch." I try to keep my cool.

"Why? Do you still love him?" he asks vehemently.

"No, Mitch." I roll my eyes. *Oh, how the fuck did we get to this place?* "I have three children with this name—I'm not changing it."

"Change theirs, too! When they're old enough, they're not going to want his name anyway. Trust me, I know. Besides, what are you going to do when you get remarried—still keep his name?" He rolls onto his back.

"Um, let's see. First of all, I don't think you can walk into Social Security and say, 'Hi, I'm here to change my kids' names because their father's a douchebag.' That may seem a little shady, Mitch, like I'm looking to leave the country with them! Second—what do you mean you know they won't want his name? Third—if I got remarried, my new husband might want to adopt them and give them his name, which would take care of the first and second. However, the third will never happen because I am not getting married again." I finally suck in some air—my lungs thank me greatly.

He turns onto his side to face me. "First—I'll have my people look into it. Third—you *will* get married again, and not that I've met your kids or anything, but the fact that they're *your* kids guarantees, in my eyes, that he'll want to adopt them." He pulls my hand to his mouth and plants several kisses on it.

"Second?" I ask.

"That's my business, Charlotte, not yours," he says sternly.

"Ah—well, since you've brought that up, I should remind you that my personal life is none of your business." I pull my hand away.

"You're my girlfriend, Charlotte. Everything about you is my business," he states, grabbing my hand again.

"On paper, Mitch!" I snap, although one would think I'd slapped him in the face. "You have say over my body and my time—nothing else!"

I watch as his facial expression changes from hurt to just plain pissed. Before I can say another word, Mitch yanks me by the hand, turning my whole body. He pulls my panties down and slaps my ass several times, then releases me and turns to sit on the edge of the bed. I scoot over to the other side, far away from him.

I'm ... I don't know what I am. I want to say something, scream maybe, but I can't control my rapid breathing to form either of those actions. I feel shocked, pissed, and oddly, a little turned on. I study his posture. He's slumped over, his head in his hands. Me? I'm fighting the urge to comfort him, slap the shit out of him, and for the grand finale— fuck the crazy out of him.

Mitch takes a deep breath and straightens up before slapping his knees upon exhale. He stands and pulls his jeans on. "Get dressed, baby. We'll leave in ten minutes." He keeps his back to me.

If a bubble magically appeared above my head, it would say "What the fuck?!" I think he senses my thoughts, because he sits back on the bed in defeat and clears his throat.

"My mother died of breast cancer when I was nine, because suffering from MS wasn't enough. My dad—well, 'the sperm donor,' really, since he stopped being my dad when I was five and he couldn't cope with my mother's illness—decided that drugs were more important than us. The only thing that man gave me that I will cherish 'til my last breath was my wonderful grandparents and the opportunity to be raised by them. They took care of my mother and me once she got real sick. He gave up parental rights to me when she died and my grandparents, per my mother's will, were granted guardianship.

"While he's spent the past thirty-four years in and out of rehab and jail, I've spent it doing everything I could to make them proud enough of me to wash away some of the disappointment they felt in producing such a menace to society. My grandfather was an amazing man. I looked up to him and had—or have—such a deep respect for him that I've always felt honor in carrying the Colton name. If he were my mother's father instead of my father's father, I would've changed my name as soon as I could have. That's why I know your kids will probably want to have a different name. Your dad sounds like the same stand-up kind of guy my grandfather was, and your kids would probably find it an honor to have the O'Brien name."

"Mitch ..." My voice shakes as I interrupt him.

"I'll leave." He stands up.

"Is that what you want?" I ask, knowing the answer. He wouldn't have made "his" business mine if he wanted to leave. He knows he screwed up—again. I know he was looking to earn a Get Out of Jail Free card. Not that he was looking for pity, and not even that he just wanted the card. It's more. *More?* Crap ... more. Imagine the power in such a small word, like a few other four-letter words. I know I'm right, though. He wouldn't have gone into detail like that if I wasn't.

"Jesus, baby, do you even have to question it?" he asks in disbelief, laced, I think, with embarrassment. "Are you okay?" he adds, and I hear guilt added to the mix.

"I'm fighting quite the internal battle over here," I say, then continue speaking when he says nothing. "I'm pissed off. I'm just not sure if it's because you spanked me, or because a part of me was turned on by it," I say, not hiding an ounce of my confusion.

"We're a perfect fit, baby, for many reasons. But as far as the bedroom, as you said, you like me to have control over you. I think it's because you have to manage so much on your own outside of the bedroom that you're relieved to relinquish it. I like having that control over you because I know it's the only place I can." He throws his shirt on.

"So you don't trust me?" I ask, reaching for my dress.

"I want to, but I'm fighting quite the internal battle myself. Charlotte?" He finally turns to look at me. "I'm sorry I spanked you."

"Are you?" I ask as I finish pulling my dress down.

"No." He smirks. "I'm just sorry I did it while I was angry. I promised I wouldn't, and I did. I just ... I didn't like what you said. I thought we got past that today." He walks around the bed and sits in front of me. "Every time I think your wall is coming down, you throw it right back up." His hand reaches up to my face and I pull back.

"You've been doing the same thing," I say, quietly.

"I know. Looks like maybe we're both experiencing some feelings neither of us signed up for."

"More," I murmur. He nods. "You don't do the kid thing. You hate them."

"Whoa—I don't hate kids! I love kids." He defends himself.

"You don't want all of the bullshit."

"I'm growing fond of your bullshit ... it's got a nice scent to it." He chuckles.

"That is the weirdest line I've ever heard!" I grab a pillow and smack him with it. "Besides, you're the one dishing out most of the bullshit around here."

"True," he concedes after laughing. "I won't blame you if you want me to leave, but you should know that the money will still be in the account every month for you."

"Even if I'm not with you? Why?" I look up at him sharply. I'm taken aback.

"Because the idea of any other man touching you makes my blood boil and every hair on the back of my neck stand." His eyes glaze over with anger at the thought.

Do I want him to leave? *No.* Do I want another man to touch me? *No.* Do I have any idea whatsoever as to what I'm doing? *Hell no!*

"Where are we going?" I finally raise my white flag. Mitch grasps my face and pulls me to kiss him, but I lean back before his lips land on mine. "Let's get one thing straight."

"What, Charlotte?" he breathes.

"You are my boyfriend, therefore, your personal life is my business as well." I look him straight in the eye and bite him back with his own words.

"You are my personal life." He smiles. "Can I kiss you now?"

Satisfied with his comment, I nod.

Chapter Seven

"REMEMBER, WE HAVE to be back at three-thirty so I can get the boys." I glance over at him quickly as I set reminders for myself for the next day. Mitch is too preoccupied with glancing at Brooklynn, who is trying to sing to The Wiggles. The laugh lines around his eyes deepen. He merges onto I-93 South then starts bopping his head with her to "Hot Potato." Brooky giggles with delight. Mitch is grinning like an idiot and sings the chorus with her (now that he's got it down pat and all). I stare at him in amazed—but delighted—disbelief. He glances at me, quickly stiffens up, clears his throat, and turns his attention to the road.

"Mittt!" Brooky bellows out. He glances at her in the mirror, then me.

He shrugs. "Hot potato, hot potato!" he sings out, bouncing his head again. Brooklyn gets lost in a sea of giggles, and I join her.

After another twenty minutes of Wiggles and giggles, Mitch gets off at the Andover exit.

"We're going to your house?" I ask, but then quickly realize he's going a different way.

"The house I grew up in," he says, then makes a final turn and pulls into the driveway of an old colonial.

"C'mon, baby." He cuts the engine and gets out, then opens Brooky's door and helps her out of her car seat. "What?" he asks as I stare at him. Brooklynn goes to him like she's known him her whole life. I turn my focus back to the garage in front of me. I've got the oddest feeling of panic coming over me. "Charlotte?" Mitch opens my door with his free hand. "Are you okay, baby?" He feels my head. "Jesus, you're clammy. What's the matter?"

"I don't feel so well." I fan myself.

"Stay right here. I'm going to get you a drink," he says and heads off to the house with Brooklynn.

Mitch

"HI, MITCH!" MAGGIE smiles. "Who's this little angel?"

"My girlfriend's daughter. Can I have an OJ to bring out to Charlotte? She's not feeling well," I ask, crooking my neck around to see where Gram is.

"She said to expect you three."

I turn to her. "I didn't tell her I was coming."

"She also said Charlotte was going to have a panic attack." She raises a brow and hands me the OJ.

"Ugh—I hate when she does that!" I shake my head and walk toward the door.

"Here, let me have your stepdaughter." She holds her hands out.

"She's not my stepdaughter." I sigh, handing her over before walking out the door. I swear I hear her murmur, "She will be."

Just as I get outside, I find Charlotte walking up the path with a sickly look about her. *What is wrong with her?*

"Baby," I say, putting my arm around her, "take a sip of this orange juice."

"Is it laced with something?" She tries to smile.

"Of course it is. Now drink up so I can take advantage of you." I put the cup up to her lips.

"Jesus, Mitch." She grabs the cup. "I'm not a baby." She drinks.

"You're my baby." I kiss her temple. She rolls her eyes at me. Actually, *I'd* roll my eyes at me. Why am I suddenly turning into mush around her? I guess it's not sudden at all, really. Right from the start, I felt this pull. I found it easy to be myself around her—a playful side most people don't see.

"Mitch, is Brooky by herself?"

"Yes, Charlotte. But don't worry, I made sure to put some knives on the floor for her to play with or stick into the sockets. I also gave her a pair of scissors and told her to run around with them." I take the cup from her.

"Good. I wouldn't want her to be bored." She smiles as we walk in.

Gram looks up at us as she bounces Brooklynn on her knee. I can't remember the last time I saw her look this happy. I sign "hello" to her. She immediately asks Brooklynn's age and name. Just as I'm about to tell her, Charlotte signs the information. I'm floored.

"You know sign language, baby?"

"Yes. I signed with all my kids, but I became fluent with Bennett because that was the only way we could communicate for two years." She signs our conversation, which I know Gram is probably thoroughly appreciating right now. She can't stand when people who can sign stop mid-conversation in front of her. She says it's the equivalent of someone talking English, then suddenly switching to another language that not everyone understands. It's rude.

Gram beckons Charlotte to sit in the chair next to her wheelchair and shoos me away. Reluctantly I comply, but first I lean down near Charlotte's ear. "Don't let her freak you out, baby. I'll make us some lunch." I kiss her ear.

"A light one, Mitch," she says. I nod.

I head to the kitchen, silently swearing to myself. Not the most brilliant idea to leave her with Gram. At ninety years old, Gram has not lost her psychic abilities, but her filter for delivery has been permanently removed.

Maggie walks in and smiles. "I'll fix you two something, honey."

"Maggie! You left her alone with Gram?!" The panic sets in at full capacity.

"Honey child ... you don't pay me enough to try to keep up with them two! Their hands is flying so fast, I got dizzy just watchin' 'em!" She shakes her head and grins as she heads over to the fridge.

Maggie's originally from the South, and though she's been in New England for over thirty years, she hasn't lost her Southern charm or the Southern pace in life. It's calming, though, to watch someone take their time with everything.

She's been with my family since before my mom died. Gram and Pop kept her on to help with the house and me. Her children are like brothers and sisters to me. We did everything together, mainly because Maggie's husband abandoned them. Well, that, and we all adored them.

Maggie has always been good to our family and worked hard. My grandparents lost a lot of friendships over her because they refused to see her color or pay her accordingly. As a matter of fact, they paid her more than the going rate for white help. That was unheard of then. People didn't like it. I remember questioning Pop about it when I was eleven.

"Pop, doesn't it bother you that your friends aren't your friends anymore because of Maggie?"

"Let me tell you something, Pally—" (I miss hearing him call me that) *"—those 'friends' were not real friends in the first place. If it weren't for Maggie just being Maggie, I would've never known. As you grow older, Mitch, you'll find that you have an inner circle of friends and an outer circle of friends. The inner circle is the most important, so you have to be very careful about who you allow in. They need to be loyal, supportive, and dependable. They're like family, and family takes care of each other. Maggie is family—she's in our inner circle, Mitch. Damn it—she's president of it, and if no one else in our inner circle appreciates or accepts her, then they don't belong there! It's that simple. Do you understand what I mean?"* I could see his passion and irritation all mixed together on his face.

"Yes, Pop." I was pretty certain I did.

"While we're on the subject, Mitch, I know I don't have to worry about it, but I need to say it." He tapped the top of his desk in the study.

"Yeah, Pop?"

"Never judge someone by how they look—skin tone, ethnic back-

ground, et cetera. You judge them by their heart and their intentions. If they have a good heart, chances are their intentions will match."

I took what Pop said to heart and follow this advice, along with all the other guidance he ever gave me, because he was the man I hoped to someday become. He was my role model, while other kids worshipped superheroes, athletes, astronauts, and rock stars. My role model never changed as I got older. It was always Pop, and 'til my dying day, it will always be Pop.

"Mitch, honey ... you all right?" I focus back on Maggie's voice and her hand at my head.

"Sorry." I smile. "I was thinking about Pop. He would've loved Charlotte." *He would've ...*

"Do you love, Charlotte?" She crooks her head at me.

"So!" I clap my hands. "What are you making us?" I rub them together. She smiles at me, head tilted to the side suspiciously, knowing I'm trying to change the subject.

"I made some of my famous chicken salad earlier. You go fetch me the crackers, baby." She turns to the fridge and pulls out a bowl.

After a few minutes, I walk back into the living room with a plate of Maggie's chicken salad on crackers. She wasn't lying; Gram and Charlotte are signing like they're trying to win a competition. Oh, Christ— Gram pulled out the fucking albums!

"Must you torture her on her first visit?" I sign and roll my eyes.

"Oh, don't pick on her!" Charlotte smacks my thigh and takes the tray from me. "You were so cute, baby," she adds.

"Were?" I ask, pouting. She giggles, and her glee hits her eyes.

"I am a little disappointed in these pictures, though." She sighs. "Not one picture of you in a bow tie—what kind of a nerd are you, anyway?"

"Apparently," I say, leaning down to her ear, "a sexy one." I nip at her lobe. Gram smacks me. I stand back up and she reminds me that she's deaf and I don't need to whisper to Charlotte.

"Gram, sometimes I forget because you're so damn loud!" I tease her. Her hands wave nonsense at me.

Charlotte gets up and pecks my lips. "Have a seat with your Gram. I'm gonna grab the backpack for Brooky's sippy cup," she says before walking down the hall.

I settle in the seat.

"So, what do you think?" I eagerly ask Gram. She clasps her hands together and shakes them while looking up to God. She brings her gaze back to me and a few tears fall down her cheeks. "Gram?" I grab her hand.

"Mitch, it's been a long time since I've seen this look in your eyes. She was worth the wait. I love her already ... just like you." She pats my hand.

"Gram, don't start!" I sign quickly. "Don't rush me into feelings I'm not sure I'm having. We've only just met!"

"You don't want to leave tonight. The idea of being away from her is killing you inside." She gives me a sympathetic look.

"Gram, knock it off. You don't know what you are talking about!" I roll my eyes and shake my head before grabbing a cracker.

"Don't I?" She arches an eyebrow in the "I know my shit" way. "You can trust her, Mitch ... she's inner-circle material."

I hold my palm out and bring my hand down hard in a karate chop to make her stop.

Charlotte laughs. "You teasing him again, Gram?"

"Don't call her that." I shoot Charlotte a look.

"Sorry ... she told me to. What should I call her, Mitch?" She treads lightly. Christ, she can read me already. She knows I'm about to explode.

"Sorry." I rub my face, trying to snap out of it.

Charlotte goes about setting a place for Brooklynn at the coffee table with her lunch. "Can you scooch?" She taps my arm, making me stop. I give her a half smile, nod, and move over to the left of the armchair. She squeezes into the small space and, crossing one leg over the other, leans back into my arms. *A perfect fit.*

Charlotte giggles as I begin my usual ritual of closing my eyes while running my nose up and down her neck, smelling her skin. *Jesus, I'm going to miss this smell.*

"I'm delaying my flight until tomorrow," I say out of nowhere. Charlotte's breath hitches in surprise. I can't say I blame her—I'm a little surprised myself. *Damn that grandmother of mine.*

"Why?" Charlotte turns her head a little as I continue to breathe her in.

"I can't fly tonight," I say.

"Don't take this the wrong way, but—why?"

"I'm too intoxicated, I won't be able to see shit." I smile against her neck.

Charlotte laughs. "I wasn't aware that you were actually the one who was going to fly the plane."

"I'm not."

"Well, you haven't had anything to drink, so what do you need to see on the plane?" She's asking in her flirty tone—she knows I'm up to something.

"Well, I'm intoxicated by your smell. It's making me want to watch you get undressed tonight. If I get on that plane, I won't be able to see shit!" I profess, then laugh with her. I glance at Gram to find that arched-eyebrow look again.

"Charlotte, do me a favor," I whisper in her ear. She nods. "Tell Gram I have a sign for her, but I don't dare do it because she'll crack me over the head with something."

Charlotte laughs and tells her.

Gram sits there looking thoughtful for a moment, then her hands fly up as she asks, "Is this the sign, Mitch?" She then proceeds to flip me off and stick her tongue out at me. Ugh! I love my Gram! And I love that these two have hit it off.

"Can I stay with you tonight?" I ask.

"No," Charlotte says quickly. A little too quickly for my taste.

"Wrong answer!" I do nothing to mask my anger.

"Then maybe you should just stick to the original flight plan," she says back.

"This is good, Charlotte. I was worried that we wouldn't have another argument today. Third one and it's only two-thirty—we really know how to pace ourselves, baby!" I snap facetiously.

Gram starts waving her arms in front of us to tell us to cut it out. Charlotte leans forward, grabs a cracker, and pops it into her mouth angrily.

"If you two don't stop, I'm gonna put you both over my knee and spank the shit out of you!" Gram's hands unload her words at us like a machine gun.

"Apparently spanking the shit out of me is the 'in' thing to do," Charlotte says, then takes a swig of her drink.

"Well, Gram and I do have a lot in common," I say in a very thoughtful, yet serious, manner. Charlotte jerks forward, her body shaking. Her hands come up as if to catch any liquid that may come out. Her beverage must have gone down the wrong pipe, causing her to choke. "Sorry ... you okay?" I chuckle and rub her back. She nods.

"Gram," I say, looking back to her, "we have to leave in a few for Charlotte's boys."

"Sorry, Gram," Charlotte adds.

"I'm glad you two stopped by. Listen to me." She gets a very serious look on her face. "Be patient with each other. You both have been hurt, and it's easier to put your walls up than to face what you are feeling for each other. Try to remember, though, that everything you went through—all the pain—helped you on the path to finding one another. Trust in your feelings—they won't steer you wrong."

"You ought to write a column in my friend's paper. 'Dear Gram,'" Charlotte teases her. Gram made her nervous.

"Okay, Gram, stop scaring her away."

"Oh, you'll do that all by yourself if you keep acting like a waspish asshole!" she signs.

"Ooh, damn!" Charlotte laughs.

"Funny, huh?" I tickle her.

"Little bit." She winces and almost pinches her index finger and thumb together.

"Well," I say, "I have been showing you too much of that side of me."

"Yeah ... ya think?" She widens her eyes.

"Stop," I mouth to her, then lean in for a kiss—the soft, sweet, short-but-reluctant kind I've noticed she's fond of. "I'm staying with you tonight, baby." I don't ask this time. She nods slightly.

We pack up Brooky, say our goodbyes and head out.

IT'S NINE P.M. I plop onto Charlotte's bed and stretch my legs out in front of me, getting comfortable. She's doing last-minute evening things: checking on the kids, ironing clothes, preparing lunches, and doing a final once-over in the kitchen. I take this time to study her bedroom. I could've picked this bedroom out in a lineup. It's soft and warm with creamy purple, green, and ivory tones. It screams Charlotte. It smells as it looks—just like her. I've made a firm decision. Charlotte is my favorite smell—it's soft and clean, like a combination of whatever lotion she uses and fabric softener.

I glance around, taking note of various framed pictures. None with Josh—good! Then again, why would there be? CiCi told me Charlotte had redone this entire room when he left in an attempt to purge her memories of him. In fact, she told me a lot of shit in the span of several minutes when Charlotte went to check on the baby. Christ, at one point, I had a flashback of the Matchbox commercials with that guy who talked crazy fast! Then I found myself trying to remember if those commercials were from the 80s or 90s. This must happen to CiCi a lot, people blanking out on her, because she whacked my arm to refocus me.

Knowing that this is not the bed Josh "yessed" Charlotte to death in brings me a strange comfort I'm not sure I want to fully accept yet. My fingers play a beat in my lap as I wait (or die of boredom) for her. Just as I reach for the book on her nightstand, her phone pings and the screen lights up. I fight the urge for a second, but decide it's a sign. I grab her phone to see who's texting her. This is not something I would normally do, but I'm bored and haven't been completely myself since meeting her.

"Madelyn St. Claire," I say aloud.

Maddie: *Holy shit! This mother-flippin' day wouldn't end! He was here again!*

Him, with his shoulder-length blond hair and chiseled face!
Him with his body of the Gods!
And he did it again!
Good Lord—he did it again!

Ugh—Christ! This one is as bad as Charlotte! What is it with these women and their epic, dramatic texting?

Me: What? What did he do?
Maddie: *The same thing he's done 3 weeks in a row!*

Ugh!

Me: What?
Maddie: *What do you mean what?*
He stared at me intently when I came out for my next client—that's what!

Huh? Client? What does she do? I decide to wait to see if she says anything else.

I felt naked.

Now we're talking ...

Me: Go on ...
Maddie: *He wants me to ride the crazy train ... I just know it!*
He wants to get me in his bed and make me yell WOO WOO!
That's what Julie says.
Me: Who's Julie?
Maddie: *Are you drunk? Our Julie, dumbass!*

Christ, there's more of them?

Me: Well what do you think?
Maddie: *About what?*

104

Jesus—this conversation may require a translator!

> **Me:** About the conductor!
> **Maddie:** *The conductor of what?*
> **Me:** The conductor of the crazy train—are you drunk?
> **Maddie:** *I think he probably thinks I'm a freak!*
> **Me:** I think you may be right!
> **Maddie:** *Suck it, bitch—whose side are you on?*

Before I can answer ...

Ugh—he looks like a hot Viking—I so want him to give me helmet.
No—I want to hold onto the horns of his helmet while he pounds me
into submission with his love sword!

Shit—I just laughed like a girl!

> *What should I do, Charley?*
> **Me:** Let him know you want to be conquered ...
> **Maddie:** *What? He's (probably) bat-shit crazy!*
> **Me:** If not—5 mins alone with you and he probably will be!
> Why do you think he's crazy?
> **Maddie:** *He's in the reception area every week, same time, same day. I just don't know which therapist he's seeing.*

Ahh ... good Lord—this woman is a therapist? I'm suddenly a little more concerned for the welfare of the mentally ill.

> **Me:** Does he look crazy?
> **Maddie:** *Crazy hot!*
> **Me:** Well, what do you do when he's staring intently?
> **Maddie:** *What I always do!*

I wait.
I'm still waiting.
And the wait continues.

Sorry—the dramatic music carried on a bit longer than it should have!

I want to throw the phone across the room. This is utter nonsense, and yet I sit here like an addict waiting for my next fix. It reminds me of all the times I've visited with Gram while her "stories" were on. I'd really want to leave, but Christ, I had to find out what happened only to be teased with a cliffhanger! There was one show she used to watch called *Passions*, and half the main characters were stuck in Hell—literally! It was the stupidest storyline ever, yet to my dismay, I found myself asking her once a week if they got out of Hell yet. This went on for months. Apparently, it's hell trying to get out of Hell!

The phone pings.

I pretended I didn't notice him. I'm busy, you know!
Me: Why don't you just look at him and smile next week?

Why do women have to make everything so complicated?

Maddie: *'Cause he may be ape-shit crazy!*
Me: Ah, he's been promoted! From bat to ape—lucky guy! You should just tell him!
Maddie: *Tell him what???*
Me: TO RUN FOR HIS LIFE!
Maddie: *Shut up, asswhore!*
Me: Asswhore?
CiCi: *Speaking of the asswhore—did she mention the new guy ramming it up there?*
Maddie: *What?! Charley, you've been holding out?*
CiCi: *No—she's been putting out! You're a damn whore, Charley—I'm jealous!*
Maddie: *Hold the fucking phone, people! Charley—who's melting his Creamsicle in your love oven?*
CiCi: *Maddie—don't say hold the phone people in a texting conversation—we're clearly all holding the phone, dipshit!*
Maddie: *Fuck off, CiCi! Who's plunging his hotdog in your cornmeal batter, Charley?*

These girls are all fucking nuts! I love 'em!
It's Tom, isn't it?! ;-)

Who the fuck is Tom?

Is it Harry?

Harry?! I feel my blood boil.

CiCi: *It's neither of them, but it's definitely a Dick.*
Me: Are you calling Mitch a dick?

I thought she liked me.

CiCi: *No, asshat—you're getting dick.*
Don't be a dumb chick!
Hey—is it nice and thick?
Maddie: *Knock it off, Dirty Dr. Seuss!*
CiCi: *Whose baby sister is getting juice in the caboose ...*
Maddie: *Ugh—gross!*
CiCi: *Jealous?*
Maddie: *Yes.*
CiCi: *Me, too.*
Maddie: *Charley?*
CiCi: *You can still text with Mitch's dick in your mouth.*
Me: Sorry—tough to text and suck at the same time.
Maddie: *Don't I know it!*
CiCi: *Don't I know it!*
Maddie: *Jinx!*
CiCi: *What are we, twelve?*
Me: Or closet whores.
CiCi: *There's a closet around here?*
Maddie: *So, his name is Mitch?*
CiCi: *And Charley's his bitch!*
Maddie: *Tell me!*

I'll play—I'm bored, remember?

Me: His dick is huge! I don't know how I'm walking!
CiCi: *That's not what you told me before!*
Me: What?
CiCi: *Well, that solves it then.*
Me: Solves what?
Maddie: *Solves what?*
Me: Jinx!
Maddie: *Yes—we're twelve!*
CiCi: *I won't take him up on his offer.*
Me: What offer?
CiCi: *He wants to fuck me.*
Me: No he doesn't!
CiCi: *He told me!*
Me: When?!
CiCi: *When you were checking on the baby. He was staring at my mouth.*
Me: What?
CiCi: *He wants to fuck my mouth, Charley. I'm sorry.* ☹
Me: He was probably thinking of a way to shut you and your Matchbox mouth up!
CiCi: *Huh?*
Me: Yeah, motormouth!
CiCi: *Mitch!*
Me: What?

Damn it!

CiCi: *Busted! Maddie, let me introduce you to Mitch.*
Maddie: *NO! I told him STUFF!*
CiCi: *You may call him DICK.*
Maddie: *I feel so betrayed ...*
Me: Sorry, Maddie. Smile at him ... he'll love you! ☺
Maddie: *Crap.*
CiCi: *Right?*
Me: Did I miss something?
CiCi: *Yeah, the memo.*

Me: What memo?
Maddie: *Don't fuck with the GEGs!*
Me: GEGs?
CiCi: *Green-Eyed Girl Club.*
We dropped the C for Club.
Me: Why?
Maddie: *Because we're really not twelve anymore—I know—hard to believe!*
CiCi: *Ashton would be proud ...*
Me: Huh?
CiCi: *Consider yourself punk'd, biatch!*
Me: Maddie—you knew it was me?
Maddie: *Uh, yeah!*
Me: No Viking then?
CiCi: *Shit—you mentioned the Viking before I got to you?*
Maddie: *And now ...*
I must kill you, Mitch!
CiCi: *U can't! He's giving it to Charley good—bitch can't keep the smile off her face.*
Me: ☺ Ahh, Charlotte ...
Maddie: *Oh, all right—you're on probation, though!*
Me: Thanks! Shit—does Charlotte know I'm talking to you girls?
CiCi: *And waste this opportunity to completely mortify her? HELL NO!*
Maddie: *Knock, knock, Mitch.*
Me: Uh, who's there?

"Mitch, what are you doing on my phone?" Charlotte asks. As I look at her, she says bye to Maddie and hangs up the house phone.

Me: Not nice Maddie—not nice!
It's on, lady! Consider yourself warned!

Charlotte grabs the phone from me just as I complete my threat. She starts reading our dialogue.

"You pretended to be me? What the fuck is that about?" she asks angrily as she skims the conversation. The girls continue to talk, pushing the screen up. I can't help but chuckle as she gets frustrated. She gives up on scrolling and sits down.

Charlotte

"YOU'RE LAUGHING—YOU THINK this is funny?" I sit on the bed and shoot him my eye daggers. His stupid grin drops. Goddamn it, would these two bitches shut up so I can read what he wrote?!

Just as I read Maddie's text, *"Don't be mad at him—we played him,"* I feel Mitch's hands hook under my knees. He yanks me down. I scoff and stare at him impatiently. The look on his face can only be described one way—aggressive lust. He whips my knees open and stares into my eyes. I know I'm not going to get away with being pissed off.

"Jesus and goddamn it, Charlotte," he says under his breath as he finally glances down.

"You like my invisible panties, baby?" I bait him. "They're edible."

"You see," he says, shaking a finger at me like he's trying to hold something back, "this is the kind of shit that's going to get your ass spanked." And with that, he slaps the inside of both my thighs, pushing me open wider for him.

I lick my lips, staring straight back at him. In the same beat, I text the girls.

Me: G'nite girls!

I'm about to get cream filling for my love muffin, with extra nuts slapped on top!

CiCi: *Lucky bitch!*
Maddie: *Lucky bitch!*

Mitch grabs the phone from me. I shoot him a playful smirk and begin to slowly unbutton my nightgown. I lick my lips again and bite down on my bottom one as I open my nightgown at a pace I'm sure is driving him mad. I make sure to graze my nipples with my fingertips as I pull the gown away and let my breath quicken at my own touch. I lean up and pull it off of myself and lay back down.

"Charlotte, close your eyes, baby." His voice is smooth and sexy as usual. I comply. The blood pounding in my ears is deafening. I'm learning to expect the unexpected with him. "Touch yourself, baby. I want to watch you. Show me what you'll do to yourself when I'm not here to do it for you." *Oh, holy hell!* "I'm not here, baby ... show me." *Yeah ... sure he's not here!*

Deep, cleansing yoga breath.
Exhale slowly.
I bring my hands up to my clavicles.
Slowly, my hands slide down.
And ...
Deep, cleansing yoga breath
Good Lord ...
Exhale slowly ...
Pull it together, Charley!
You're a sexy bitch—you can do this!

My inner sexy bitch nudges my hands along. They stop at the top of my breasts and glide down the sides, following the soft curves. Further down my torso, my hand plants itself quietly on its side. My fingers trace swirly circles around my belly, up the center, over my sternum, and back down. The fingertips of my other hand travel up and over my breast and lightly circle my nipple.

"Ah," I gasp as I roll and tug at my nipples. I can hear Mitch's breath hitch as I continue and arch my body into my touch. I dare to open my eyes to watch him watching me. His gaze locks onto mine. Just when I think I've had the most erotic moment of my life ... he goes and gives me another one. "Baby, please ..." I beg in a whisper.

"Keep going," he encourages me breathily.

"No." I stop.

"No?" he asks. The heated glaze leaves his eyes and is replaced by confusion.

"Mitch, I will do this for you ... another time." I sit up and grasp his face. "I only have tonight with you. I don't want to spend it touching myself. I want your hands on me, your touch driving me crazy," I plead.

His eyes soften as a small smile graces his lips.

"Okay, baby." His lips sweep mine. "Okay," he whispers and gently pulls my hands away from his face. He plants a kiss in the center of each palm. "Three months ..." he whispers, as if those two words are the most painful thing he's ever said. I'm right there with him. My heart clamps down painfully and my eyes fill up. "Baby ... no." His voice is so soft and nurturing. His thumbs work diligently at pushing my tears away.

"I'm sorry." I shake my head. He pulls my face closer, and his lips graze over mine with such aching reluctance I can sense his impending need to devour me. Mitch slowly pushes me onto my back. His lips taste every inch of my face and kiss away my tears.

Why? Why have I fallen so quickly, so hard? I feel like I can't breathe. The thought of not feeling his touch, seeing his smile, taking in his scent ... it's killing me. How did this happen?

"I need you," he says, his voice giving way to the torture he must be feeling. I raise my knees at his sides. My hands climb up the back of his neck and I urgently pull his mouth to mine.

"Mitch," I cry against his lips as I feel him stretch me harshly. Our mouths stay open against each other's as we absorb the sensation of our union.

"Charlotte," Mitch says with such tortured need.

Nothing else is said. All efforts are directed toward getting as close to each other as possible. This is it. We're savoring every touch, kiss, and thrust of closeness. This is it—for three months—no physical contact. It feels like a sentence, some punishment for feeling things we should have never felt for each other in the first place.

Mitch laces his fingers with mine and pins my hands down on either side of my head. With his forehead against mine, he grinds deeper into me at an agonizingly slow pace as we climb together. It's sweet and painful all at once—and so intense.

"I can't," I whimper. *Can't what? Be without him? Not feel his touch—can't what?*

"Shh ..."

Even the way he shushes me is sexy.

Mitch and I lay still, still connected, still wanting more. Still in the moment. I open my eyes and stare into his hazel ones.

"Kryptonite," he whispers. *Yeah... Kryptonite.*

Chapter Eight

"YOU READY FOR yoga, bitch?" CiCi walks through my front door, her Hallmark greeting followed by a loud belch.

"I just don't understand why you're single, Ceese." I roll my eyes.

"Holy shit ... who the fuck died?" She looks around, ignoring my comment.

"I think he misses me." I smile shyly, looking at the several dozen roses Mitch sent me. It's been three weeks since he left, yet it feels like months.

"I think you must have a platinum pussy you've failed to tell me about!" She pulls out her phone, hits a few buttons, and brings it to her ear. I grab my hoodie, but swiftly turn back when I hear her bark Mitch's name. "Dude, knock it off with the flowers already! It looks and smells like a fucking funeral home in here! Besides, Charley's not all that fond of roses. She likes fancy little delicate flowers. I don't know what they're called, but I'm sure you have people to figure that shit out! Okay, well ... Okinawa and samurai swords! Later, bitch!" CiCi ends the call and I stare at her, dumbfounded, until I realize I've rolled my eyes so far back in my head they may be stuck.

"Okinawa and samurai swords?" I yell.

"He's in Japan, right?" She shrugs. "I thought it'd be fun to give him a Japanese greeting."

"Very thoughtful." I shake my head. "But I'm pretty certain no one uses that particular greeting in Japan ... or planet Earth."

"Well, they should—it sounds cool." She repeats it again and takes a ninja stance.

"C'mon, let's get to yoga. I desperately need to talk to Maddie." I shake my head again.

"About what?" She pops her gum and zips her tracksuit jacket.

"About getting you electroshock therapy—there is something wrong with your head!" I grab my keys. "Mom, we're heading out now!" I yell before closing the door behind us.

"Charley." CiCi's face suddenly looks serious. "Have you noticed Mom fumbling a bit?"

"Yeah, I have. A few weeks ago. I've been meaning to talk to Dad about it. He gave me 'The Look.'" I start up my SUV.

"He's so worried about burdening us." She shakes her head.

"That's so silly! We're family ... we take care of each other," I grumble as we head down the street.

"Speaking of all that shit, they're behind on a lot of bills."

"How do you know?" I look over at her.

"Really?" she asks. Right ... she knows because she's a nosy bitch. "I grabbed the bills without them knowing to see what I could pay. I thought we could all chip in." She pulls them out of her purse to show me the stack. CiCi is probably the most abrasive person I know, but she's also got the biggest, kindest heart. Don't tell her I said that, though—it would totally ruin the front she puts up.

"Stick it in my bag. I'll take care of it." I sigh.

"Uh ... how?"

"I got a big advance."

"I bet you did!" She laughs.

"Shut up, whore!" I snap playfully.

"You sure you got this?"

"Yeah ... besides, do we want to involve our sisters?" I shoot her a sideways glance.

"Oh hell fucking no!" She throws the bills into my bag.

Colleen, Caitlyn, and Caroline are fantastic people. They are good daughters and wonderful sisters ... most of the time. However, they've all moved away, leaving CiCi and me here to hold the fort with Mom and Dad. It always amazes CiCi and me how quick they all are to tell us what we should be doing or that we're doing something "incorrectly." Yet, they never seem to get their asses out here to help us. Not that our parents need a lot of care, but they are getting up there in years and with Mom's multiple sclerosis, we need to pitch in more when she's out of remission.

"Mitch's mom had MS too," I say aloud as the thought occurs to me. I never mentioned to him that my mom has it. We were in the middle of another issue at that time. Since then, the topic hasn't come up.

"Sucks," she says. "Oh well ... let's go find our fucking Zen." She opens the door as I pull into a space. "You two look like fucking freaks walking next to each other!" CiCi bellows. I look up to see Maddie and Julie heading our way and can't help my chuckle—she's right!

Maddie is a little thing, at just a smidge over five feet. Her hair is dark brown, almost black. It sits just above her shoulders, and lately she's decided on bangs. Quite frankly, her hair is so thick and her face so little, it looks as if the former may swallow the latter. Maddie would totally love that I called her "little"—it's a daily uphill battle to keep her curves at bay.

Next to Maddie is Julie—or "that fucking bitch," as we refer to her. You see, Julie is just a pinch under six feet thanks to her never-ending gorgeous legs. They find themselves attached to the most perfectly shaped body that knows not how to retain fluid no matter how much greasy, fattening crap Julie throws in her mouth.

Julie is gorgeous and her long, dark, strawberry-blonde hair makes her look exotic. She models, as one does when they look like that. I think it's some sort of contract: *We will give you this amazing body and good looks but you must use it in a way that makes every other woman on the planet feel like shit.* That she-devil signed it!

"We don't look like freaks ... we look like a conversational piece," she says before slurping the rest of her Coffee Coolatta down, along with its calories. Fucking bitch!

The four of us plow through the door of Ava's yoga studio, causing—I'm sure—an inward cringe on Ava's part.

"Hey, Ava, go easy today for Charley's sake," Julie says immediately—and a little too loudly—as she throws her stuff in a cubby hole. "Her ass is still sore from the massive pounding it recently received."

"Go easy on us, too ... we're having sympathy ass pains," CiCi chimes in, throwing her bag in another. "Jesus Christ, Julie! Maybe you'd get a little ass pounding if you'd stop letting shit die up there!" CiCi complains, waving at the air as she walks away.

"CiCi repellant," Julie shrugs before walking over to a mat.

Yessiree, my friends are some classy bitches—there's no denying it!

"Maddie, can't you prescribe them something?" Ava shakes her head.

"Give them a little shock therapy?" I add.

"Sorry, ladies, we can't fix their kind of crazy." She throws what she can of her hair into a ponytail and gets a mat.

"How are you doing?" I ask Ava quietly. She's been going through round after round of hormone injections to help her and Trent conceive.

"Better today." She nods. "Yesterday I was a raving lunatic and sick as a dog. I don't think I can do too much more of this. The point is to add to our family, not break it apart." She fans her eyes a little and shakes her head—her routine to hold back her tears.

Ava and Trent have been married for ten years, and trying to have a baby for nine of them. They've been on an adoption list forever, and are involved with the foster-care system. They came close to adopting a few times, but the biological parents changed their minds. It's been heartbreaking to sit on the sidelines and watch them go through this over and over again, and I can only imagine how it's been for them.

"Charley, now's not the time to really mention this, but Trent and I have been talking ..."

"Good. It's good to do that in a marriage." I try to lighten the mood. She gives me a half smile.

"We're considering taking you up on your offer, if you're still serious about it. It would mean the world to us. I just don't know how much more we can take." She sighs, shakes her head, and walks away. I decide to stand in place until I'm sure my legs won't give out.

Ava finds her mat at the front of the now-packed class and ties her medium-length blonde hair into a ponytail.

"C'mon, Charley." She waves for me to get on my mat. *Right* ...

"CHRIST, CHARLEY, WAKE up!" CiCi kicks my leg. "Ava, why did you have to do the effin' yoga nidra? You know that shit sends her right out!"

"I'm up. I'm up." I wipe my face.

"Dude, stop taking it up the ass so much," Julie suggests.

"Julie—Christ—shut up!" Ava snaps vehemently at her.

"What crawled up your twat?" Julie looks at her as if she's smelled something foul.

"Julie, know when to stop!" I throw my hands out for emphasis as Ava walks away, pissed or in tears—quite possibly both.

"What?" She widens her eyes.

"Stop being so fucking pretty! You know what she's going through!" I say in a low voice as I roll my mat with more force than the task requires.

"Shit! Ugh! Why am I so dumb?" She smacks her forehead.

"We can't all be the brains behind this operation." Maddie pats Julie's arm.

"Yeah, thanks, short stack ... I guess." Julie nods and heads over to Ava, hopefully to apologize.

CiCi watches as the last yogi leaves. "You know what the problem is? There's too many of us. I mean, who else runs around constantly in a posse with four other bitches? Outside of us, I don't know any other woman our age who still hangs in a large crowd all the time! Hormones are raging, we rag at the same time ..."

"First of all, no, you did *not* just call us a 'posse' like it's 1990," I start.

"Second, what do you suggest? Should we start voting people off?"

Maddie adds.

"Yeah. You first, bitch." CiCi smirks at her. Maddie replies with a hand gesture—it's not "I love you."

"The problem is that you guys forget sometimes that other people are walking this planet. You need to tone it down with the 'ass pounding' and 'asswhore' comments around people who are not only strangers, but have no idea we're actually kidding. It's funny to us, but these people look at us as if we're wearing capes with 'AW' for 'asswhores' on it." As soon as I say it, they stop and look up, pondering.

"I call dark purple with turquoise initials," CiCi says.

"Lime green with purple initials," I say.

"Red, white, and blue, because I'm the captain, bitches!" Maddie smirks.

"Sure, Maddie ... you can be captain of the asswhores." CiCi laughs.

"Yeah ... it's all you, babe," I chime in.

"Faaaaaccckk! You two are irritating!" She shakes her head and walks over to her cubby, leaving us to continue laughing.

"We all better now?" CiCi asks as Julie and Ava come back out from her office.

"Yes," Ava sighs, pushing away nothing with her hands.

"Dinner ... girls?" Julie asks.

"That was hard for you, wasn't it?" Maddie asks sympathetically.

"Bitches!" Julie says in a quick cough.

"Whores!" Ava says in the same manner.

"By the power invested in me, by the plaques on my walls," Maddie announces, "I now diagnose us all perpetually twelve!"

"We should've never swapped spit," I say, then cringe.

"It was just that one time, Charley, and it's still hot in my mind," Ava teases.

"There the fuck you are!" CiCi bumps her with her hip.

We decide to get Mexican after everyone agrees that CiCi will not have to sit next to Julie

Mitch

MY PHONE ALARM vibrates violently, nearly sending it off the edge of the nightstand. I grab it and turn it off. I don't know why I bothered to set it; I haven't slept well since I've been here.

"CiCi." I read the voicemail alert aloud and suddenly feel nervous. Is something wrong? I quickly hit the button and listen. "Okinawa and samurai swords?" I laugh. She is one crazy bitch! How can you not love her? This is almost as good as the simple text she sent me yesterday—a picture of her flipping me off. I decide to text Charlotte before I head out.

What are you up to, baby?
Out with all the girls. It's been eventful!
Oh ... how so?
Well, apparently, we're a posse of super asswhores diligently working on color schemes for our capes. Maddie's is red, white, and blue because she's our captain. We have a severe case of Tourette's between the five of us. Ava and I swapped spit at some point in our lives—the memory still burns hot in her mind. CiCi finds Julie's ass offensive and Maddie has diagnosed us all perpetually twelve!
And, oh yeah ... some yoga was performed in the midst of all of that!
So just another typical day for the GEGs?
Yeah ... basically! ☺
I hate how much I miss you!
We need to talk about something very serious.
I miss you too!
And ...
I hate it ...
You can't do that!
What?
Say we need to talk about something serious and leave me hanging.
Not on text!
And not when you're running out the door!

I'm calling you now!
No! I'm with the girls.
CHARLOTTE!
Nah nah nah nah
U
Can't
Spank
Me!
Maddie's diagnosis is correct! ☹
Not nice! ☹
I will call you after my meeting!!
♥

Kiss kiss ... possibly a spank or two!
Tsk, tsk, Mitchy!
No more to drink!
☺

Ugh! Why did she have to say that? Not a chance in hell I'm going to be able to concentrate in my meeting now.

"Uh ... Mitch, you all right?"

I turn to face Kyle as I finish buttoning my cuffs. "Yeah, man. Everything set for the meeting?"

"Yes. Don't forget the change we talked about in the PowerPoint presentation," he says. I stare at him blankly. "The problem that will hinder production at the pace they want for their model?" he questions, apparently hoping to spark a memory. "Shit, Mitch ... what's going on with you?" he asks.

What's going on with me?

Charlotte McKendrick. And she needs to tell me something serious.

"Mitch!" Kyle practically yells. I'm like a deer in the headlights. Shit. This is not good.

"Kyle, can you run the meeting today?" I shake my head, trying to snap out of it.

"Uh ... yeah." Kyle's eyes widen. I understand his confusion—I never hand over the reins! "Are you okay? Are you sick?"

"Um ... no. Yes. No. I'm okay. I'm not sick," I try to clarify. "C'mon, let's go." I grab my jacket and lead us out.

Kyle remains quiet the entire time we're traveling to the meeting. What's there to say besides stating the obvious? I'm off.

"Do you want to talk about it?" he asks before the elevator reaches the floor.

"Nope," I say quickly.

"HEH—UP—OH." CHARLOTTE GIGGLES.

"Baby, how much did you drink?" Great. I just listened to Kyle chew me out for twenty minutes—something he's never done before, me being his boss and all. Now she's tipsy. Too tipsy to tell me what she meant earlier.

"Uhh ..." she trails off like she's thinking, then giggles again.

"Go to bed!" I yell and hang up. Just as I throw my cell down on the chair in my office, there's a knock on my door. It flies open barely a second later, warranting my full attention.

"Mitch, goddamn it! Talk to me!" Kyle snaps after closing my door. Shit. I knew he had a pair—I've seen it plenty of times in the board-room. But he's never used them toward me.

"Twice in one day. That must be some sort of record." I give him a smile fully laced with the respect he deserves.

"Cut the shit, man! I have been your right-hand guy for ten years, and I have never seen you off your game like this! What *the fuck* is going on?" Kyle stands in front of me with his tie loose, his top button undone, his sleeves rolled back, and his hands on his hips like I'm his kid brother or something. He kind of looks like a politician who's been out greeting "the people" in an attempt to get their vote. I chuckle slight-ly—he'd make a great politician. "You think this is funny, Mitch?" he yells. "This meeting was not only to go over the production issue, but to pitch our latest innovation in emissions control, and you were spewing out information on technology that's two years old!" His face actually turns red.

This is why I trust and respect Kyle. His loyalty, drive, and devotion to my company cannot be competed with. One would think this was his company too, what with all the blood, sweat, and tears he's poured into it. Because his dedication is as solid as mine, I presume he's in the same lonely predicament when he goes home at night.

And just like that, it hits me. All at once.

"I want more, Kyle," I state with steadfast determination.

"More? Mitch, I can't give you any more than I have. I don't think it's humanly possible." He stares at me, his eyes wide and mouth agape.

"No, man. I want more for *us* ... both of us." I try to clarify, though I don't think I've done a good job, seeing as his eyes look like they could blow out of their sockets. "Relax, man! I'm not saying I want to bend you over my desk and make you my bitch!" I laugh, lightly at first, but then can't hold back when I see him calm down. "All I'm saying is, we need to do a massive overhaul on how we handle shit! I don't want to live like this anymore. And, no offense, but you're not really the person I want to grow old with." I pick up my phone and sit in the chair.

"I don't know what to say, Mitch, except, well, that hurts my feelings. I always try to look nice for you." Kyle sounds sincere before he laughs at my expression. He sits down across from me and inhales deeply. "What are you thinking?" He exhales forcefully.

"Well, first things first, no more three-month tours! We're businessmen, not rock stars!" I say, pulling up my schedule.

"Yeah, but we rock at business," Kyle states.

I raise an eyebrow. What's up with him? He's a little off, in a good way. Relaxed, actually. He's a good guy to be around, but he's usually very serious. He never jokes, never relaxes, and his mind is usually on the next five things he has to do.

"You're different," I say.

"Pot, kettle, man." He smirks.

I furrow my brow. "What do you mean?"

"So far, you've been acting differently this entire trip."

"How so?"

"The truth?" His eyes widen in a challenge.

I nod. "Nothing but."

"Lack of focus aside," he starts. I shift in my seat, prepared to interject, but he raises his hand. "You've been more relaxed, more approachable. Dare I say ... more human?" He smirks.

"What the hell does that mean?" I snap. He laughs and shakes his head. We're silent for a moment.

"Sorry. Go on." I nod again.

"Mitch, I've been working with you for ten years. Given that, I'm probably the only person in the company who's ever seen you let your guard down naturally and joke around, but ... it doesn't happen often. You're serious, ultra-focused ... normally." That same stupid smirk returns. "She must really be something, that Charlotte."

Thoughts of Charlotte and her sexy little smile, her girlish giggle, and her oh-so-soft skin dance around in my mind. I'd give anything to run my nose up her neck right now, as pathetic as it sounds. I bring my attention to Kyle as I hear him chuckle.

"What?"

"Throw the towel in, man—your bachelorhood is over. The mere mention of her name and you get this glazed-over look." He smiles broadly. He's genuinely happy for me.

I'm glad to have Kyle in my life. Sure, our relationship began as strictly coworkers. Over the years it's morphed into a very comfortable friendship, mainly because of our similar drive, focus, and ridiculous hours spent working together in a day. We've both done our fair share of alienating, pushing aside old friendships. I'm not sure of his reasons, but I'm well aware of mine.

Being with Charlotte, even for such a short amount of time, and getting to know her friends, I feel a part of me coming back to life that I thought was long gone. The part of me that remembers the simple joy of laughing at—or doing—stupid shit with good friends. Good, lifelong friends like Chip McGregor and Pete Sullivan, whom I slowly pushed out of my life to focus on business, to ignore my memories, my loss. I couldn't be around them anymore—not without Kelly.

Kelly.

"Mitch?" Kyle's voice sounds strange. I look back at him. "What's going on, man? Your mood just went south."

"Nothing." I quickly shake my head and refocus. "So, do we have the numbers and logistics plans ready for the Nusaki meeting on Friday?

We don't need any fuckups, albeit mine or anyone else's." I get up and pour some scotch to ease the tightening in my chest.

"Mitch?"

"Well?" I ignore his confused look.

"Yeah, man. Everything is set. Mitch, go home," he adds. "I got this. Take a week or two. Go be with her, man. That's where your heart is right now, not here." He slaps my shoulder.

"I'm Mitch Colton. Mitch Colton doesn't take time off, remember? Especially for a piece of ass." I cringe as I say it.

"Yeah, I remember. What I don't remember is Mitch Colton speaking in third person, or ever saying something so disrespectful toward Charlotte in the past three weeks. I don't get it, man. One minute you're grinning like a lovesick puppy, and the next you're like ice." He stares at me, waiting, I think, to see which way my mood will go.

"It's nothing."

"Dude, it's something! Is it because I reminded you about her? Did you guys get into an argument?"

Christ, why won't he drop this?

I swirl the cubes around in my scotch. "No," I say, before taking one swig, then another, as blue eyes dance across my memory. "I'm always thinking about Charlotte," I say. Another swig.

Scent of vanilla.

"I know you are. That's why your behavior doesn't make any sense."

"I was thinking about someone else ... remembering ..." I trail off and take the last swig.

Hair the color of sunshine.

"Who?"

Little freckles all over her round, beautiful face.

I take in a shaky breath and close my eyes, trying to remember the sound of her laughter.

"My wife." I breathe out and feel my heart drop.

"What?" he asks in disbelief.

"Kyle, I need to be alone now. I'll see you tomorrow." I put my glass down and grab my suit jacket before stepping out of the office. Kyle stares at me, dumbfounded. Then again, why wouldn't he? He had no idea I was ever married.

Chapter Nine

Charlotte

DEEP BREATH.

I cut the engine, staring at Gram's garage. I open my door, fighting the urge—my cowardice, really—to rev the engine back up and leave.

No. I need answers.

She must know where he is, or at least that he's safe. Christ, let him be okay.

Two weeks.

Two weeks of no communication on his part. I've called. I've texted. I've emailed. I've Skyped. I've Face Timed. I've done everything short of sending a fucking pigeon.

No reply. Nothing.

Before I can knock on the door, Maggie opens it and gives me her welcoming smile.

"Hi, Maggie!" I hug her.

"Hello, baby girl ... we been expectin' you!" She pats my shoulder.

"You have?" I pull my head back from the hug.

"Child," she says, like it's the longest word in the dictionary, "she done told me this mornin' you was fixin' to come up here." Her eyes look up to the Heavens.

"Right," I say. Gram the Great and her magic crystal ball have struck again!

"You'd think she be givin' me my numbers by now, so I can gets me a lady in waitin'." She bats her eyes at me and I can't help but chuckle.

"Oh, but Maggie, where would that leave her?" I say, horrified in Gram's defense.

"See—that's exactly why she won't give me my damn numbers!" She shakes her head as she leads me to Gram.

Gram welcomes me with a gracious smile, only it doesn't hit her eyes. They are sad. Sad, I bet, because she knows why I'm here. This is exactly why I wanted to leave the moment I arrived. I could feel it in my bones—she's going to tell me something I don't want to hear. My tears have manned their stations. My chin quivers, allowing the first wave of drops to fall out of their respective pools.

Feeling paralyzed, all I can do is stand there, signing "Why?" She waves me over and pats the chair Mitch and I snuggled into the last time I was here. My legs—though they feel like Jell-O—finally move. I sit and she takes my hands in hers. She squeezes and rubs her soft, mani-cured thumbs across the top of my hand before releasing. "I'll start with this," she signs, then lifts a large scrapbook from her lap and places it on mine. She gives me an encouraging nod when I show my confusion.

I look down and open it.

The first page has a baby picture of Mitch that I've seen before in her albums, but I don't know who the other baby picture belongs to. I look up at Gram. She waves her hand for me to continue. The next pages have toddler pictures, then elementary school. I don't get it. Who is this girl? *Sister?* Ah—sister!

I ask Gram. She shakes her head. "Who?" I ask. She signs "Kelly." Turning the page, I find high school pictures.

The prom.

They were together. Kelly was his girlfriend.

Turn the page.

From his MIT sweatshirt and her Tufts, I guess college years. They stayed local. Well, those are two of the best schools in the country.

Turn the page.

They graduated from college. She also graduated to fiancée. My breath hastens to keep pace with my rapid heartbeats.

Turn the page.

Kelly became his wife.

They were so young.

I study the various photos.

They were so in love.

Turn the page.

Wedding reception.

Turn the page.

My breath hitches.

An ultrasound picture, next to a photo of Kelly holding up a sign that says "six weeks" next to her flat belly. She's smiling from ear to ear. *She's so beautiful.* Weeks seven ... eight ... nine ... so on and so forth, all the way up to week twenty-four.

"Is there another book?" I ask Gram, looking up. Her eyes are full of tears as she shakes her head and hands me an envelope. I give her a quizzical look. She takes in a hiccup-y sigh and grabs a tissue.

I look down at the envelope and carefully open it. Pulling out a yellowed, folded-up newspaper article, my belly clenches, telling me I don't want to open it. My fingers don't listen.

Oh God.

PREGNANT ANDOVER WOMAN KILLED BY DRUNK DRIVER

Kelly Colton, 24, was driving home from her parents' house when her car was allegedly struck by Craig Taylor, 35, of Wilmington. Mr. Taylor was going approximately 85 miles per hour with a blood alcohol level of 1.6; twice the legal limit. Mrs. Colton died on impact, as well as her unborn child. She was five months pregnant.

I put the article down. I couldn't read anymore if I wanted to. My tears won't let me. I close my eyes and suddenly flash back to the night

I spent with Mitch at his house. His behavior upon my earlier-than-expected arrival all makes sense now. *"How fucking fast were you flying? ... If anything ever happened to you, baby."* I gasp. Oh God, does it all make sense now! But ...

"Gram, I haven't heard from him in two weeks. I don't understand why he won't talk to me. Everything was fine, and then ... nothing." I search her eyes for an answer ... an idea ... anything. She nods in agreement and inhales deeply.

"Kelly," she signs, "was his world. They were crazy in love, and settled into that love. They were very young, but their love was old," she says. I stare at her blankly. She rolls her eyes at me. Wait! She rolled her eyes at me? *Ouch, Gram.*

"By the time they wed, it was like they had been married for years already," she explains. "They were comfortable and settled into their feelings for each other." I understand now, thinking of my parents. "When Kelly died, and the baby ... it changed him. Understandably so, of course. Instead of pulling strength from family and friends, he pushed everyone away. Eventually, everyone gave up—except us, of course. He poured himself into work—successfully, as you know."

I half smile and wait for her to continue. I don't know how it's possible, but apparently, sign language comes equipped with its own brand of "awkward silence." Gram seems content, though, as if she got a load off of her chest.

Me?

I'm still waiting ... like a fucking asshole.

"What does this have to do with him not talking to me?" My hands show my frustration, flying into action with the words I spit out.

"Oh," she mouths, and chuckles at herself in embarrassment. "Sorry," she signs, and adjusts herself in her seat. I give her a curt smile because it's much more polite than what I want to do for forgetting the "me" part of this story. I'm not mad at her, really—just frustrated with everything.

"He came to visit me after he met you, and I knew." She smiles. "I knew he met the one ... well, the other one." She winks at me. I humor her with a smile. "I saw something in my grandson I haven't seen in almost twenty years." Her eyes fill up.

Christ, I didn't even do the math before. My Mitch has been alone for almost twenty years. Well, in the affairs-of-the-heart department. She continues to tell me how she interrupted him mid-sentence to ask my name, and after saying it, he went right back to what he was talking about. I was the only girl he'd brought home since Kelly. How happy he's been since I walked into his life. That he's his old, genuine self again.

"Then ..." she signs.

"Then what?" I ask.

"Two weeks ago, he started talking about Kelly and Isabella, wanting to start another foundation in their names." She shakes her head.

Isabella? Oh. I think of how he was with Brooky, and my heart breaks a little more.

"I said that was nice, and then I asked about you. He gave me a quick 'she's fine' and carried on. For the past two weeks, all he's talked about is Kelly and all their memories. I ask him about you, and he changes the subject. Finally, the other day, I asked him why he didn't talk about you anymore. He just said, 'Gram—it's over—let it go.'"

I gasp at this and look around frantically. I'm pretty sure a brown paper bag should magically appear at this point, as I am in the beginning stages of hyperventilating.

"I don't get it! I don't understand!" I look at her, bewildered. "I don't think I did or said anything wrong." She shakes her head and grabs my hand.

"It's guilt," she says. "I think one day, probably weeks ago, he realized he was thinking more about you and less about Kelly."

"So, he's pushing me away?"

"Yes."

"What should I do?" I shake my hands frantically. I don't want to lose him. I ... I care deeply about him.

"Don't let him get away with it. Be patient. Be persistent. Be his light out of the darkness. Please, Charlotte, he loves you. Don't give up on him."

"Love?" I shake my head.

"Yes! He's loved you from the moment he met you. I know my grandson."

Mitch was right—she can be so loud.

"You know, I know a thing or two about a thing or two, so don't scoff at me when I say that you love him, too!"

I scoff.

She smacks my legs and stares daggers at me. "If you didn't love him, you wouldn't be here!" she adds.

I look at the floor, and despite my efforts, feel my face contort into "ugly cry" face. Once you've converted to "ugly cry" face, there's no coming back from it for at least an hour. Gram smacks my knee and I glance up.

She smiles. "I've got a plan!"

"What is it?" I ask, feeling some hope resurface.

"Wednesday night—take me to bingo!" She taps my lap, her smile huge.

"Gram, no offense, but you're ninety. Going to bingo is not a plan—it's a staple."

"Smartass!" she signs, then adds in an extra gesture.

I'll pretend to not have noticed—ahem.

"What's this brilliant plan of yours?"

"I usually talk to him on Spike during intermission, remember?" She taps my knee again.

She's a tapper.

"It's Skype, and yes, I remember." I remember being confused as hell when she started playing this "Horse" game. I started marking my board and she tapped me to stop. "Horse" is a separate game from bingo, but has to do with it and the little cards they get people to buy stacks and stacks of. I'd explain it to you, only I'm still confused by it!

"Well, we're going to plant a seed." She smiles and winks.

I fight the urge to ask "What'chu talkin' 'bout, Willis?" because it may lose its thunder by the time I'm done signing and she may not get it anyway. "Seed?" I question instead.

"You'll see." She rubs her palms together with a smirk. No Dr. Evil laugh ensues, though it would be perfect timing.

"FUCK ..." I say under my breath as I stare into a sea of curly white-haired ladies. I pull my cell out and go into my grocery list, suddenly remembering something to add.

19. *Q-tips*

I bring my focus back to pushing Gram's wheelchair as she is convulses in it, pointing out prime seating for us.

I see the reason for this state of urgency.

Agnes McAlister of the Andover McAlisters (she actually introduced herself that way last time) is breaking a sweat pushing her tennis-balled walker, with her new hip and an abundance of determination.

And ...

She's making a beeline for our hot (I can't believe no one snatched these puppies up yet) seats. My heart races as I map out the quickest way to cut Agnes off and get there first.

Oh, the pressure ...

We dash! Well, I dash ... she rolls. We weave in and around people. "Sorry!" I say as I turn my head to a gentleman after having almost knocked his plated pretzel from his hand. I turn back, just in time to barely swerve around a lady with an oxygen tank. She's not happy with me. I got that much from all the words she spewed at me. Well, my foot *did* get caught in her tubing and—not being able to stop—I *did* yank her nasal cannula off her face.

This is one of those moments in life that requires slow-motion instant replay—I look that ri-goddamn-diculous!

It's worth it, though, to beat Agnes. Gram declares victory by raising her right fist and slapping her bicep with her hand. *Gotta love Gram!*

"So, what's the plan?" I huff as I collapse into my seat.

"First stage of the plan," she says, spreading out bingo packets, "is we play bingo."

I stare at her blankly.

Blink ... blink, blink.

"Brilliant ... that's brilliant! Why didn't I think of that?" She's fucking senile! *What the hell am I doing here?*

She taps my arm and gives me an encouraging smile. "First bingo ... then seed," she signs.

"Okay, Mrs. Miyagi." I sign, then bow. She stares at me, thoroughly trying to understand what I said. I roll my eyes and stand up. I turn to her and perform the famous crane kick to perfection. Gram stares at me as if I'm bat-shit crazy. I must be—I just channeled CiCi. I notice the awkward silence around us and look up to find I'm the cause of it.

"Spasm," I mumble as I sit. Most nod, and some yell out their ailments to me like it's a competition.

Thankfully, the bingo caller comes over the speakers. His voice is loud and words incoherent. The sea of Q-tip heads hang on to every incoherent word like their lives depend on it. This must be the geriatric version of *Survivor*.

Charley, stop! You love old people. You love their Q-tip heads. You love bingo! You just don't love the situation you're in right now. When I'm right—I'm right. Pure frustration. *Sorry sweet, elderly people, with all of your ailments that I'd prefer to not repeat, I'm done taking it out on you.* Except you, squeaky walker lady! That shit was squeaking three weeks ago! Take your winnings and buy some damn WD-40 already! Okay ... now I'm done.

"O 69!"

Oh ... 69. Mmm ... Mitch ...

I smack my head.

"B 4!"

Yes, before Kitty starts aching.

"HIT THE CONCESSIONS," she signs after tapping my arm.

"But ..." I say, trailing off. "The last game isn't done yet." She shakes her head and shoos me away with a wave of her hand.

"You're so bossy!" I tell her before giving a disgruntled sigh she won't hear. She winks.

Sometimes, it's hard to believe we've only known each other for five weeks. I feel like she's always been a part of my life. You know that feeling you get when you meet somebody for the first time, but they're so familiar to you? I had that feeling with Mitch, too. *Mitch.* I choke back my tears. Oh, how I miss him. How I want to rip his ball sack off and throw it to Loxy and Vader to play with!

If I can't resolve this with him somehow, I'm taking myself off the market for good. He's ruined other men for me anyway! Besides that, I'm pretty content with my track record of having two men abandon me in one year, through no fault of my own. I don't think three will be a charm in this specific case. No, I'm done. I'm going to spend my free time finding Jesus. *Mitch helped you find Jesus.* Jesus Christ, inner Charlotte ... shut up! *See?!* That was a different Jesus! That was sex Jesus. That was orgasm Jesus. That was "pray for my vagina to make it through another night with him" Jesus! *Jesus, that was good!* Hail Mary, sister! *Amen.* I do the sign of the cross.

Within ten minutes I head back to Gram, silently thanking her for shooing me out ahead of the crowd. The stampede is both impressive and brutal. I crouch down beside her as she's fixing her tablet to go in her stand. As I unwrap her pie and place it in front of her, I hear a gasp. I look at Gram and she's flipping someone off. I follow the path of her eyes and my breath hitches.

Mitch.

He's angrily staring at her through the tablet. His eyes dart to me and I watch them soften, looking ... remorseful.

We stare at each other in silence for what seems like an hour. I half expect tumbleweeds to roll between the tablet and me.

Sensing he will do something cowardly, like ending the Skype call, I speak up.

"You need to apologize to Brogan for being a complete fucking asshole. He didn't ask you to be a part of his life. You bonded with him. You made him feel important, like he mattered. Unlike his father. You took this poor, innocent kid, built him up, and then shattered him. No explanation, nothing. You just tossed him aside, like he didn't matter to you. He didn't do anything wrong. Oh, wait—he trusted you. Big mistake, huh?" I ask, my voice dripping with condescension. I do nothing to push my tears away. I'm just glad for the ability to articulate my words.

Mitch's eyes are so sad, and they look tormented—*good*! "He deserves an apology, Mitch," I reiterate. "If you could stop being a selfish prick for one minute to call him, I'd appreciate it greatly!"

"Baby—"

I cut him off. "No! You don't get to call me that!"

He nods, a defeated look on his face. He leans forward and ends the call.

I exhale and gasp.

I look at Gram. She's grinning ear to ear. "That went well," she signs and taps my hand.

"You. Are. Crazy!" I sign dramatically.

"I'm a gardener who planted a seed. Now watch it grow, dear."

"What are you talking about?"

"Out of sight—out of mind? Not exactly true for him, but it has helped. He needed to see you, to see your eyes. He needed to remember what—who—he is pushing away. He loves you. It was all over his face when he saw you. Now for phase two." She rubs her palms together.

"What's phase two?"

"The second half of bingo. Sit. They're getting ready." She points to my seat.

She must be senile!

Chapter Ten

MY EYES SHOOT open. I'm not sure why. I glance at my alarm clock. Six a.m. glares at me in all its green glory. The doorbell rings. Ah, that's what woke me up! I jump out of bed and make a mad dash out of my room and down the stairs. There are only two reasons somebody would ring the doorbell to a house with small children at this hour: an emergency, or that person has a death wish.

I shush the dogs and jerk the door open.

"Stop!" I push her hand down just before she touches the bell again.

"I'm so sorry, Charlotte," she says quickly. "I assumed everyone was up, since I was told to arrive at this time." I can tell she feels bad. I just don't know who the hell this woman is.

"I'm sorry, who are you and who told you to arrive at this time?" I ask her flippantly, which I don't mean to do, but I am *not* a morning person.

"I'm Pauline. Maggie's daughter. Mitch hired me to nanny for you," she says slowly, as if trying to spark some recollection of this plan.

"Mitch? He hired you? When?" I'm so confused. It's only been two days since our cyber stare down.

"Um ... yesterday." She tightens the grip on her purse strap. "He told me you've had a difficult time finding the right person. The family I was working for just relocated, so it's perfect timing." She smiles, but there is a flicker of hesitation in it. "Charlotte?"

"Yes?"

"Did Mitch not tell you I was coming today, or at all? Have you found a replacement? Do you want me to leave?" She turns her shoulder to head back down the stairs.

"No, no, and most definitely no!" I widen my eyes, shake my head, and smirk. "I'm sorry, Pauline, I'm not at my best this early in the morning. Please come in." I stand back and finally act like I grew up with some manners.

"You sure?"

"Oh yes, please!" I give her my warmest smile. She lets out a sigh of relief and a nervous chuckle. "Would you like some coffee?" I ask as I head toward the kitchen.

"Love some," she says, following me.

"Make yourself at home," I say, pointing to the table in the kitchen nook. She sits. "Feel like an omelet?" I ask, probably with too much excitement. Pauline laughs. "What?" I ask as I ready the coffeemaker.

"Mitch said you would try to feed me the moment I walked through the door. He said it was your 'thing' and that you're good at it, so I should just let you."

"He said all that?"

"Oh, he said a lot of things about you and the kids." She waves her hand. "Just about talked my ear off last night." She unzips her purse, shaking her head.

"What sort of things?" I ask as nonchalantly as I can while starting breakfast.

"Hold on." She shuffles through her purse. "Most of it was notes for me to write down." She pulls out a notepad. "He gave me your schedule for the week, but told me to double-check with you for any changes." She looks up at me. "What?"

"Uh ... nothing," I say and start moving about the kitchen again.

"Oh, that reminds me!" she says quickly. "Mitch booked you a spa day today since Friday is your slow day. You need to be there by nine sharp." She smiles. I work diligently at the eggs while holding back my tears.

"He told me all about Bennett's disorders. Vest ... vestibular processing disorder and proprioceptive disorder. He gave me the names of all his therapists at the school and Easter Seals. Gave me the links to several really good websites that explain what he's going through and how to help him."

"Pauline?" I stop her successfully, unlike my tears.

"Charlotte? Are you okay?" she asks when she looks up.

"He, um ... he gave you all of that information?" I blow my nose.

"Well, yes." She looks at me strangely.

The man I met only six weeks ago, only spent three days with in person and spoke with for three weeks via technology, the same man who hasn't uttered one word to me via any method in two weeks besides calling me "baby" the other night, has told this woman everything about my son as if he were his. If it were the million-dollar question on *Who Wants to Be a Millionaire?*—Josh would've lost.

I wipe my tears. "What else?"

"Uh ... he gave me Brogan's baseball schedule and asked me to have him read to me every day, even if it's just one chapter. I guess they just finished the first *Harry Potter* a couple of weeks ago."

"Wait, Broge read to Mitch every night they Skyped?" I knew they spoke every night for an hour or so, but I thought they were just discussing baseball and video games.

"Yes. He said it's the area he's been struggling in at school. Brogan reads him a chapter or two and then they discuss it to check his comprehension." She looks back down to read more from her notes. I stare, dumbfounded, until the popping sound from the bacon pulls me back to the stove.

I get lost in the rhythm of clanking pans and dishes, coffee percolating, et cetera. Pauline just becomes background noise. I really don't know what to make of all of this.

"I don't think I've ever seen a man so head over heels." She laughs. *That* I heard. "Poor Isaiah." She shakes her head as I bring her coffee. "I was so grumpy toward him last night after listening to Mitch going on and on about you."

"Isaiah?"

"My husband. Thank you." She grabs the mug.

"Do you have any children?" I ask, heading back to the counter for our omelets.

"Twin boys—Cale and Colton. They're three." Her eyes twinkle at the thought of them.

"Colton?"

"Yes, in honor of the Colton family. They have always been good to us. Cale is named after Isaiah's father."

"That's so nice, Pauline. I'm sure it means a lot to Gram and Mitch. Where are the boys now?"

"Home. My husband will drop them off at daycare." She sips her coffee.

"Wait." I place her plate in front of her. "You're putting your own children in daycare to spend the whole day with mine?"

"Well, I have to work, Charlotte, or I'd be home with them." She's more sad than defensive.

"Bring them with you! Well, I mean, if you want to. Brooky would love to play with them, and so will the boys!" I sit next to her.

"Charlotte, no, I wouldn't want to impose." She shakes her head, then takes her first bite.

I watch.

Her eyes close and a slight moan escapes her throat.

I smile.

"I insist, Pauline! Besides, you'll be imposing if you don't."

"How so?"

"I'll feel terrible and make you leave early to go get those babies of yours."

She laughs. "It's crazy how well he knows you in such a short amount of time."

"What do you mean?"

"Mitch told me not to bother with daycare—that you wouldn't hear of it."

I don't know how to respond, so I say nothing. I put my efforts into eating instead.

"Charlotte." She places her hand on top of mine. "Give him time. He's just a little scared. He needs time to sort through his feelings."

I look up at her. "I'm just terribly confused."

"Time, baby girl, just time." She taps my hand and goes back to eating.

"Your mom calls me 'baby girl.'" I smile.

"My mom calls everybody 'baby girl.'"

"Well thank you for popping my 'I feel special' balloon." I smirk.

She laughs. "Well, thank you for being just the way everyone has described you."

"They forgot to mention the 'cranky morning bitch,' though, didn't they?"

"Yup!" She elongates the word and glances to the side. I laugh and smack her hand. She echoes my laughter.

You know that feeling you get when you meet someone you know will become a lifelong friend? Yeah—that's the feeling I just got.

I SETTLE INTO my pedicure chair, letting my feet soak. Maybe he'll at least reply to my text now that he's gone out of his way to do all of this for me. I pull out my phone and take in a deep breath. Here goes nothing ...

Thank you for sending Pauline to me. Thank you for knowing my kids so well.
Thank you for my spa day.
I hate this, Mitch.
I know I didn't do anything to deserve this.
That's what's making it so hard.
If you can't speak to me on the phone, at least text or email me.
I need to talk to you about something important!
I've been trying to tell you for over two weeks now. I have to make my decision this weekend.

We don't have to talk about anything else but this.
I'm not telling you over text. I need your point of view ... your input.
This decision will affect us ... if there even is an "us" anymore.
If I don't hear from you by Sunday, I will make the decision as if you weren't in the equation.
Kind of like what you've done to me the past two weeks.
Hope you are well.

Mitch

"UGH!" I THROW my phone down.

"What's up, man?" Kyle looks up from the proposals he's going over.

"Nothing."

"The same nothing that's been going on for three weeks?" He eyes me.

I ignore his question. "How are the proposals looking?"

He ignores mine. "Did you and Charlotte break up, Mitch?"

"No. I just need a break from her," I say, rubbing my face. If I give him a crumb maybe he'll shut up.

"Of course you do, man. All of that happiness was overwhelming the shit out of you! You must feel better now that you're a miserable fucking prick again." He aggressively opens another folder to make a comparison.

"Dude—when the fuck did they become brass?" I ask and push the folder I was looking at down to him. I should have thrown it at him.

"I'll tell ya when! The moment you told me you didn't want to 'grow old' with me and that things needed to change around here. The 'we're not rock stars' speech—remember that?" He pushes himself away from the table, stands up, and starts pacing. "You gave me a glimpse of hope! I thought all my hard work had paid off, and maybe, just maybe, I could find a woman that makes me feel and act the way Charlotte makes you feel and act. Stupid me, huh? You yanked that hope away as soon as you showed it to me." He sits, defeat on his face.

"You're not a prisoner here. I'll give you a good reference," I say.

"Fuck you, Mitch!" he snaps, grabbing the folder I shot down to him.

"Who the fuck do you think you're talking to?" I yell. "I'm your boss, Kyle, not some punk down the street! I will send your ass packin' if you talk to me like that again!'

"Send my ass packin', Mitch! How many guys did you go through before I came along? Do you think there's another poor shmuck out there that will put up with your shit and still respect you at the end of the day?" he yells back.

I think for a moment. "No," I say truthfully.

"Right—so fuck you, Mitch!" he snaps again. "Punk," he adds under his breath.

I try to keep a straight face, but despite my attempts, I start to laugh. Kyle is unsuccessful as well.

"I fucking hate you, man."

"Yeah—I hate you too." He smirks.

After a few minutes, I toss the files onto the table. "It looks good to me. Did you find anything?"

"Nah, man ... it's solid." He tosses his as well and leans back.

"I'm sorry, Kyle." I clear my throat.

"Forget it, Mitch. I don't think there's a future Mrs. out there for me anyway," he states, staring at the wall opposite him.

"Don't say that, man. Look at me." I shrug. "Never in a million years did I think there was a Charlotte out there for me."

"And what are you doing about that, man, besides acting like an asshole and pushing her away?" Kyle scoffs.

"I'm ... I ... don't know. It's been a long time since I felt this way. I'm scared. I was excited. Now I'm just scared." I lean my elbows on the table and bury my head in my hands.

"You're a fucking pussy!" Kyle spits out.

I jerk my head up and hold my hands open. "Dude!"

It's all I've got. *I am a pussy.* Fuck—what's wrong with me?

"You're going to lose her, Mitch! I'm talking to you as your friend now. You are going to lose her!" He straightens up the folders. "I don't know what happened with your wife."

"She died," I say, cutting him off.

"Shit." His tone becomes remorseful. "I'm sorry, Mitch. When? How?"

"Twenty years ago. She was hit by a drunk driver. She was pregnant. I lost her and Isabella that day." I take in a shaky breath. I've never told this to another soul. No one, outside of the people in my life at the time, knows.

"Christ," Kyle says under his breath.

"Kelly was the love of my life. No one held a candle to her. No one ever occupied my thoughts, my heart, like she did," I continue, feeling as if a floodgate has opened. I don't think I could stop now if I tried.

"Until Charlotte." Kyle half smiles.

"Until Charlotte," I agree. "I didn't realize it until that day you told me I was 'done.' It was then that I also realized I had forgotten to remember Kelly. The guilt hit me so hard—I couldn't breathe."

"Guilt?" His brows snap together. "Guilt for what? I didn't know Kelly, but if she loved you as much as you loved her, I doubt she'd want you to be miserable and alone for the rest of your life. Which do you think she'd prefer—for you to have one-night stands, or to go home to somebody who loves you as much as she did? Someone worthy of your love in return."

"You don't understand. I was supposed to be with her that night. I worked late." I stand up and head over to the window, our last conversation playing in my head.

"Hey, Mama, I'm leaving now."

"Oh, good! I'll have Mom pack up dessert and I'll meet you at home. Wink wink." She giggled.

"Again, sweetie? You're gonna kill me!" I laughed.

"He's twitching, isn't he?"

"You have no idea." I shifted in my chair.

"Oh, I think I do. Don't worry, baby. I'll massage that right out for you." I could hear her smile.

"Mmm ... and how's my other girl?"

"Kicking like crazy. She's going to be a Rockette, I tell ya!"

"She can be whatever she wants to be. Kelly?"

"Yes?"

142

"Thanks for letting me hold your hand at the ice-skating rink."

"Thanks for telling me I was cute like Debbie Gibson."

"I knew right then."

"Knew what?"

"That one day, I may not marry Debbie Gibson, but I was definitely going to marry Kelly Foster."

"And since Debbie was able to shake your love, I thankfully have not."

"You never will, Mama. I love you so much, Kelly."

"I love you, Mitch, with every breath I take. Until my dying day—I love you."

"See you soon, honey."

"Bye, babe."

Little did we know—that *was* her dying day. Thinking back on the conversation is almost eerie.

"Mitch. Mitch!"

I snap back and look at Kyle. "Sorry."

"It wasn't your fault. You didn't make that douchebag drink and drive." He walks over to me. "Man, you've lived with this a long time. Maybe Kelly sent Charlotte in your direction."

"Kelly would've loved Charlotte." I smirk. They're a lot alike.

"Mitch, you suffered long enough. It's okay for you to be happy again, and have that happiness with Charlotte." He pats my back.

"Yeah, I guess. I just ... I need time."

"Don't take long, Mitch. A woman like Charlotte may not wait around." He heads back to collect the folders off of the table.

"Oh, she'll wait," I say, secretly thanking God there's a contract. "But I will make sure to slowly remind her again of my intentions."

"What are your intentions?" He grabs his jacket.

"To make her mine—permanently." I turn and pick up my coat as well. "Kyle, we're going to bust our asses in Germany and try to get this trip shortened significantly." I open the door.

"Are you telling me we're not rock stars, Mitch?" Kyle stops and raises his brows at me.

"This tour is ending sooner than planned. Hopefully refunds will not be necessary." I chuckle.

"Good. Let's start brainstorming over dinner—I'm starved." He heads out.

"Me too—I'm fiending for a burger."

"Mitch?" He hits the button to the elevator.

"What?"

"I fucking hate that you're the best date I've had in years."

"Uh ... thanks?" I laugh.

"Don't back out of this!" He shakes his head and pushes past me onto the elevator.

"I won't." I follow him.

Chapter Eleven

Charlotte

I GET OFF the phone with my doctor's office and immediately call Ava.

"My appointment is canceled," is how I greet her when she picks up.

Ava gasps and lets out a sob. "Are you sure, Charley? And Mitch doesn't mind?"

"I'm positive. Mitch left it to me to decide. Besides, Ava," I say through my own tears, "ever since that conjured-up day we supposedly swapped spit, I knew I wanted to have your baby."

"I love you, you crazy bitch!" Ava screeches, though I can hear both laughter and tears in her voice. "You are an angel. I ... we could never thank you enough."

"Stop." I sigh. "What's the next step after the birth control is out of my system?"

"I will call and make an appointment with my IVF doctor. They'll do a vaginal ultrasound, physical, and Pap smear, unless you've just had one. Then there's the hysteroscopy to check your uterine wall. They'll go over the medical instruction of the IVF cycle, injections, medication use, and embryo transfer, then all the other stuff. It's basically everything we've done, except our bun's going in your oven," she says, then finally pauses to take a breath.

"I'm sorry you know so much about this." I choke on my tears. Ava and Trent could write a book and perform all of these procedures by themselves ... with their eyes closed.

"Charley, we're so blessed to have an incredible friend like you." She starts crying again.

"I will throat-punch you if you don't make me godmother!" I change the subject—sort of.

"No throat punch required." She laughs.

"The girls will be pissy," I warn.

"The girls aren't lending me their vag like you are!"

"Ava?"

"Yes?"

"We both seem to have a problem saying things that don't come out quite right, don't we?" I giggle.

"Eh—yep!" She laughs.

"You make me feel like a dirty whore, Ava," I add.

"You're welcome! Oh, hey ... my next client is here for her foil. See you at yoga tonight?" she asks.

"Yep. I'll bring my vag with me."

"I love your vag, Charley," she says with a hint of dreaminess.

I'm speechless.

"Too far?" she asks after a beat.

"Just a smidge over that there line that shouldn't be crossed."

"Well, I don't care. I'm gonna leap over it. I love you, Charley, and I love your vag! I don't think I will ever see a vag more beautiful than yours the day my kid's pushing through it! I gotta go!" she adds quickly.

"Me too—to vomit—so thanks for that!" I say, feeling my eyes widen even though she can't see me. We hang up. I decide to text Mitch.

Two things!
1. I've made the decision without you.
2. Wilson hasn't fixed the account yet, nor have you.
There's a shitload of money in there you need to put somewhere
else.
I have an idea!
Put it in your new girlfriend's account!
Or ...
You can shove it up your ass!

I put my phone down. I don't know why I bother. It's not like—*oh shit.* I pick it back up.

1. It better not piss me off!
2. There's nothing to fix. It's accurate, so start doing stuff with it.
You are my new girlfriend.
And ...
I can think of something I'd love to shove up your ass. ;-p

I sit and stare at his text for—Christ, I don't know how long. This one text has me speechless for so many reasons. First, he texted me! Second, he's acting like my Mitch. Third, I have almost five hundred thousand dollars in my account. Fourth—

How's Kitty?

Fourth, what the fuck?!

I Skyped with Brogan last night.
I apologized.
I'll Skype with you tonight after the kids go to bed.
9:30 okay?
Wear something sexy.
Definitely wear your invisible edible panties.
Smacks lips
My favorite.

Fifth, no, really, what the fuck?!

I know you're staring at the fucking phone, Charlotte!
Answer me!

I look around. How does he know?
My phone rings.
I hit ignore.
My phone rings.
Goddamn it—ignore!

Do not embarrass me!

Huh?

"Here, Charlotte." Pauline walks into the kitchen and hands me her phone. "It's Mitch. He couldn't get through to you on your phone. You may have to get it checked."

"Yeah, I'll do that. Thanks." I take the phone and slowly bring it up to my ear as she walks back out to the living room.

I breathe deeply. "What?"

"Charlotte, you have ten seconds to come up with a better greeting than that!" he snaps.

"Fuck you!"

"Well there, see, now that sounds promising." He chuckles. I'm not laughing.

"You know what I've realized over the past few weeks, Mitchell?" I choke back my tears. Damn it—I will not fall apart!

"You're calling me by my full name, baby? Sounds like you need to have an orgasm or two to rectify that situation." He tries to reel me in again.

I ignore his comment. "You're no better than he is."

"If you're talking about Josh, you better take that fucking shit back right now!" he yells.

"Or what?" I challenge him.

"Don't fucking test me, baby ... don't do it!" I think he's trying to calm down, but yelling through teeth is just as loud.

"What are you going to do, Mitch—break my heart? Well, sit back and relax, 'cause you've already done that. More like crushed it to smithereens." And now ... I cry. Damn it!

"Oh, baby, no ..." he trails off.

"Bye, Mitchell," I gasp between sobs.

"Stop! Don't hang up!" he pleads. "I'm coming home two weeks from this Thursday. Be at my house, please." He sounds so calm now.

"Okay," I agree, knowing it's the only way to get him off the phone so I can have a proper cry.

"Charlotte?" he breathes.

"What?" I'm barely audible.

"I ... I never meant to hurt you. I haven't been thinking clearly. I just ... I have a lot to tell you when I come home. I asked you to have patience with me before I left," He lets out an exhausted sigh. "I didn't realize the depths of that request until today. I have a lot to work through, Charlotte. I want to work through it with you by my side." I cover my mouth as a sob escapes my throat. "Baby ... I'm so sorry," he says, an ache in his voice.

"I have to go now." I wipe my tears and try to pull myself together.

"Baby?"

"Mitch ... I have a lot to think about."

"Two weeks then?"

"Yeah."

"I miss you, baby."

"Bye, Mitch."

"Charlotte?" My name sounds like a plea.

I hang up.

I pick up my phone and dial my go-to girl for all matters of the mind.

"Hey!" Maddie says quickly.

"Maddie, you've got to fit me in today. I will pay you. I need to talk," I say hysterically. Luckily, Maddie is fluent in hysterical.

"I have a slot in one hour. Everything is going to be okay. I gotta go." And with that she hangs up.

I sit back and take to deep breathing. My phone pings.

You are my favorite smell.

I close my eyes and think about the way he sniffs me. *Oh, how I miss that sniffer of his sniffing around ...*

I push myself up from the table and take Pauline's phone with me. I find her folding towels and hand it back to her.

"Thanks, Charlotte." She grabs it from me.

"Pauline, you don't have to do that." I try to take the basket from her.

"Nonsense." She shoos me away.

"So, Bennett doesn't have therapy until one o'clock. Do you mind if I run some errands?"

"Go. We'll be fine."

"Thanks!" I half smile before grabbing my keys.

"You okay, baby girl?" She gives me a suspicious once-over.

"Uh ... well ... I will be," I say. "Be back in a couple of hours. Call if you need anything." I wave my phone. She nods and I head out.

I PLOP IN the chair across from my best friend, who seems to be losing the battle with her bangs as she continuously blows them out of her eyes.

"Spill it," she says, then sips the coffee I brought her.

"I will, but you have to promise you won't utter a word of this to the other girls." I know I don't have to say this, but I do anyway. Maddie has been good about secrets since the day I met her in middle school. If you tell her not to say anything, she will go to her grave with it. Good Lord, I don't know how she keeps it all organized in that brilliant mind of hers. Never—not once—has she slipped up! The look she's giving me right now is a simple reminder of that fact.

"Okay, here goes nothing." Slowly, I begin to explain what's been going on the past few weeks. Mitch's avoidance of me. Him declaring us "over" to his grandmother. The new knowledge of the wife he had—

and lost—that he never told me about, and how he still doesn't know that I know. Bingo and my confrontation. His renewed interest and efforts. I tell her about everything except, well, you know.

"Break up with him," she says.

"I can't." I blow out a big puff of air.

"Why?" she asks flippantly. "You don't need another Josh!"

Because I signed a contract. Of course I can't say so aloud, though.

"Because I ... I've fallen for him, and I know he feels the same way about me. I know he feels a lot of guilt over his wife. I'm the first woman he's developed feelings for since she died almost twenty years ago. So, I know where it's coming from. Does that make it hurt any less? No. But I really need help trying to work through this with him, Maddie. I ... I've never felt this way about anyone before. Josh was a joke. My feelings were crap compared to how I feel about Mitch. I need help knowing how to act around him. I'm so pissed. I can't control myself, even though I know what he's going through." I attack her tissue box and blow my nose.

"Actually—that's good. Charley, you are reacting just how you should. He's using his wife's death as a crutch." She pushes her glasses up the bridge of her nose.

"Maddie!" I gasp.

"Let me finish, please." She holds up a hand. "He's been using his wife's death as an excuse to push everyone—as well as his feelings for them—away. Then you happened, and he forgot to push until something triggered him. A thought, a memory, who knows? And he pulled his crutch back out because he got scared. Gram knows her shit! She did the right thing. Twenty years is a long time to use the same crutch. Seeing you reminded him, or maybe made him realize that he doesn't need it anymore." She takes another sip. I join.

"Charley, he needs to be held accountable for his actions. If you baby him, it tells him his behavior is excusable. You essentially give him a new crutch, and that wouldn't be good for either of you. No—he needs to own how he's behaved. He needs to deal with your anger and disappointment. He needs to be able to figure out how to rectify the situation. In the long run, you will be helping him find closure and move on with his life in a healthier way than he has." She chugs her coffee now.

"Your secret is safe with me, Maddie." I smile at her.

Her smile hits her eyes and she laughs. "Eh—it's no secret that I'm the brains behind this operation."

"I love you, Captain. Thank you." I get up and hug her, ignoring her eye roll at my nickname.

"I'm glad I'm able to help. I like him a lot, Charley. I especially like how happy he makes you—well, you know, before he became a pussy."

"Stop!" I smack her arm.

"Well, I have my next client. I'll send you my bill." She nudges me with her hip.

"Hey, is today 'Viking' day?" I raise my brows.

"Nope—tomorrow at three."

"Smile at him," I say in encouragement.

"Actually ... I did."

"And?"

"He asked me why I was carrying so many books at once."

"Huh?"

"Oh, I had several huge psyche books I was borrowing from a colleague. I was going to leave them at the front desk, except I dropped them all before I got there. So ... he jumped up and helped me." She blows her bangs out of her eyes.

"So he speaks?" I raise my eyebrows.

"And goddamn it—even his voice is sexy!" she says with frustration.

"What else did he say?"

"He asked me if this week's plant survived, or if it will meet its demise next week."

I can't help but laugh at this. "Very observant, isn't he?"

"Yes, he knows I'm a plant killer. Everyone knows! If a plant last two weeks with me, it's a miracle!" she says and heads over to water her latest to-be victim.

"Just so you know, I do expect a weekly report on this matter. The Viking, not the plants." I pull a barrette out of my purse, walk up to her, and clip those goddamn bangs out of her face.

"Thanks," she says with relief. "These bangs are driving me nuckin' futs." She hugs me. "Yes, I will give you a report if there is anything to report."

"I'm sure there will be." I pat her back and head out the door.

9:35 p.m.

I stare at the screen of my laptop. Yup, it's still there—$478,533.22. In two more weeks that number will jump by a quarter of a million. I grab my cell to text CiCi.

Mitch has confirmed.
My pussy is platinum.

My laptop starts singing to me. *Crap.* I ignore the incoming Skype call. After a few minutes, my phone pings. I shouldn't look, but I do.

Get to your laptop, baby.
I want to see you!
No.
Why?

I don't bother with a reply because, well, when you have nothing nice to say ...

Please ☺

My Skype starts going off again.

Answer it!

I get offline.

I'll see you in two weeks, Mitch.

And with that, I turn my phone off. But then my house phone rings.

Of course. Why wouldn't it? I sigh audibly and pick up.

"Charlotte?"

I can hear him clench his teeth, and I wonder how that's even possible.

"Mitchell," I reply coolly.

"So, you want to play a game now?"

I can tell he's straining terribly to keep his voice level.

"Sure, let's play phone Monopoly!" I unleash my inner smartass.

"What?"

"Yeah, it's real simple! You monopolize our phone conversation, and I pretend to listen while painting my nails." I can't be too sure, but it sounds like I hit the steam-release button on Mitch.

"Charlotte," he says after a moment or two. *Damn him and his sexy voice!* "Be careful, baby. You don't have a Get Out of Jail Free card."

"Don't I?" I challenge him.

"No. You don't." His calm and sexy voice is now actually freaking me out a bit. "Now get on your computer so I can see your pretty face."

"Mitch, I'm hanging up now. If you call back tonight, I will just turn all the ringers off, so don't bother. I will see you in two weeks," I say with strength and confidence.

"Charlotte, you are about to make a very bad decision. I'm giving you one last chance to do as I say like you're supposed to, or there will be consequences," he states clearly and slowly, like he's talking me off a ledge.

"Good night." I sigh and hang up. I can't believe him! He honestly thinks that after everything that's happened, he can go back to the way he behaved our first night. Hell no! He can try it all he wants, but it's not going to work. Our relationship has morphed into something completely different than what we planned on that first night.

I wait a few minutes. Sure that he's accepted my threat regarding the ringers, I finally settle into bed. Not that I'll sleep or anything!

Three days later...

"WHAT ARE YOU talking about?" I snap at the guy on the phone.

"Your card has been declined," the guy from the mortgage company repeats.

"No way!" I yell and pull up my bank account. $1,118.55. My heart sinks. "I'll have to call you back," I say.

"Okay, ma'am," he says, and I hang up.

I scroll down. *Transfer $475,000.00 July 1, 2013.* Gone. He took everything but the first month's originally agreed-upon payment.

Deep breath.
Exhale.
Deep breath.
Exh ... oh, fuck this shit!

My fingers fly across my phone's keyboard.

Sometimes I really hate being right!
You owe me half a month!
So ... back to work!!
Thanks for "breaking me in," Mitch! ☺ Have a nice life!

I hit "send" then proceed to wipe the snot away from my nose.
Ugly cry.
Ugly, messy, disgusting cry.
Fuck you, Mitch!

Mitch

YUP, LOOKING DOWN at my phone in the middle of this meeting was a big mistake. The very same meeting in which we're having a tough time closing the deal.

Her entire message silently screams at me, and my stomach twists.

If I don't leave this room now, I may lose my lunch—followed by my reputation.

"Kyle!" I stand up. Everyone gives me their undivided attention. "Pack it up," I say. He stares at me, dumbfounded. "Gentlemen, we're not going to waste any more of our time, or yours." I look around at the five of them. "We have gone over this line several times. No one else has what we are offering. Mentioning these other companies in comparison is a great tactic. That is, of course, if a single one of them was worth comparing to us, which none is. They do not have anything similar to our product, nor our commercial standing. They most certainly are not in the position to walk out the door when a meeting is clearly wasting their time and money. However, we are, gentlemen." I throw my stuff into my briefcase. "You have twenty-four hours to decide, or the deal comes off the table." I close my briefcase. "Kyle." I nod.

"You have our number," he says. "Have a good day." He follows my lead out the door. "What the fuck?" he asks, following it up with a surprised laugh when we get to the elevator.

"Get the jet ready," I say before I connect to Mr. Wilson.

"Where are we going?" He pulls his phone up to his ear.

"Home. I just lost Charlotte. I, uh ... fucked up big time." *Man, did I fuck up!* "Wilson!" I snap before he finishes his name.

"Mr. Colton!" He greets me in his creepy-enthusiastic way and I suddenly feel like I've dropped my bar of soap in the jail shower.

"I need you to transfer that money back, please. Immediately!" I try to keep my voice down, but am not too successful.

"Uh ... um ... Mr. Colton," he stammers.

"Now, Wilson, or I will pull every cent from your bank!"

"Uh, yes, sir ... it's ... it's done," he says nervously.

"Good." I say and hang up.

"So ... what happened?" Kyle smirks. *Him and his fucking smirking!*

"I tried to rule her with an iron fist." I pace. *It worked in the bedroom ...*

"And?"

"She beat me over the head with it." I lean back against the elevator wall and close my eyes.

"You are going to make me best man, right?" He laughs.

"If she doesn't make you a pallbearer first." I open an eye. "Faaaac-cck!" I yell and pound my fist against the wall.

The doors open and my phone hits my ear again. This time, my assistant is on the other end. "Erica, gather all of our things and meet us at the airport. We're flying home."

"But, Mr. Colton—" she starts.

"Cancel all of it. I have a family emergency. Kyle does too."

"You both have an emergency?" she asks, sounding confused.

"Just do as I say, please." I hang up. "Kyle, wipe that effin' grin off your face!" I yell as we get in the car. "Should I call her? Do I text her? Do I just show up? What do I do?" I glance back and forth between him and my phone.

"Hell if I know!" He shrugs, leans back into his seat, and closes his eyes. A few moments of silence pass before a slow smirk comes across his face. "Maybe you should pass her a note during study hall," he practically mumbles.

"It took you that long to think of that, asshole?" I fight the urge to whack his leg with my knee in order to not prove his point. He just chuckles ... him and that smirk. I'd like to wipe it off his face.

I hop out of the limo as soon as we hit the airport. Erica jumps off the courtesy golf cart that has our luggage piled high in the back.

"I want a goddamn raise!" she snaps, walking past me.

"Done." I nod, a little shocked at her aggressiveness. I turn to Kyle. "So, did everyone in the company gain a new set of balls this past month?"

"Apparently," he answers, just as awestruck. We all climb onto the plane and settle in. I give Charlotte a quick text before the wheels go up.

I fixed it, baby.
And ...
I'm going to fix us, too!

With that, I turn my phone off and begin working on my game plan. I hope I come up with a solid one in the next several hours.

Chapter Twelve

Charlotte

CRAP! IN FIVE ... four ... three ... two ... one.

"What the fuck's going on with you?" CiCi bellows as she barges into my bedroom. "You haven't picked up the damn phone all day and you had Mom call me to take the dogs? I sat on the fucking phone with her for a goddamn hour listening to her conjure up every goddamn ailment known to man to diagnose you with! Your fucking fingers broken—you couldn't call me yourself?" She plops onto my bed.

I raise my left hand up in the air and flip her off. "Nope ... still workin'!" I inform her.

"Charley, what's going on?" She pushes at my shoulder. I sigh and turn to her—better to get this over with quickly. "Hmm ... red, puffy eyes and nose, a mountain of old used tissues, favorite ugly-ass comfy pajamas, and shipping kids and dogs off to somewhere else for the night," she says and taps her lips with her index finger. "It seems to me that you've come down with a case of 'Mitch is a motherfucking dickhead who should have his balls cut off and fed to him.' Am I right?" she asks. Her eyes are wide—ready to strike. It's moments like these when I thank God this crazy bitch is on my side!

"Ding, ding, ding, ding—you are correct!" I shake a finger in the air (not the same one from before, of course).

"Do I need to fly to Germany to kick his ass, Sis?" She lies next to me.

"Nope, don't bother wasting your frequent-flyer miles. We broke up, Ceese ... it's over," I say, trying to keep my composure and steady my quivering chin. I fail miserably at both.

"No way!" She sits up. "Who broke it off?"

"He did."

"Why?"

"Um ... he's been dealing with personal stuff and it's made him act differently toward me. I don't know, exactly. He wouldn't talk to me for almost three weeks and then, one day, he decided he's going to go back to the way things were with us. Apparently, I was supposed to jump on board with that!" I cry and take the tissue she hands me.

"You didn't, and ...?"

"And that's it—over. I had to return the funds I had left in my account."

"Wait! He fired you from your job, too?" she yells. "That's illegal!"

"Um ... well ..." *Shit!* "It was sort of under the table for now, so I have no documentation."

"That's a little shady." Her eyebrows knit together.

"Well, it was a trial thing. If they felt it was working out, they would've provided me with a contract." *Contract* ... I hate that word! "I couldn't pay my mortgage this morning." I sniffle.

"We'll figure that shit out—don't worry!" She hugs me. "This explains why I haven't heard back from that pussy-ass motherfucker."

"Huh?"

"Yeah, he hasn't texted me back in weeks!"

"You text Mitch?"

"All of the time. I like fucking with him." She shrugs. "Not the way you liked fucking with him, of course," she adds, which makes me start crying all over again. *Damn, did I like "fucking" with him!* "Sorry." She winces. "Okay, well, I've got the dogs and Pauline dropped the kids off at Mom and Dad's, so rest up and get yourself back together."

"CiCi, what are you going to do?" I sit up as she walks to the door.

"Nothing—what are you talking about? I'm good." She continues on with her calm façade. Anyone who knows CiCi knows that "Calm CiCi" is really "Psycho-Bitch CiCi." This normalcy she's displaying— this is the shit that tells you to run for your life!

"Ceese!" I yell as she leaves. Fuck it. He deserves the wrath of CiCi O'Brien! Good luck, dude!

I shuffle out of bed and dig out some Xanax I have remaining from my time with Josh. I've decided this moment requires a good night's sleep. Popping two of them, new marketing slogans come to mind. *Xanax—the little pills in a bottle that helps you with the fish that slips out of your hand!* Nope. *Xanax—helping you not panic through the suck pump that is life!* Yes! I should've gone into marketing!

Shuffle, shuffle, shuffle ... plop.

"My pajamas are not fucking ugly!" I mumble before drifting off.

Mitch

6:00 p.m.

"WHERE'S THE KEY, Pauline?" I talk low into the phone.

"In the hanging plant there."

"Thanks. I'll catch up with you later," I say before hanging up. Slowly, I unlock the door and walk in.

Silence. Dead silence.

I search the rooms downstairs and finally make my way up. She must still be in bed. I open her door and creep in. Ugh ... bed. *Bed and Charlotte.* Before I realize what I'm doing, I'm down to my underwear. Cautiously, I climb in next to her and move her hair away from her neck.

I lean down.

And ...

I sniff.

I sniff again ... long and hard. *Mmm ... Charlotte.* I take in the sight of her: her long wavy hair, her cute little ear, her lovely curves, and her ... ugly-ass motherfuckin' pajamas. What the? As if the baby-shit gold wasn't enough, there are sea turtles swimming around the circles of tie-dyed art. I can't help my silent, shaking laughter. Charlotte gasps and turns her body in a panic.

"Mitch?" she asks, sounding completely confused by my presence. She rubs her eyes.

"Yeah, baby ... it's me." I lean forward and grasp her lips with mine.

"What are you doing here?" She pushes me away and turns her head.

"I'm following through on what I said." I take her hand off my chest and plant soft kisses on each knuckle.

"What you said when?" She pulls her hand away.

"My text."

"What text?"

I grab her cell phone off the nightstand and lie on my back. "This text." I show her.

"So your plan to 'fix us' is climbing into bed with me almost completely naked and scaring the fucking shit out of me?" She makes the face that means a smartass comment is going to fly out of her mouth.

"Whoa ... wait a minute!" I cut her off. "At least I have the decency to be naked! Nothing says *scary* like these pajamas, baby." I pull at them and laugh a little.

And there it is ... her sexy little smile.

"God, baby, I've missed you," I whisper and lean forward to kiss her again.

And there it goes ...

"Mitch." She sighs.

"Is there a story behind these, baby?" I tug at them again.

"They were a gift from a friend of mine."

"Some friend." I push her hair behind her ear.

"Well, we do this on purpose. For birthdays and holidays, we buy each other the most hideous gift we can find. It's become quite the competition." She laughs nervously. "I actually like these, though. They're the most comfortable PJs I've ever had, and the softest. Feel." She holds the material out to me. I give it a better feel this time. Wow ... it is crazy soft.

"You're softer." I lean toward her ear as my hand goes under the shirt. My knuckles skim over her belly, and she gasps. "That sounds promising, baby." I nip at her earlobe.

"Mitch, stop." She pushes my hand away. I open my mouth to say something, but her phone pings in my hand. Out of habit, I look down to read the message from Jay Baby. *Jay Baby?*

> *CiCi gave me the cliff notes and she's calm.*
> *Cue the psycho music, please!*
> *So listen ...*
> *Imma be over in 10 min.*
> *Mouth shut.*
> *Legs open, Charley.*
> *Imma face-plant into your pussy.*
> *Girl—Imma do the alphabet.*
> *Imma A, E, I, O. O. O ... U!*
> *Imma be a plumber and plunge my tongue into that shit.*
> *Imma hide my face in there like it's in the Pussy Protection Program!*
> *Imma smack it up*
> *Flip it*
> *Rub it down*
> *All niiiight!*
> *Imma make your legs shake gurrll.*
> *Then Imma listen to you whimper as I make you accommodate my girth*
> *And get lost in the rhythmic beat of my balls slapping that fine ass.*
> *Love you, baby!* ☺

"Mitch, what's wrong? You look like you're gonna murder some-body," she says as she reaches for her cell. I smack her hand away hard. "Ow! What the fuck is the matter with you?" she yells. I jump out of her bed and pace as I look at past conversations with this Jay guy. It's one sexual comment after another.

Your ass is begging to be fucked in those jeans!
Nobody's tits fill my hands like yours.
You know that time when I didn't think about fucking you? Me neither!

I can't read anymore. I go out of the text and see his picture. I tap it. He's behind Charlotte making a "hell yeah!" face. His hands are cupping her tits and she's laughing while kissing his cheek. I toss the phone on the bed next to her. I feel like I'm going to vomit. I grab my pants and throw them on. Charlotte looks at her phone then up at me, panic on her face.

"Wait, Mitch, this isn't—"

"How long?" I yell and pull my tank top on over my head.

"Wait, it's not what you—"

"How long?" I ask again through clenched teeth.

"He's been one of my best friends since we were kids!" She jumps up and races to me. "Mitch, please listen!" She palms my face. I rip her hands off and push her away.

I feel nothing but raw anger crushing my chest. My heart is aching. How could she do this to me? To us? *Us?* I'm fucking delusional! There was no "us"!

"Mitch," she cries, "can you pass me my phone and that towel over there?" I look down at her. She's on the floor holding her right arm up. Blood pours down it. *Shit!* I forget my anger and race the towel over to her. "Phone, please," she says through her tears. I pick it up and hand it to her.

"You're going to need stitches," I say, wrapping the towel around her forearm. I reach down and pick up the frame she cut herself on when she fell. When I pushed her. I didn't even hear her crash into this table with the framed pictures—I was so mad. I turn the frame over. It's us. *Us.* CiCi took this picture in the backyard. I pick up the other frames. The kids, and two more of ... us. *Us.* I'm so confused.

"I want to show you something, since you won't listen." She holds her phone out to me. "This is Jay and his boyfriend, Victor."

I take the phone and look at the picture of Jay kissing Victor. I swipe to view the next picture. One photo after another of a gay couple very much in love. I look up at Charlotte.

"What you read is part of an inside joke I have with Jay. He's the one that bought me these PJs. We have this opposites game—well, that's what we call it. I ... forget it. I just wanted you to know." Her chin quivers. "You can go now. I'll call CiCi to take me for stitches."

"Baby ... I'll take you." I don't even try to hide the ache in my voice.

Charlotte slowly shakes her head while looking down. When her gaze finally moves back up to me, I see tears streaming down her face. "I think you've done enough to me, Mitch."

And there it is again—the crushing in my chest. I came home to fix us, but have managed to permanently destroy us instead. "Please, baby ... I don't want to lose you." My voice cracks. I bring a shaky hand up to her cheek to wipe her tears away, but she jerks her head back. I'm trying everything I can to hold it together here, fighting back the stinging in my eyes of my own impending tears.

"I don't want to lose me either, Mitch. Please go." Her eyes plead with me.

"I'll fix this. I'll make it right," I say, but she ignores me as she brings her cell to her ear.

"Ceese, I need you to drive me to the hospital. I fell and sliced my arm on the glass frame I broke." She doesn't even mention me—the reason she fell.

I get up, grab the rest of my things, and leave. I'm pretty sure leaving is the wrong thing for me to do. I'm also pretty sure I don't know what the right thing is.

ONE HOUR.

I've been sitting in my car, staring at my white knuckles fisting the wheel.

I'm a coward.

When did I become such a fucking coward?

When I had someone to fight for, not something.

Fucking coward.

And—where the fuck is CiCi?

I wasn't bad at this the first time around. I was actually pretty good at it. Then again, I was young and naive. I thought Kelly and I had our whole lives ahead of us. I know better now.

God, I never thought I'd feel this way again. I was so sure Kelly was it for me. Until Charlotte walked into my life, I'd never been so unsure about being so sure—again. I'm afraid I'm going to lose her. So, I handle it by pushing her away. The irony chokes me and tonight's episode has me gasping for what feels like my final breath.

I'm a coward.

I'm scared, so I run.

She's right.

I'm just like him.

I know what it feels like to be abandoned. Kelly abandoned me—not her intention, of course, and it certainly was not her fault. Still, I can't help but find my grief travel down this road every so often. She left me. It's a God-awful pain. I can't imagine how much more intense it is for Charlotte, now that this has happened to her twice.

How could I do that to her? I just dropped her like she was nothing. It killed me to do so. I know why I did it, but ... she didn't.

Hours.

Phone calls. Texts. Skype.

Days. Weeks.

Investing in us, our hearts.

Her mind—*it intrigues me.*

Her laugh—*it centers me.*

Her heart—*it swallows me.*

Her voice—*it calms me.*

Her smell—*it intoxicates me.*

I abandoned her.

I got scared—am scared.

Because I love her.

I am a coward.

"Shit!" I hit the wheel. "Find your fucking balls, Mitch, and reattach them!"

With a new sense of purpose, I get out of my car and head back inside. Fuck—what if she's passed out from blood loss? I close the door quietly and release a sigh of relief when I hear her on the phone.

"No, Jay, I didn't laugh, because once again, you've proven that you have the worst timing!" I hear her snap. "Mitch was here. He was holding my phone so he could show me his earlier text about fixing everything between us. Christ, he flew here from Germany to work things out with me!" she yells. "And then you and your perfect-timing skills send the mother of all obscene fucking texts to me!" She pauses. "No, I don't feel better that you threw up in your mouth texting that shit! He went ballistic! Could you blame him? He wouldn't let me get a word in edgewise! That is, until he pushed me away and I fell. Sliced my fucking arm up." She pauses again. "No. Actually, I fucking tripped over my sneaker. That's why I fell, but he didn't see or hear me. He was so mad." Pause. "No. He was mortified that I got hurt. He thinks he caused it. I didn't even correct him because I was focused on explaining how you and I are, and that you're gay. No. He left. I told him to. Jay," she sighs, "he's got me on this crazy roller coaster. I can't keep up. I need to slow down." Pause. "No. I haven't told him about the baby."

The loud pounding in my ears drowns out anything else she says. I think it may have something to do with my racing heart. The baby? *A baby? My baby?*

My baby.

My Charlotte.

My future.

I pull my phone out and text her.

Please get off the phone.

"Hold on, Jay," she says, and pulls the phone away from her ear. "Um ... I have to go. I'll call you tomorrow. Okay. Love you, too." She hangs up.

"Charlotte," I say as I walk into the kitchen. She turns quickly. Within seconds, I'm practically nose to nose with her. "A baby?" I ask her in a whisper, with my hand already under her shirt and my fingers splayed across her belly. She gets that panicked look on her face again. I touch her face. "I won't run. God, baby, I promise. My feet are cemented to this floor." I try to reassure her, confident that this is the cause of her panic.

I'm such an asshole.

For three weeks, she begged me to talk about this. We would've had she not been drunk that night. Wait!

"Charlotte, you got drunk knowing you were having my baby?" I can't help the spark of anger in my tone. She gives me a look of confusion, then it appears that a lightbulb flickers on.

"You think I'm having your baby?"

"I just overheard you, Charlotte." Is she going to try and lie about it?

"I'm not."

"You're not having my baby?" My stomach twists in knots.

"No."

"Whose baby are you having?" I ask vehemently.

"I'm not pregnant, you asshole!" she spits out at me. "God, Mitch," she says in a sob, "that's twice in one day! I can understand why you thought that earlier, but—"

I don't let her finish her sentence. I just attack her mouth with mine. She fights me at first, but I relentlessly lick into her mouth with a hunger so fierce, it makes me moan at the taste of her.

Backing her up to the counter, I kiss her harder. I'm so starved for her—I can't get enough. I reach down and yank at her bottoms. She tries to pull away, but I kiss her harder and she whimpers in delicious defeat. Her efforts start to match mine. Bringing my hands to the back of her upper thighs, I hoist her up onto the counter.

"Mitch, no." She wiggles, trying to get down. I crouch and wrap my arms around her legs so my hands come up between them. In one swift move, I grab her wrists, spread her wide, and yank her so her ass is at the edge.

"I'm gonna make you come hard all over my face, baby," I say in that voice I know drives her wild.

"Mitch!" she gasps.

"It's nighttime, baby ... you know, freaks and all." I smile mischievously before I lower my face and slowly run my nose up her center. I inhale and release a groan that I swear came all the way up from my toes.

Taking my time, I taste the skin adjacent to her groin on both sides. She shivers and I run my tongue along her lips—her plump, sweet lips. She whimpers and wiggles. I lick up her center and listen to her gasp. I raise my face. "Baby, do you like feeling my mouth on your pussy?"

"Ye ... yes," she stammers.

"Do you want more?" I return to her warm center, inhaling her again.

"Yes." Her voice trembles with desire.

"I want to feel Kitty purr against my mouth, baby." I lick again. She moans. "I'm going to release your hands. Don't push me away." I bring my face up to hers and nudge her nose with mine. "Okay?"

"Yes," she pants.

I smile and grasp her lips as I release her wrists. She leans back on one hand and brings the other up to palm my cheek. She stares into my soul. Her jade eyes are almost olive, darkened by desire. I rub my lips against hers, enticing them to part.

"Mitch."

"Baby, don't." I shake my head slightly. "I need you. You need me." When I beckon this time, her lips open for me. Her hand slips back to my neck. She fists my hair and kisses me hard, knocking the breath out of my chest.

She rips her mouth from mine and brings it to my ear. "I want your tongue in my pussy, Mitch, licking it the way you're licking the inside of my mouth. I want to ride that hot, strong tongue of yours." She bites my lobe and my cock twitches so hard, my balls ache from it.

"Fuck," I grunt.

"I want that too, baby ... please." She licks the shell of my ear.

"Yes, ma'am." I groan and move my head down to where she wants me. At the sight of her glistening pussy, Morale painfully stretches the material of my pants. I press my thumb against her clit and watch her hips rise off the counter, begging for more.

"Mitch ... baby, please!" she begs as she gyrates her pelvis. I slide my tongue slowly up her center again, then lift my thumb and replace its pressure with my teeth. She yelps. I bite. I tease. I blow. I savor. I slip two fingers into her, my pace cautious to avoid detonating the bomb that is about to go off. It will explode only when I want it to. *When I say.*

"Mitch ... now, goddamn it!" She pulls at my hair. *Or ... when she says.* I'm all about equality.

I massage the wall of her sweet, tight ... mmm ... there it is.

Toes curl.

Mouth opens to a perfect "O."

And she gives it to me.

She looks me square in the eye and gives me her orgasm. *Fuck!*

Once she finishes her last quake, I slowly pull my fingers from her warmth. Sliding them into my mouth, I suck her taste off.

Charlotte pulls them from my mouth, grasps my lips, and proceeds to take the same two fingers into her mouth. She sucks them purposefully. I feel her tongue sliding between them, lapping up her taste. I am awestruck.

"Fuck, baby, that's hot," I say, feeling breathless. "You been catching up on porn while I've been away?"

She pulls them out of her mouth and gives me that sexy little smile I love so much.

"Am I making you nervous, Mitch?" she teases.

"No, baby. I don't joke when I'm nervous. That's your thing." I palm her face and graze her cheeks with my thumbs.

"What do you do when you're nervous?"

"Apparently ... I run." I lower my eyes.

"What did I do to make you nervous?"

"Nothing. You didn't do anything." I gaze into her eyes. She gives me a look of confusion. "My feelings for you made me nervous."

"Made?"

"Yes. Now, I'm more nervous about losing you." I rest my forehead against hers. "I'll never abandon you again."

She takes in a sharp breath.

"Don't make promises you can't keep, Mitch." She pulls my hands from her face and pushes me away before hopping off the counter.

"I *can* keep it, baby." I use the tone that always gets to her as I slide my hands onto her hips. She turns away from me and starts spraying the counter down. "OCD much?" I chuckle near her ear.

"I prep our food on this counter, Mitch. You think I'm gonna leave sex residue on it?" she asks, sounding aggravated as hell. Between spraying and wiping, she continually pushes my hands from her hips. It makes me laugh.

"We didn't have sex yet, baby," I remind her as I grasp her again and shove myself against her.

"We're not going to, either!"

"Oh, yes we are. Especially since you're pissed. Pissed-off Charlotte equals off-the-charts-hot sex." I push into her again.

"Get off of me!" She bucks and yanks my hand away from her breast. I grab her wrists and wrap both of our arms around the front of her.

"That's it, baby. Keep fighting me. I know the harder you fight, the harder you want to be fucked." I bite at her lobe.

"You. Are. Hurting. My. Arm!" she yells. I release her but seize her arm to look at it.

"Why didn't you get stitches?" I gently strip off the stained bandage.

"It doesn't need it. I put a few butterfly stitches on the questionable areas, but it's fine." She inspects it with me.

"I'm sorry I was such an asshole earlier." I sigh and throw the bandage away.

"Only earlier? Not the past three weeks, or just now?"

"I'm sorry for all of it ... except just now. I wasn't being an asshole just now." I turn her and slap her ass. "Let's get you upstairs for new bandages."

"Watch the slapping, Mr. Colton!" she warns, looking over her shoulder.

"Yeah, don't act like you don't like it," I say, calling bullshit.

"Puhleeeease!"

"You admitted it to me, baby. You can't take it back now."

"When?" She stops at the bottom of the stairs and turns.

"One night on Skype. You had a few glasses of wine and spilled the beans, lady, like it was your job or you were in confessional." I smile.

"Shit. I thought I dreamt that." She winces and turns to head up the stairs first. Of course, I let her go. I am a gentleman. It has nothing to do whatsoever with the fact that she is buck naked from the waist down.

"Baby, go slow up the stairs. Really, really slow," I say with concern. Of course, I'm mostly concerned with not being able to enjoy this view for long. *The word "man" does come after "gentle," does it not?*

"Why do I have to walk slowly for an arm injury?" She looks over her shoulder. "Oh, Mitch!" She whacks my shoulder. I growl and bite her ass. "Stop!" She laughs and tries to push me away, causing us both to lose our balance and fall on our sides, onto the stairs.

"Oomph," we say in unison.

"Damn it, Mitch," she complains.

"Shit, baby, keep your arm up." I raise it with my right hand—while my left lifts her shirt.

"What are you doing?" she asks, then laughs when I take her nipple into my mouth.

"Preventing blood loss."

"What?"

"If I suck here, the blood will pool this way instead of your arm." I bite. She gasps.

"Dr. Colton, you should submit your barbaric findings to a medical journal. I'm sure you will receive great recognition for changing the field of medicine forever."

"You think?" I give her a goofy grin and kiss her.

"I think you're stupid." She grabs my chin.

"I like being stupid with you. It feels good. I haven't felt like this in twenty years." I Eskimo kiss her.

"I'm supposed to be mad at you." She pouts.

"Yeah? How's that working out for you?" I ask as I doodle circles on her belly with my fingers.

"Not well. Gah ... Mitch." Her voice shakes as my fingers trail down between her legs.

"What, baby? I'm just touching what's mine," I say softly as I circle her opening. "Is this mine, Charlotte?" I slide one finger into her and back out, then swirl her wetness around. "Say it."

"Yes. It's yours." She closes her eyes, taking in the sensation.

"Upstairs, baby." I pull my hand away and grasp hers, yanking her up with me. We go up and to the left, into her master suite. "Now, bathroom," I say quickly. I flick on the light and grab a new bandage for her arm. Charlotte works diligently at my pants. I rip the tape with my teeth. "Fuck," I grunt as she wraps her hand around me.

"You better concentrate, Dr. Colton." Her seductive tone is absolutely fucking wicked.

"What happened to my good-girl Charlotte?" I ask as I try to get the fucking bandage on her.

"Oh, baby, I'm gonna be so good for you. You'll never want to leave me again." She bites down my neck, and my cock feels ready to explode in her hand. All I can concentrate on, though, is how my chest tightens at her words.

"Charlotte! I didn't leave you because of you!" I push away from her. She stares at me blankly, looking unsure. I quickly and silently finish with the bandage.

I hold her arm up to my lips and lay a prolonged kiss over the now-covered injury. She leans down and her soft lips work their slow, agonizing way up my neck. I lower her arm and run my hand up to the back of her neck. She brings her face to mine. Our mouths barely touch. We breathe each other's breaths.

The anticipation kills us at the same time.

Finally, our lips touch in a petting motion. Our tongues meet briefly, then come back out for a full caress. Our mouths make love like they're playing a symphony—a slow, savoring rhythm 'til we finally hit the climax. It's urgent. Painful. Freeing. Binding. Expressing our hearts—our love.

Mouths connected, I back her into the room and onto the bed. I pull my mouth from hers and trail my lips down her neck.

"Sweetie, please, I just need you." She brings my face back up to hers and raises her hips.

I nod and grasp her lips again, then pull her leg so it loops around my waist. Charlotte's head arches back, her mouth open as she tries to accommodate the boost of my morale.

"Damn, baby," I groan near her ear.

"Damn," she repeats.

I pull back almost all the way and then sink in at an agonizing pace. I love the sounds she makes. The whimpers, the gasps, the moans ... but mostly, her deep breathing. It has an echo of something—always hitching, aching.

"You feel so good ... so right," I breathe into her ear. She turns her face to mine and kisses me fiercely. My hips pick up their pace.

"More," she breathes into my mouth. "Harder." Her hands grasp my ass, helping me. "I need you, baby. I need to feel the ache from you."

Fuck ... she knows just what to say.

"You sure, baby? Like our first night?" I mutter against her ear.

"Yes. Oh God, please ... yes!" she begs. I grasp her lips quickly before bringing her legs up and then down on either side of her head. *Goddamn, her flexibility kills me.*

"Ready, baby?"

"Mmhmm." She licks her lips.

I take in a slow, deep breath, and then—unleash the beast. I'm in the zone, pounding into her so relentlessly, that I can barely comprehend anything that comes out of her mouth other than her whimperish moans. That is, until she reaches between us. Her index and middle finger spread into a "V" at her opening, adding to the sensation I'm already experiencing.

"That's it, baby. Stretch my little pussy with that big cock of yours."

Charlotte, my Charlotte, just said ... *that*?!

This confirms my earlier suspicion: Charlotte has been watching porn. I slow down because I can't chuckle and fuck hard at the same time. With her, though, I may have to master that at some point.

She opens her eyes. "What?"

I can tell she's a bit self-conscious now.

"I just love you, baby." I smile and collect her lips as I release her legs. She stills.

Shit.

The words fell off my lips so naturally, like I've said them to her a million times. But I haven't. I've never said them to her at all. I pull my mouth away and stare into her eyes. Her widened eyes. And ... *I love her.*

Ever have that moment where you fully embrace something you've known and felt all along? I'm having one right now—and embracing the hell out of it.

I love her.

Sadly, I have to admit, my timing sucks. Not the best—or most romantic—idea to tell your woman "I love you" for the first time whilst impaling the crap out of her. It just doesn't help validate your feelings.

I listen to Charlotte's slow, steady deep breathing. Our hips matching her breaths. I bring my hand up to cup her cheek. Her jade eyes stare into my soul.

"I do." I kiss her. "I am," I say against her lips, "so in love with you." I pull my head back as she takes in a long, shaky breath. "I'm sure there could've been a more appropriate time to say it, but my heart blurted it out before my head could stop it. I shouldn't have said it while—"

"While you were stretching my little pussy with your big cock?" she teases.

"I'm making you nervous?" *Damn it!*

"Always." She leans up and plants a kiss on my lips.

"I always make you nervous?"

"A good nervous." She smiles.

"A good nervous?" I raise an eyebrow.

She nods. "It comes with one side effect."

"What's that?" I kiss her.

She takes my hand off of her cheek and places it on her heart. I feel it beating rapidly.

"It makes my heart race. You make my heart race." She smiles softly as her eyes fill with moisture. She blinks and shakes her head. I'm not quite sure what this reaction is. I don't know the meaning behind all her looks and reactions yet.

"Baby, you don't have to say it back to me. I don't want you to feel pressured, especially if you're not certain you feel the same way." That's the only meaning for this reaction I can think of.

"Oh, Mitch." She takes in a sharp breath. "You are the only man I will say that to, and for the first time in my life, mean it with every fiber of my being. I have never been more certain of how I feel—with the exception of my kids." Before she can ramble on—and she will—I kiss her. Hard. She moans into my mouth and slowly rolls her hips, cueing me to finish what we started.

"Mmm ... yes, ma'am," I murmur against her lips.

Charlotte rolls me onto my back. She pulls herself up, her knees at my sides, and moves her hips. She throws her head back, enjoying the fullness this position gives her. I sit up, placing my arm around the small of her back. My free hand grasps her right breast and guides her nipple into my mouth.

"Ah, Mitch." She moans and fists my hair as she rides me at a more intense pace. "Oh, Mitch ... baby," she breathes.

"I'm with you, baby. Let me hear you. Let me hear you come for me." I plant one hand on the mattress, giving me the leverage and balance to reach deeper ... higher.

"Fuck ... oh, Mitch ... Jesus ... oh, Christ ... God ... oh." She pulls tighter at my hair. And then she does it again—whips her head out of the arch it was in and looks straight into my eyes. She gives it all to me. *Fuck, that's hot!* It's just the thing that pushes me over the edge. My balls tighten and a surge of pleasure shoots up my shaft. I explode deep inside her. The heat and intensity of our locked eyes matches our orgasm.

"Ugh!" I bellow, grabbing her hips and thrusting into her one last time. Forehead to forehead, we sit there, still connected, panting.

"You're amazing, baby."

"We're amazing," she corrects.

Chapter Thirteen

Charlotte

"MITCH," I SAY with a sigh. He's been staring at me for the past ten minutes or so, his fingers tracing and doodling little designs over my skin.

"What, baby?" He nudges my nose with his.

"We're doing a great job avoiding some major conversations ... at least two, don'cha think?"

"We are," he agrees. "Can we keep it that way until tomorrow?" He pecks at my lips. "I don't think I can emotionally handle what I need to talk to you about. I have a bad feeling I'm gonna be pissed about whatever it is you need to tell me. Please, baby, it's gotta be almost nine, which means it's nearly three a.m. for me." He rolls onto his back. "I'm tired ... not to mention starved."

"Let's go downstairs and eat." I pat his chest and get up clean off in the bathroom.

Oh, shit.

Oh no!

I stand there frozen. I'm pretty sure all color has drained from my face.

"Are you okay, Char?"

Char?—that's new. I'd answer him, only I think I may have stroked out—nothing's moving!

"Baby?" His hands slide onto my hips.

"Um ... I'll be out in a minute," I finally pipe up.

"Oh no ... uh-uh ... what's going on?" He turns me to him.

"We're discussing things tomorrow, right?" I smile shyly and start walking backward into the bathroom. I close the door and lock it before he utters a word or moves a muscle.

"Okay—now you're making me nervous!" He states loudly on the other side.

You and me both, Mitch!

"NO. I DON'T like eggplant." He shakes his head at me while I plate some for him anyway.

"You've never had mine." I nudge him away from the drawer I need to get into.

"It doesn't matter. I don't like it! Make me something else," he snaps.

"Well, I might have if you'd finished that sentence with 'wench,' but since you didn't ... " I shrug.

"Smartass!" He slaps my butt and goes into the fridge to see what's there.

"Uh, no! You will try mine! If you still don't like it, I will make you something else." I shut the door on him and pull the first plate out of the microwave.

"I'm a grown-ass man, Charlotte! I know if I don't like something!" And at that, I shove a bite in his mouth.

He rolls his eyes in irritation.

I wait.

He chews.

I wait.

He rolls his eyes in pure enjoyment.

I smirk.

He chuckles.

I stick a fork in the center of his eggplant parm and hand it to him, my "I told you so" face fully intact.

After I get some for myself, I join him at the table. His plate is nearly empty.

"Gee ... I really wish you liked my eggplant parm," I say sarcastically.

"Well, I don't know what to tell you—it's disgusting." He smiles.

"I'm on to you, Mr. Colton!" I shoot him a look of suspicion. "You're just with me for my culinary skills."

"Yep, but that's okay—you're only with me for my irascible behavior." He winks. "I have to make sure I get to the gym more. You're gonna make me fat."

"I doubt that, what with the amount of sex you like to have." I smile, then think about the news I have for him. "You probably won't want to have sex with me after tomorrow," I say in almost a whisper.

"Why? You plan on throwing out your vagina?" He chuckles.

"Vagina?" I raise an eyebrow.

"That's what they'll call it."

"They who?" I giggle.

"The private detectives who find your thrown-away vagina. It'll be on the six o'clock news," he says.

"It will?" I play along.

"Yeah, it'll be a big story about the mystery behind the tossing away of the most perfect vagina anyone has ever seen."

"Sounds like you've got my vagina on a pretty high pedestal, Mitch."

"Kitty likes her heights." He shoots me a full-wattage smile. I shake my head and giggle.

God, I love him.

"All right, no more doom-and-gloom talk. Let's enjoy the calm before the possible storm." He holds his wine up to me. I clink his glass in agreement.

Mitch

I GLANCE AT the clock. *Damn.* Nine a.m. I inhale the smell of Charlotte's hair. She feels so good in my arms. My hand glides down her back. *She's got a great ass.* I feel myself growing hard under her thigh, and I caress her with more intent.

"Mmm," she moans lightly. She lifts her head and softly teases my nipple with her mouth. My hand dives into her hair, pulling her lips off so I can attack them. Charlotte straddles me, then abruptly pulls away as she sits up. I lay my head back on the pillow and drink in the sight of her. She moves her hair so it flows over her shoulder. *Christ, the way her eyes stare into my soul.*

"Mitch," she starts, "we have a lot to talk about today. We can't keep doing this."

"Making love?" I cup her hips.

"Avoiding the conversation." She tries to climb off.

"Just where do think you're going with my Kitty?" I ask playfully.

"Kitty needs to shower and get ready for the day." She taps my hands just as my cell starts ringing. I grab it.

"It's Kyle. I need to take this," I say. "But when I'm done, Morale's got some lotion he wants to dispense into Kitty." She snorts, slaps my hand, and climbs off. I admire her lovely ass as I answer my phone. "Hey, Kyle."

"Mitch—holy shit!"

"What's the matter, man?"

"I just met the woman of my dreams!"

"What?"

"She came in here looking for you. Well, to rip your head off. Christ, she's gorgeous! She's got long, dark brown hair, a nose ring, and those eyes, Mitch—her fucking eyes. They're green like fucking emeralds, man! Shit, I bet she has a hot tattoo in a hot place! I want to find that tattoo, Mitch." He finishes rambling. I think for a moment.

"CiCi?" I ask.

"CiCi," Kyle sighs. I laugh. "Mitch, this is no joke. She left here not five minutes ago, and I'm completely obsessed," he says in awe.

"What did she say to you?"

"Man ... I don't know. She had me by the balls—literally had her fingers wrapped around my balls! Her hand fit them good, Mitch." I can hear desire in his voice. "At times it was a little painful, I have to admit, but my balls were made to fit in her palm. Mitch," he says, all too seriously, "I have found the keeper of my balls, Mitch. I'm ready to hand them over." I'd say something, but I'm too busy gasping for air from my laughter. He ignores my reaction. "Who is she? An ex of yours?"

"No," I say as I pull myself together. "She's Charlotte's sister."

"Did you patch things up with her? Please tell me you did."

"Yes. Well ... sort of."

"What do you mean, *sort of*?"

"We haven't discussed things yet." I slide to the edge of the bed to get up.

"Well, discuss, make up, and tell me where I'm meeting you guys for drinks tonight," he says quickly.

"Drinks?"

"Yes, drinks. You, me, Charlotte, and CiCi."

"A double date?" I ask with a hint of apprehension.

"Yeah! Shit. Mitch, is CiCi involved with anyone?"

"I don't know, actually—I don't think so." I rub my temple, trying to wrap my head around this. "You sure you want this, man? CiCi's sort of different. I mean, in a good way—like crazy or eccentric." As I'm trying to clarify, I realize—how can one truly explain CiCi's personality? "She has no filter, man. You're kind of straitlaced."

"Yeah, I'm boring, Mitch—thanks to you!" he says. "I wasn't always like this, by the way. Maybe I need someone without a filter."

"All right, man, I'll see what I can do." I take in a deep breath and blow it out. To say I'm unsure about this union would be an understatement.

"Great! Call me and let me know!"

"You got it. But before you go, I want to get one thing straight."

"What's that?"

"What's my name again?" I ask, then laugh.

"What?" he asks, then catches on to my teasing. "Oh, that's easy. It's dickhead!" His sarcasm flies freely. I should care, being his boss and all but, I don't. I've recently realized that Kyle is my best friend. It's been a long time since I've had one of those. So ... free pass on the "dickhead" comment due to friendship status, right? *Friendship status?* Shit. I think I've sniffed too much "Charlotte." I'm starting to think like a chick.

"Dude? You there?" Kyle pulls me out of my thoughts.

"Yeah. Sorry. So, I'll text you the time and place."

"Thanks, man! Later!" he says, and we hang up. I rub my face before I get up. I head into the bathroom just as Charlotte turns the water off and steps out of the shower.

"All yours." She smiles.

"I know you are." I grab her towel. "Now get back in there."

"I'm done." She snatches it back.

"Charlotte, that was only ten minutes. You always take longer than that. Now get back in there." I seize the towel again.

"That's because you interrupt me," she states. "I'm done. Take yours. I'm going to make us breakfast." She grabs a different towel and wraps it around herself.

"I'm trying to take what's mine." I pull her by the hips, bringing her closer.

"No, Mitch." She pushes against my chest and looks me straight in the eyes. "Not until after we talk."

"We have a contract, Charlotte," I remind her.

She takes in a breath and nods slowly. "Playing that card again, are we?"

"Yes, I am. I've kept my part of the contract. It's only fair of me to expect you to keep yours." As I say this, I can see her wall building back up, anger flicking in her eyes.

"Good of you to keep me in check, Mitch—ell." She lowers towel. I scan her body slowly, then look back into her eyes. She stares at me blankly. The wall is completely up now. Of course it is. One minute I tell her I love her, and the next, I remind her of something I myself want to throw out the window.

I touch her cheek. "Go make us breakfast, baby. I'll be down in a few." I lean down and sweep her lips. She shoots me a look. "Go. I'm done being a jerk." I shrug.

"Okay, but I think it should be known that I had a much harsher word in my mind for you." She wraps herself back up.

"I'm sure I deserve it." I pat her toweled bottom, urging her to move out of my way so I can get into the shower.

Charlotte

THE SMELL OF corned beef hash and bacon hangs heavy in the air. *Mmm* ... if any morning calls for comfort food, this is it. I bring the fried hash over to the large electric skillet, making two good piles. I flatten the piles and pour my egg mixture over them, then lower the heat. Watching the eggs slowly fill every nook and cranny of open space, I start to think about what I'm going to say. He's going to flip out. He may—no—he *will* tell me to pull back on my offer. I won't. This could be our last breakfast together.

A very small—miniscule, really—part of me wants to say *good riddance*. I can't believe he threw the contract in my face again. I'm so confused. Yet ... I don't think he meant to. Maybe he just doesn't like to be told no. Who does?

"What do you have going on in here, baby?" He startles me, pressing his face to my neck for a sniff, then a kiss.

"It's almost done." I flip the omelets over and sprinkle some cheese before folding them. "Coffee should be ready," I add.

"Okay," he says, but encircles my waist with his arms instead of letting go.

He sniffs up my neck.
Down my neck.
Damn it.
My anger has now been snuffed. *Damn him and the way he sniffs*

182

me with that sniffer of his!

"Plates, please." My voice cracks as I point to them on the counter. He reaches over and grabs them. "Thanks."

"Charlotte, you are going to put a bra on later for Brogan's game, right?" he asks as his fingers glide across my bare back.

"No. I don't have to with this dress." I look down at it quickly as I plate the omelets. "Shit, I almost forgot about Brogan's game." *Good job, Mom!*

Mitch's hands come back around my waist and up my Jersey-cotton dress until he fills them with me. His thumbs circle my nipples. He turns me around to him and inspects my breasts. I stand still, feeling every shade of hot and bothered.

"Bra or sweater, Charlotte." He flicks my tightened buds gently.

"It's going to be ninety degrees out today! I can assure you, they won't show!" I push his hands away. "Stop being so damn controlling—I'm not a child!" I bring the plates over to the bacon and toss some on aggressively. *Damn, I hate how he affects me.*

"Coffee?" he asks, sounding almost cheerful.

"Yes," I mumble and bring our breakfast to the nook.

"So ... speaking of a child," he starts, then settles into the chair across from me.

"Is that my cue?" I bite off a piece of bacon.

"Pretty much," he says, bringing a bite of omelet up to his mouth.

I wait.

He laughs at me.

I shoot eye daggers, then an encouraging nod.

I wait.

In very slow motion (accentuated by slow-mo sound effects), he brings the forkful to his mouth.

In slower motion, he makes an exaggerated face of pleasure.

"I'ma smack you in a minute!" I announce.

"I'ma?" He chuckles. I throw a piece of bacon at him. It bounces off his nose and hits his plate. He picks it up, shrugs, and eats it.

"Hey!" I reach forward.

"Uh-uh!" He taps my hand. "Come on now, O'Brien. Spill the beans."

I sigh with irritation at his name reference.

"Charlotte." He gives me "The Look."

"Okay." I take in a deep breath. Here goes nothing—or everything. "Ava and Trent, as you know, have been trying to have a baby," I say. He nods. "Before you and I met, I offered to be a surrogate for them." I take a sip of my coffee and swallow hard. I can see Mitch has started putting two and two together—he closes his eyes and massages his temples.

"Go on, Charlotte."

"About a month ago, Ava asked if the offer was still on the table. She just couldn't go through another round of the vicious IVF cycle."

"So, you said yes," he states instead of questions.

"No. I said I needed to talk to you first." My heart is beginning to pound.

"Good." He nods. "The answer is no." He starts on his omelet again.

I try to keep my cool. "Oh, Mitch, that ship has sailed. You no longer get a say."

"How do you figure? You're not pregnant, so you haven't done the procedure yet—correct?" He sits back and crosses his arms.

"How do I figure?" I scoff.

"Yes."

"Three weeks, Mitch! I begged you to at *least* talk to me about this! You ignored me. I didn't think there was an 'us' anymore."

"I'm here now, and I say no," he says, his voice calm. He goes back to eating.

"I've already said yes." I grit my teeth.

"Take it back." He shrugs. I can't believe he's being so cavalier about this! We're talking about a baby and people's lives here!

"I won't," I say as I stab my omelet with my fork.

"You will. End of discussion." He slams his coffee mug down. "We will help them find somebody else. Christ, I'll pay for it! But I'll be damned if I let you carry another man's baby!"

"Their baby. I'm just the incubator," I correct him. "The decision's been made, Mitch."

"Yes, it has—it's a *no!*" He's all teeth and anger. "We will find somebody else!"

"There's nobody else!" I yell. "There's nobody else they trust! I am a sure thing."

"Yeah, you are, aren't you?" he snaps.

I gasp.

He shakes his head. I'm sure he's disappointed in his mouth. I am, too.

"We'll do everything we can to get the best person for them. Somebody local so they can be very involved. I'll pay double. Whatever it takes, baby, we'll do." He reaches across the table for my hand. I pull it away.

I stare down at my plate, unable to take another bite. I wipe away my tears before they plummet down my face.

"Baby." He sighs.

"No! You shut your mouth and listen to me right now, Mitch!" I bring my eyes up to look him straight in the face. "*You* are the only man I have ever done that with. I'm not a whore, and I'm not a gold digger, which is what you implied last time!"

"Baby—" he tries to cut in.

"Don't *'baby'* me!" I stand up. "I don't deserve to be treated like this, Mitch! I made an unselfish decision and I would do so again, because it's not about me—it's about my kids and making sure they have everything they need! I will, though. I will be a whore and lay down with a hundred men if it keeps a roof over their heads," I say through my tears. "If I mean more to you than that fucking contract, I wouldn't go waving it around in my face if I were you!"

"You will lay down with another man over my dead body!" He shoots up out of his chair, catapulting it across the kitchen and onto the floor, and charges around the table. I back up to the wall. His hand dives into my hair, pulling my face to his. "No other man will ever touch you again," he breathes into my face. "No other man will ever kiss you again." He pulls my bottom lip into his mouth and sucks—I swear to God—the plump right out of it. "No other man will ever get the chance to love you." Forehead to forehead. My pounding heartbeat will surely burst my eardrums.

"Mitch," I pant.

"I wasn't looking for this, Charlotte. It wasn't even a thought. But here it is, and I want it. I want it all. I'm not afraid of it anymore. I think I knew," he says as he opens his eyes to find mine, "from the moment I first laid eyes on you. The first time I touched you."

"At the table?"

"You felt that, too?" He smiles and kisses me.

"Yes."

"Baby?"

"Yes?"

"When I get mad, I say stupid shit just to one-up you. I'm sorry. What I'm not sorry about is the way you kick my ass over it. And ... I care, baby. I care about how my words affect you." He strums my bottom lip with his thumb.

"I'm not changing my mind about the baby," I say, before I drop all my defenses. He tenses up.

"Let's just stop discussing it for now," he says with a sigh.

"There's no discussion, Mitch. You bailed. I made a decision that I will not go back on." I place my hand on his chest to give myself some distance.

"I didn't bail." His tone is biting.

"You did."

"Give me time to see how I feel about it." His voice lowers as he calms down.

"Take your time, but you will not waste Ava and Trent's." I try to push away from him, and he just pulls me closer.

"Charlotte, goddamn it." He rests his forehead against mine. He lifts his away and lays a prolonged kiss on mine. "I'm going to go for a walk."

Well. That's it, then. He's leaving me—again. I knew that the chance of this happening was greater than it not happening.

"Can you at least leave me the half for this month to tide me over? It'll give me time to figure out what I'm going to do." I quietly mourn my pride as the words come out.

He looks at me strangely for a moment before I see a flicker of comprehension in his eyes, followed by disappointment and sadness.

"I'm not walking out, baby—just going for a walk. I need to sort my head out." He palms my face and brushes my lips with his. "I promise."

"I won't change my mind."

"You've said that." He nods.

"And you're okay with that?" I glance up from under my lashes.

"No. No, I'm not. You know I'm not. But I'm not okay with losing you either—hence the walk. I need to calm down." He kisses me again

186

and lets go. I watch him as he leaves the house.

"Pfbbt." I blow some hair out of my face. The best way for my thinking to stay on a constructive path is for me to keep moving. I can't sit and marinate in my thoughts; I need to feel the ground beneath my feet.

I'm noisy as hell. Clatter and chaos helps me to focus clearly. I know ... it's odd.

Clank of the dishes in the sink.

Faucet on at its highest capacity.

Disposal chewing up unwanted food.

Each sound represents a "loud" thought in my mind. Slowly, I pull one thought at a time, lining them up in order.

The worst is over. I've told him. I was about ninety-five percent sure he would respond the way he did, though I wasn't expecting the passion he backed it up with. I feel the guilt of my choice slowly rise as I realize the stubbornness behind it.

He's right. Nothing medical has happened—yet. Well, I did stop my birth control (probably should've mentioned that to him). But I haven't done anything else. I could hold off.

No!

Ava has been my best friend more than half of my life. I've watched her emotional suffering for years, all over trying to have something I could easily give her.

It's nine months. If he's being honest about his feelings (and I hope he is) about me, then nine months is not a big deal. Hell, he'll probably be away for most of it! Besides, love or not, he's only been in my life a few months. And because I'm a woman, I must mention again—he was M.I.A. for one of them. (Us women folk can't help it!)

That aside, I'm sure this is going to play at his psyche a bit. Deep inside, he probably wants a baby. Not a replacement of Isabella, but a chance to have what was ripped from him so tragically. My being pregnant with some other couple's kid may prove difficult for him.

Since I've gone and traveled down this road already—do I even want more kids? I take in a very deep breath and ponder the idea.

My three fill my cup so wonderfully that I would be perfectly fine with not having any more. Yet ... I can't ignore the feeling that someone is missing. Maybe even two someones. I've always wanted five. My pregnancies weren't the easiest, but man do I love being pregnant. Yes, I'm one of *those* girls.

What if Mitch actually doesn't want his own kids? I think for a moment. No, he does. I got that much from his rant. I'm not waiting. It doesn't matter what he wants now. What if I put this off for five months and Mitch leaves me again—permanently? That's five months longer Ava and Trent may have to wait for their dream. No. I won't delay them.

Mitch's hand reaches past me and turns off the faucet, then the disposal. His arm encircles my waist and I feel his cheek press against mine.

"Okay. I'm on board. Not that I have a choice, but I thought about it and I came up with a very good reason for you to do this now." His voice is steady and calm. I turn around to face him, encouraging him to continue. "At first, I thought maybe you could hold off. Let us have a baby, then do this for them," he says. I feel my eyes widen with shock. "Then I realized that wouldn't be good for us. Any of us, including your kids. It's too much to throw at them, never mind us." He takes a break and my expression, I'm sure, matches the warmth for him I feel in my heart. "I told you I want it all with you, Charlotte. That doesn't mean we need to act with haste, possibly sabotaging ourselves. I want us settled with each other and our feelings, and to have a stable home for your kids. A baby now would just force the transition rather than properly nurture it. You know I'm already very fond of your kids. I want this to be smooth for them, too." He pauses to take another breath.

I stand frozen, amazed ... flabbergasted. I may ask him to pinch me. I may pinch him!

"I realized this would be the best way to do things," he continues. "You have a baby for them first. That's it, though. Then you are mine. If you get pregnant again, it will be ours. If they want another, we will find someone else to carry it for them." He stops.

"Are you real?" I ask.

His smile crooks sexily, as it always does. "What do you think?"

"Are you sure?"

"Yes."

"Thank you." I smile and cup his cheek, then lean up and kiss him. "Uh ... there is something else I need to tell you. I should've mentioned it last night, but honestly, I didn't think about it 'til after the fact."

"What is it, baby? Am I going to need to take another walk?" He chuckles nervously.

I wince. "You may."

"What?"

"I'm not on birth control anymore. I didn't get my shot. We may be in the clear, though, because I only just skipped it."

"Grab your purse and whatever else you need." He pats my ass.

"Why?"

"We're going to BJ's or wherever the hell you have a membership."

"Okay. Why?" I ask again.

"Condoms."

"But ..." I trail off and gesture with my hand. I'm about to mention the local CVS. But before I can finish, he shoots me the "are you kidding?" look.

"Bulk, Charlotte—we need to buy in bulk."

"Right. Bulk," I agree, then say a silent prayer for Kitty.

Chapter Fourteen

"SO, WHERE'S THAT dickless pussy?" CiCi bellows to me as I slice oranges for Brogan's baseball team. I look over my shoulder to find her followed by the other super asswhores. I silently thank God the bleachers haven't filled in this section yet.

"Maddie, I thought you were captain?" I ask playfully, then turn my focus back to my sister. "Ceese, aren't all pussies dickless?"

"Cut the crap! I know you were with him last night!"

If anyone seeing us didn't know us, this would be where the switchblades came out, if they had that sort of imagination.

"Sorry, Charley," Jay pipes up from behind the girls.

"No surprise seeing you bringing up the rear, Jay!" I bark at him.

"What, Charley?" he shouts obnoxiously, "you want me to give it to you in your rear?" he asks. Everyone laughs except for CiCi and I, who snarl. Except not really—we're just fighting ... fighting the urge to laugh along, that is.

I give in first. "Damn it!"

"Can I get a woot woot?" CiCi cheers in victory. Collective "woot woots" ensue. I start slicing oranges again. "Yes, he was with me last night. We've made up. We're working things out, so please don't be an asshole toward him."

"I have to be an asshole toward him."

"Why?" I wave the knife in irritation. Mitch and I are already on shaky ground; we don't need any more crap blocking our path to happiness.

She points. "Watch it with the knife, killer! If I'm not an asshole to him, he'll think I hate him. I don't hate him. I'm just mad at him." She shrugs.

"Well, that's true." I shrug along.

"Where is he?" Julie asks.

"He went to pick up Gram. They'll be here soon. Don't tell Brogan, though—he wants to surprise him."

"Aw ..." A collective asswhore sigh, plus one Jason—the original and still reigning champion asswhore.

"I nominate Jay as our mascot," I announce. The girls look in his direction.

"All those in favor, say aye," Maddie states, then does so. Julie, Ava, CiCi, and I follow suit.

"I don't know what you crazy bitches are up to, but I'm in! Aye!" Jay holds up his hand. We take turns congratulating him on his promotion, then follow it up with a slap on the ass from each of us.

"Mom ... what are you guys doing?" Brogan asks, looking a little embarrassed.

"Oh, one of those silly things you do when you're twelve," I say, pushing the air around me away gently.

"You guys aren't twelve, though." He looks at us, confused.

"So we didn't get the memo, yet," CiCi says. "Sue us!"

"Hey, your team's getting ready to do warm-ups!" I point past his shoulder.

"Oh, okay." He smiles and shakes his head at us before jogging over to join the other kids.

"That kid's going to commit me the minute he turns eighteen," I say, watching him meet up with them.

"Well, they'll have to get through us first," Ava says.

I give them all another once-over and sigh. "Well ... that's comfort-ing."

The five of them stand side by side in a "Care Bear Stare" stance. Though their signs demand presence, they aren't pretty, and they aren't meant to give me the warm fuzzies. But in the end, it always makes us all laugh—nobody else does, but that's par for the course.

"Okay, take your warm fuzzies and go sit down." I throw my knife into my bag.

"Oh, it's warm," Julie says. "Never fuzzy, though."

"Oh my God, go!" I point.

"You know, I knew you were a twisted bitch the first day I met you," CiCi says to Julie, dragging her away.

"It was on that playground right over there, Ceese." She points. "And we've been in love ever since," she adds in a dreamy fashion.

I giggle—*assholes.*

I continue organizing the refreshment table for the boys. Just as I throw the last Gatorade in the ice, a pair of hands greets my hips.

"Damn, Charley—your ass looks hot in these yoga shorts," Josh says next to my ear before kissing it. I fight through the sudden, over-whelming need to vomit and throw his hands off my hips as I turn. "Shh ... shh, sweetie ... don't cry." He touches my face, speaking softly. *Is he for real?* Apparently when he pictured this moment, I was crying, and his ego left no room for improvisation in case my weeping wasn't in celebration.

Asshole!

"Get your hands off of me!" I snap and pull away.

"It's going to be okay, Charley. I'm ready to give you a second chance." He smiles. Not a regular smile. Not a happy "glad to see you" smile. No, it's an "I forgive you" smile.

I stare at him blankly.

I blink.

Is he on something?

He tilts his head to kiss me. I know that in the future, when I replay this moment in my mind, it will be completely in slow motion. His head will ricochet backward with bionic sound effects from the slap I deliv-ered to his face. However, we are in real time, and Josh is holding his cheek with a look of anger in his eyes I've never seen before. He steps toward me.

"You take one more step toward my daughter, you son of a bitch, and I'll brain ya!" my father yells. We both turn our heads in his direction. "Happy" Jack O'Brien looks like a force to be reckoned with, and he's got a Louisville Slugger as his sidekick.

My daddy. My hero.
God love him.

"Sit down, old man!" Josh says flippantly. "What do you think you're going to do with that bat?" He chuckles.

"Same thing I'm gonna do with mine, asshole—just at a different angle," Mitch says angrily from my right. We turn our heads toward him. He also has a bat in his hand.

"Mitch," my dad says calmly, then nods.

"Mr. O'Brien." He returns the gesture.

My future recollection of this memory may or may not involve some tumbleweed rolling around at this very moment. It should also be mentioned that it's high noon. I don't know what they meant by that back in the day, but for me, the time is noon and I believe Josh is definitely high.

"Okay, well, I think my wife and I can handle this conversation alone, since it pertains to us and neither of you." Josh reaches for my hand.

"Ex-wife!" Mitch snaps, yanking me back a smidge quicker.

"I don't know what she's told you, man, but we are not divorced."

"It was finalized last month, Josh," I say, but am distracted by Brogan making his way over to us.

"As a lawyer, you should know that your signature and permission were not needed in the state of New Hampshire. You should also know that you have no rights to the house, car, or any custody of the kids. You chose to give everything up. We made sure it's a permanent fix," Mitch continues to inform him.

"Dad?" Brogan asks from behind him. Josh turns. "What are you doing here?"

"Buddy!" he says, sounding overexcited and most definitely unnatural.

"What are you doing here?" Brogan asks again—so bravely.

My other hero.

"I'm home, buddy. I wanted to see you play today."
Oh—so awkward.

"You don't belong here," Brogan says nervously.

"Broge, go back to your team. Mom and I will handle this." Mitch smiles curtly and nods. Brogan makes a beeline for Mitch, throwing his arms around his waist.

"I didn't think you would make it to any of my games." He looks up at him.

"I told you I would. I promised." He taps the bill of his hat and hugs him.

"That is *my* son!" Josh yells. "Buddy, aren't you gonna give me a hug?" Josh holds his arms out. Brogan just stares at him, and Josh looks at me in disbelief. "You just let him steal my son from me?"

"He didn't steal me, Dad. You never wanted me." Brogan's chin quivers.

"I'm your dad. I love you, Brogan. He doesn't know you like I do."
Yep, that's validation enough for me—he's definitely high!

"I don't know him?" Mitch almost laughs.

"No. You don't!"

"What position does he play?" Mitch asks.

"Uh ..."

"Third base." Mitch answers for him. "Here's an easy one. Who's his favorite team?"

"Red Sox."

"Now, who's his favorite player?"

"Ortiz."

"Wrong—Pedroia. What's his favorite subject?"

"Science." Josh nods for emphasis.

"History. What's his favorite video game?"

"Uh ..."

"*MLB 13: The Show*. Who's his favorite character in Harry Potter?"

"Harry."

"Ron. What does he want to be when he grows up?"

"An astronaut." Josh rolls his eyes.

"A robotics engineer. What's Brooklynn's favorite song?"

"'Twinkle—'"

"'Hot Potato,'" Mitch cuts him off. "What's Bennett's favorite animal?"

"Dogs."

"Horses!" Mitch yells. "Just because you signed a piece of paper that says you're the father doesn't mean you're a dad, asshole!"

I'd say something to break all this up, but I'm too busy giving this man babies in my mind. I can't help it—my ovaries are bursting over here!

"I think you should leave, Dad." Brogan says. Josh stares at him, and I think I might see a flicker of remorse in his eyes. Oh—nope, false alarm.

"You don't deserve to be called that, either!" my dad pipes up. "What kind of man leaves his family without concerning himself with how they'll keep a roof over their heads or food on the table? You should be ashamed of yourself! You won't be pissing in their stew ever again!"

"I think you should go now," I say to Josh.

"I'll be in contact." He sighs, finally defeated.

"I won't hold my breath," I say as Mitch tightens his arm around my waist. Josh shakes his head and walks off the field.

"Hey, Josh!" Mitch calls out. Josh turns. "I owe you a big thanks."

"For?"

"You're the reason I now have everything I hold dear in life." Mitch looks down at me, then Brogan, as he says this. He gives us each an extra squeeze.

Josh stares at us, seemingly taking it all in. I have a feeling that in all the scenarios he came up with, this one wasn't even a thought. No, of course he thought I was just sitting around, waiting for him to give *me* "another chance." I'm so grateful for my ability to see what a complete asshole he is; otherwise, I would be feeling bad for him right now. Josh shakes his head and walks away. It's odd not seeing Josh fly into action. He's never speechless.

"You guys okay? Brogan?" Mitch looks down at him.

"Yeah, I'm okay. That was weird," he says, still watching his father's back. "He never wanted to come to a game before. Do you think he's changed, Mom?" He looks up at me.

Oh, dear ...

"Honestly, Broge, I don't know. I don't know if he's changed, if he's trying to change, or if this had nothing to do with that at all. Do you understand what I mean?" This is so overwhelmingly awkward. I want to be as straightforward as I can with him, but by the same token, he's only nine. Sometimes it's easy to forget his age because he's such a little old soul.

"Brogan," Mitch says, kneeling down, "this stuff is confusing for all of us. The only thing your mom and I can tell you is to listen to your gut. We don't know why your father showed up here out of the blue. I think we all need to sit back and see what happens. See what he does next. Mom and I won't keep him from you if he wants to visit, but if you don't feel right about it, we won't make you do it. You need to do whatever you feel comfortable with at the pace you feel comfortable. Do you understand?" He places his hands on Brogan's shoulders. "Don't do anything you don't want to do because you're worried about your dad's feelings. You need to worry about yourself first. Your mom and I will always put you first. You should, too. Okay?"

"Okay. I don't think I want to spend time with him yet, not that he'd want to." He shrugs.

"Okay." Mitch nods and pats Brogan's shoulder. "Now, let's shake this off and get to your team. The game you're going to win for me is about to get started." He nods over to the team.

"Oh, yeah!" Brogan smiles and runs off. Mitch stands up. Just as he turns to me, he's almost knocked over by Brogan's tackle hug. "I'm glad you're here, Mitch. I love you." He hugs him tight. I choke on my slight gasp.

Mitch hugs him back. "I love you too, Brogan, and I'm so proud of you." He pulls his cap off and plants a kiss atop my son's head. Brogan looks up at him, squinting from the sun, with the biggest smile. "Now, go! I want to yell at some umpires!" Mitch chuckles as Brogan runs off.

"Mitch, you make your mother proud," Dad says to him, holding out his hand.

"Mr. O'Brien," he says as they shake hands, "Thank you, sir." Mitch seems a little *verklempt* by Dad's words.

"Call me Dad, Mitch. It would be an honor." Dad's other hand covers Mitch's. Dad has only allowed one son-in-law to call him "Dad"—Colleen's husband Zach. And that didn't even happen until after they were married for five years.

Colleen had ovarian cancer and Zach was amazing throughout it all. He was her rock. We all loved Zach already, but not one of us had much faith in him to handle what Colleen was going through. He proved us all wrong without ever knowing we doubted him. That's the amazing part ... for us, at least.

Rambling aside, Dad loves his girls. As he sees it, no one will ever love and appreciate us the way he does. For him to tell Mitch to call him "Dad" after only a few months—wow. I'm in shock *and* very proud of Mitch and the man he is.

I haven't told him.

I need to tell him now, more than ever, that I love him. My heart is exploding with it. I can't believe how he just talked to Brogan. I know he's going to be a wonderful father, because he's already becoming that to the kids. They're all crazy about him. He makes them feel good about themselves. He reminds them that they're important and appreciated. Amazing, with the exception of three weeks (*yes, Charley, beat the dead horse again, why don't you?*), he's managed to give my kids more in this short amount of time than their father has their entire life.

And ...

He knows just what they need. He knows what they need to hear, whether good or bad. He knows they need to tell him stuff and have his full attention. He knows they need him to feel excitement over the things they're excited about. Feel disappointment over the things that disappoint them. He knows they need to know he remembers stuff about them and thinks about them. He knows because he was that kid with a father like Josh (to a degree), and he needed those things, too.

I told Dad about Mitch's father one day when he asked about his family. I told Mitch that Zach was the only one my Dad's ever respected enough (by that, I mean above and beyond ridiculous standards) to let him call him "Dad." This is so huge for both of them. I watch them, hands still grasped, talking to each other, mutual respect just beaming out of their eyes. It's weird, but all just seems right with the world.

"When are we going fishing, Dad?" Mitch wastes no time trying out his new privilege as they let go of each other's hands and start walking. Mitch looks back at me and extends his hand. I grab it and jog a little to catch up. He leans down and sweeps my lips sweetly.

"I don't know." Dad shrugs. "When do you want to go, baby doll?" He looks over at me.

"Daddy, why don't you and Mitch go without me? Maybe take Brogan and have some guy time?" I ask. They both agree and, as we head over to greet Gram, Maggie, and the rest of my family, make plans for the following Saturday.

"Mom, I'd like you to meet Mitch. Mitch, this is my mom, Shannon."

"Mrs. O'Brien, it's nice to finally meet you." Mitch reaches for her hand when she stands up.

"I'm a hugger, Mitch," Mom says as she opens her arms wide. "Come on in."

"Be careful, dude ... that's how my dad ended up with five girls," CiCi chimes in.

"I don't think it was just the hugs, Ceese." Mitch smiles and goes in for one of Mom's specialty "I'm never gonna let you go" hugs. "I see your girls got their looks from you, Mrs. O'Brien," he adds.

"You don't think I'm cute, Mitch?" Dad asks. "I'm hurt ... just hurt." He shakes his head.

"And their humor from you, Dad."

They both chuckle.

"How come he's Dad and I'm Mrs. O'Brien?" Mom pushes away and holds him at arm's length.

"Mrs. Dad?" he asks. She smacks his chest. "Mom? I can call you 'Mom'?" He crooks his head a little.

"Yes. That is, of course, if you want to."

"I would love to. It's been a long time since I had somebody to call 'Mom,'" Mitch says thoughtfully.

I pat his back softly. "C'mon, baby, let's sit down now. The game is about to start."

"Yeah, before I start to cry, goddamn it," Mom says, all teary-eyed from Mitch's statement. She knows he lost his mom at a young age. Just as she releases Mitch to sit down, she gets a bad spasm and loses her balance. Mitch grabs ahold of her quickly. "I'm okay, goddamn it!" she snaps. Mitch ignores her and helps her into her seat. "Stop fussing. I'm fine—just lost my balance. Stop looking at me, goddamn it!" she snaps at all of us now. You know Shannon O'Brien is not feeling up to snuff when "goddamn it" starts flying out of her mouth like this. We pull our collective stares away and find our spots on the bleachers. "And don't none of ya talk behind my back, goddamn it," she throws in for good measure. We all sit in silence.

HAMPSTEAD 15 VS. SALEM 5

"YOU GUYS NEEDS to be a little quicker on your feet, Broge. That was some skin-of-your-teeth action there," Mitch teases.

"Dude, are you kidding me? We slaaauuuughtered them!" Brogan brags as he jumps into the backseat.

"All right ... get your seat belt on there, slugger!" Mitch chuckles. He closes the door after him and turns to Gram. "So, we'll be by to-morrow with the kids around four, okay?" he signs to her. She nods and opens her arms for him.

"What can I bring?" I ask Maggie.

"Just this man with a smile on his face." She nods to Mitch.

"Will do." I kiss his cheek when he stands up.

"I've got a few ideas about how you can do that." He winks at me. I turn several shades of red, as we're still standing in front of Maggie and Gram.

"On that note, ahem, we'll be leaving now," Maggie says, then giggles. I turn redder and Mitch smiles, putting his arm around me and hugging me sideways.

"Bye, guys." I wave, then swing to slap Mitch. He flinches and mouths "ow" while he rubs the area on his chest I just whacked.

"We'll see you at the house, baby doll!" Dad yells from behind us.

"Okay!" I yell back. "C'mon, let's get the kids home."

"Does it always take you guys thirty minutes to leave these games?"

"Yes." I groan and roll my eyes. "The stupidest part is we end up at my house anyway. It's goddamn retarded," I complain as I open my door. Mitch heads around to the driver's side.

"I have to agree with you there, babe," he says as he climbs in. "So ... your mom?" he asks as he starts up the SUV.

"Same as yours."

"I thought so, but I wasn't sure." He looks over. "Why didn't you tell me?"

"I was going to. I just hadn't gotten around to it. When you told me about your mom, it didn't feel like the right time to jump in and make that announcement. She was in remission, but it seems like it's back." I glance at my parents as we drive away, giving them a final wave.

"My mom used to get pissy, too. Who can blame them? MS sucks. You sure they'll be all right to watch the kids while we're out tonight?"

"Yeah. It'll be fine. So, do you plan on telling CiCi that Kyle's going to be there?"

"Uh ... *no*."

"That's a good idea."

"He's a good guy." He grabs my hand.

"That only means he's going to have to work harder, because she won't believe he really wants to be with her."

"Why?"

"My sister only dates douchebags," I say, with a lowered voice so the kids don't hear. "A guy she went out with in college really fucked her up ... mentally. Or emotionally. Whatever's tied in with your self-esteem."

"Both. But she seems so confident."

"Yeah ... she's a great actress. Truth is, she's very awkward around good guys, especially if she likes them."

"Baby ... CiCi is awkward around everybody." He laughs. I snort. He's right.

Chapter Fifteen

"I CAN'T BELIEVE you invited everybody," Mitch says for the millionth time as we pull up to Mick & Marley's Pub.

"I'm not going through this again, Mitch!" I snap as I open my door.

"Hey! C'mere." He pulls me toward him.

"What?"

"Stop. I don't want to argue." He caresses my left cheek. Slowly, he leans in, nudging my nose before his lips entice mine to part for him. Just as I give in to his advances, the girls pound on the hood of his Benz, making us both jump. "What the fuck?" Mitch yells at them.

"Let's get our drink on, bitch!" CiCi bellows.

"Kyle really doesn't know what the fuck he's getting into."

"Maybe CiCi won't go for Kyle anyway." I shrug. We both let out a big exhale to prepare ourselves, then climb out of the car.

"You know we're totally gonna hump your girl on the floor when the band starts, right?" Julie asks him as he puts a protective arm around my shoulders.

"I'm looking forward to watching that." He bites back his smile.

"We're gonna give it to her, Mitch—like really, really give it to her." She widens her eyes.

"Whatever you guys do, Julie, is no competition for what I can do, so I'd stand down if I were you," he says, trying to be serious.

"Nobody can pound her ass like we can, Mitch." She opens the door to the pub.

"Oh my God—shut up!" I laugh.

"Pretty sure Charlotte would disagree with you, Julie," Mitch continues.

"Mitch, you've never pounded me in the ass." I turn back to look at him as we walk in.

"Yeah, Charlotte, and I'm pretty sure Julie and the other girls haven't, either." He says in an exasperated tone. "It's just a joke."

"Oh my God! We need to leave now, guys!" CiCi turns around and makes a beeline for the door.

"Why?" I ask, eyeing Mitch.

"Because the guy over there waving us down?" She jerks her head in his direction. "I had his balls in my hand earlier."

I grab her by the arm and pull her back. "Why do you think we're all here, Ceese?"

"What?"

"He wanted us to meet him somewhere. He's into you." I waggle my eyebrows at her.

"How can he be into me? I grabbed him by the balls and twisted them!"

"And now he's obsessed." I laugh.

"He's not my type." She shakes her head.

"He's cute."

"He's hot as hell."

"What's the problem, then?" I lower my voice and lean in toward her ear.

"He's not my *type*," she repeats.

"What are you talking about?"

"He has his shit together. He's not going to want a fuckup like me." She tries to pull away.

"You have your shit together!" I yank her back.

"Stop it! I'm not the kind of girl he's looking for." She fights against my hold.

"Maybe *he's* not good enough for *you*, Ceese!" I snap and stare daggers at her. "Stop being such a pussy and get in there!"

"What's going on here?" Julie walks over to us. CiCi's eyes go wide, pleading with me not to say anything to Julie, who intimidates her the most because she's just as bad as she is, if not worse.

"Nothing, we were just heading over." I smirk at CiCi, who rolls her eyes and lets out a sigh in irritation.

The three of us head over to meet up with everyone. Kyle stands as CiCi approaches and pulls a chair out for her. He seems nervous, and she's a little fidgety. I pull out my phone and take a picture. They both look at me.

You know when you're in the middle of a moment you wish you could somehow capture and keep forever? I did just that. I captured the moment I realized my sister met "The One." Of course, she doesn't realize this yet.

She finally sits as the waitress brings our drinks.

"Mitch said you like Malibu Bay Breezes." Kyle points to her drink.

"Uh, yeah ... thanks." She picks it up. Kyle grabs his beer to take a swig. "How are your balls?" CiCi asks, as if this is a normal question. Kyle spits his beer out as he chokes on it. I facepalm, then elbow Mitch, whose shoulders are shaking in an attempt to hold in laughter.

"Um ... chilly, now that they're not being warmed in your lovely palm." He gives her a half smile.

"If you're just looking to fuck me—you can forget it!" she says, challenging him.

"Is that all you've got?" Kyle quips.

She thinks for a moment. "For now," she finally says, then grabs his beer. She takes a swig and leans back in her chair. Kyle signals the waitress to ask for another round of beers. When she brings them, Kyle grabs one and leans back in his chair as well, his eyes glued to CiCi. And so begins their stare down. I've never seen anything like it.

Swig.

Stare.

Swig.

Stare.

There goes that imaginary tumbleweed rolling through again.

The local band that was setting up when we arrived finally starts playing.

"Let's go, girls! I can't watch these two eye fuck anymore!" Julie gets up and looks at us. We all get up. "Did you climax yet, Ceese?" Julie asks, extending a hand to her.

"C'mon, Julie, you know it takes a lot of work to get me to climax," she says, not taking her eyes off Kyle. He licks his lips and takes another swig of beer. CiCi grabs Julie's hand and stands.

Kyle stands, then grabs her free hand as she walks away and turns her back toward him. He pulls her to him 'til they're nose to nose.

"I'm a very hard worker, Ceese," he says over the music. "There are no limits, no boundaries that I won't push to get the sweet end result I'm looking for." Kyle sweeps her lips quickly. CiCi stands there—paralyzed, I think. I've never seen my sister speechless. "Go dance with your friends, beautiful," he says before leaning near her ear and nipping at her lobe. I stand in a trance, like I'm watching my fucking soaps, 'til Mitch smacks my ass to get me going. I grab my sister and drag her to the floor.

"Holy shit, Ceese, that was hot as hell. That was like a Mitch move." I look back at them and see Ava and Trent walk in. The men shake hands and Ava runs up to us.

Mitch

"SO, YOU'RE THE guy who's going to impregnate my girl?" I ask Trent as we sit.

"Wait. *What?*" Kyle turns his attention away from CiCi.

"Yeah, this dude's gonna get Charlotte pregnant." I'm trying to tease, but it's hard. I'm still pretty pissed.

"Mitch, Ava told me you were cool with this," Trent says, sounding unsure.

"I'm cool with it, man. I'm not as cool with Charlotte being the incubator. That's the selfish prick in me, though. I'll get over it." I reach across the table and slap his shoulder.

"Again ... *what?*" Kyle whacks my shoulder.

"Charlotte is going to be the surrogate for Trent and Ava," I say, then drink some beer.

If it weren't for the band, you could have heard the faint sound of crickets. Kyle is speechless, his eyes wide, and Trent looks uncomfortable as hell. "Trent, what do you do for work?" I wave at the waitress for another round.

"I'm a computer scientist. I—"

Kyle cuts him off. "Dude, for what company?"

"Gen-Tek in Boston," Trent says. He seems a bit taken aback.

"You like it there?" I ask.

"It pays the bills."

"So you hate it there?" Kyle asks and smacks me on the arm. I see the wheels a-turnin'.

"I have been passed up five times for promotions that should've been handed to me on a silver platter," he finally says, giving in. "Motherfuckers!"

Okay. I think he's pissed off.

"Trent, polish up your resume and bring it in to us! We're always looking for computer research scientists," Kyle offers.

"What company are you guys with?"

"Colton Technologies," we say at the same time.

"You think you can get me in there?"

"We may be able to pull a string or two." Kyle shrugs. "As long as you can show us that you can bring it. Colton Technologies only hires the best and the most dedicated."

"I'm their man then, Kyle!" He nods and glances at the dance floor. "Ha! Looks like CiCi's nabbed a real winner there." He jerks his head in her direction. Kyle and I both turn to look.

"What the fuck?" Kyle asks angrily and jumps up from his seat, knocking his chair back.

You know that moment when you ask yourself why the fuck it has to be *your* friend who causes a bar fight? Yeah, I'm having that moment right now. I jump up and run after Kyle. Too late!

"Get the *fuck* off of her!" He pulls this huge lumberjack-looking dude away from CiCi.

"Fuck off and mind your own damn business!" CiCi yells, trying to act like she was okay with this dude manhandling her.

"You heard the lady," Lumberjack says, and grabs Kyle's shirt. He pulls his fist back—only Kyle goes all ninja on his ass. Within two minutes, the guy is down and out. Kyle is still in his tae kwon—*who the fuck is this dude I've been working with for ten years?*—do stance, just waiting for somebody else to attack. Apparently, nobody is dumb enough to join their buddy on the floor. Kyle straightens himself out and walks over to CiCi.

"When you're ready to be treated like a real woman and not a fucking lady of the night, call me!" He pulls a business card out of his wallet and flings it at her. "I'm outta here, Mitch." He heads to the bar, where he throws down a few hundreds. "For your trouble," he says to the bartender.

"Man, what are you doing?" I grab his money.

"That's what they do in the movies when a fight breaks out," he says. He looks flustered, cursing under his breath with his chest heaving as he glances back at CiCi.

"This isn't the movies, for one. Two, you didn't destroy any property. C'mon, man, you need to walk this off. Actually, we should all leave before the cops get here." I slap his back and wave for the others to come with us.

"One thing is for sure, Mitch," he starts when we get outside.

"What's that?" I grab his keys.

"We're no longer boring." He watches CiCi walk out.

"I guess not." I nod. "Let me drive you to Charlotte's so you can cool off."

"Fine." He sighs and climbs into his Lexus GX 460.

I throw Charlotte my keys. "Take her to your house."

"Okay," she says, then mouths, "Sorry." I wink at her.

"Mitch, what the fuck kind of game was she playing?" he yells.

"I told you to buckle in with her, man. She's going to give you a run for your money." I start the car.

"I just don't get it."

"Okay. This is between you and me—you got it?" I glance over at him.

"Yeah, of course!"

"CiCi tends to go out with guys that don't really deserve her. I guess some supposedly nice guy in college really did a number on her, so she trusts the good guys less than the bad. Do you understand?" It's hard speaking "chick" to my buddy.

"I guess. I don't know. Should I be a badass, then?"

"I think you covered that back there, sensei. What the fuck was that shit? You went all ninja warrior on that guy." I still can't believe what I saw. "I'm gonna call you 'Bruce' from now on!"

"I've trained in karate all of my life. I'm a 10th-dan black belt."

"Whatever that means." I chuckle.

"It's the highest level. Listen, what am I going to do about her?"

"You still want to pursue her?" I ask in disbelief.

"You ever know me to quit on something? I want her, man. I know she wants me, too." He lays his head back against the headrest. I pull up to Charlotte's, and she drives around me and into the driveway.

"Drive CiCi home." I turn his SUV off and hand him the keys. We both get out and head to my car. CiCi closes her door and turns, only to realize Kyle and I are both there.

"I'm going inside," she says quietly to Charlotte.

"No, you're not." I gently grip her wrist. "Kyle is taking you home," I say when she turns back to me.

"No, he's not. If I were you, Mitch, I wouldn't push it with me right now. You're still on my shit list!" she snaps and pulls her arm away.

"I don't care what fucking list I'm on, Ceese! Kyle is bringing you home. You are not spending the night here—that's final!" I put my hand on her back and steer her toward Kyle.

"Charley, are you gonna let him talk to me like this? What happened to 'chicks before dicks' or 'sisters before misters'?"

"Mitch, I'll take her home," Charlotte says.

"No you will not." I grab her hand. "Ride with him or walk, CiCi."

"I'll have my dad drive me."

"Forget it," Kyle says. "What is wrong with you?" he asks CiCi, his voice laced with annoyance.

"Kyle!" Charlotte gasps. She looks pissed—something I'm well-acquainted with. Her nose does this little scrunched-up flarey sort of thing. *It's fucking hot.* I look back at CiCi. She just stands there, not saying a word. She seems so un-CiCi-like. When she starts shaking her head slowly, I think she may be trying to stop her eyes from tearing up.

"Please take me home, Charley." She tries to steady her voice.

"Let's go in, Charlotte. Let them sort this out."

"No, Mitch. I'm taking her home."

"This is ridiculous!" Kyle says. "CiCi, I will take you home and not say a word to you, okay? Just tell me where you live. We've all had a crazy night, and we should just put an end to it before everyone starts arguing. Let's go." He holds his hand out to her.

"Ugh—fine!" She throws her hands up in the air and walks past him, ignoring his gesture. Kyle shakes his head and follows her.

"Good night, guys! It was fun! Let's do it again!"

"Shut up, Mitch!" they say in unison, but CiCi extends the courtesy of flipping me off as well.

"C'mon, baby, let's go in." I squeeze Charlotte's hand.

"I don't like the way you just handled that! I'm never going to hear the end of it!" She pulls her hand away. Deciding it's best not to say anything, I open the door and allow her to go ahead of me.

"What are you two doing home so early?" Dad asks. *Dad.* I'm still overwhelmed by this. It's a good overwhelmed, though. Amazing how a few months ago, I didn't know any of these people, and now it's like I've been around them my whole life. Funny how that happens.

"Not really our scene tonight," I say.

"Well then, we're gonna head home if you guys don't mind." He stands up and walks over to us. "Mom's not feeling so hot today," he adds in a lower voice.

"Anything else happen?" Charlotte keeps her tone low as well.

"No, but I think it's time for a checkup." He frowns slightly.

"What's going on out there?" Mom walks out into the living room. "What's with all the hushed voices?"

"We were talking about you, Mom, what else?" Charlotte smiles and hugs her. "You and Dad can head home now. We didn't feel like staying out tonight."

"You didn't leave early on account of me, did you? 'Cause I'm fine, goddamn it."

"No, Mom. Stop it. Although, I am going to give you a 'what for' if Brooky is walking around here tomorrow saying 'goddamn it' to everything." She kisses her mother's cheek.

"Well, then, I'll expect that phone call tomorrow." She giggles, her eyes full of mirth.

"Mom!" Charlotte complains.

"It could be worse! I own 'goddamn it,' but CiCi will own anything said after that!"

As much as I'm enjoying this exchange between Charlotte and her parents, I can't help but wonder if this is going to be another half-hour production. Christ, why can't they just say goodbye and head out? I'd bet my eyes they'll see her tomorrow. The O'Briens are lingerers. I've never seen anything like it. They stood on the field today—lingering—in a large O'Brien circle, discussing lunch and God knows what. It wasn't like we were deciding where to go; we knew we were all coming back here. It was so odd. Do all families do this? Do they all just stand around after events like they are figuring out what to do next, even though they know already?

"Mitch?" Charlotte nudges me out of my train of thought.

"Huh? Oh. Sorry. Bye, Mom. Bye, Dad. See you tomorrow?" I ask and go in for a hug.

Dad hesitates. "Eh, I don't know. We'll see what tomorrow brings."

"Jaccckkk." Mom shakes her head, sounding annoyed.

"Let's go, Shannon." He gives her a curt nod.

"Call me tomorrow!" Charlotte says and widens her eyes at her dad.

"Will do." He kisses her cheek.

I watch Charlotte as she locks the door behind them and sets the alarm. She seems somewhat melancholic. It has been a long, exhausting day for us both. The surrogacy debate. The Josh incident. Her mom's MS. And for the grand finale, the bar fiasco. I haven't even discussed Kelly with her. Not tonight. I don't think either one of us could handle another thing.

"Would you like a glass of wine, baby?" I rub her arms and kiss her hair.

"No. I just want to head up and get into some comfy PJs." She turns to me and plants a soft peck on my lips.

"The invisible kind, right?" I smirk and raise an eyebrow.

"Seriously? You're not exhausted from today?"

"I'm never too exhausted for sexy time with my lady." I wrap my arms around her waist, lean down to her neck, and ...

I sniff.

"Sexy time?" She giggles and tries to pull away from my vicious sniffing.

"Yes. Sexy ... very sexy ... time." I nudge her nose with mine before capturing her lips.

She pulls back. "Mitch?"

"What?"

"I need to tell you something."

"What?" My hands slide up her legs, bringing her dress with them.

"I love you," she murmurs against my lips.

"I know, baby." I kiss her again.

"I know, but I hadn't actually said it yet. I wanted to. I wanted to shout it out today on the field." She pulls back again. I lean in. "No. Please, let me just say this." She looks serious, so I nod. "What you said to Brogan today. How you handled the whole Josh situation. What you said to Josh ... "

"Hey ... what, baby? Tell me." I chuck her chin.

"I've just never felt so proud, so in love. My heart felt like it was exploding. It's a wonderful feeling, Mitch. It's also scary. I'm scared." She looks away. Her teeth feast on her lower lip in an attempt to control her nerves.

I stare at her. I stare long and hard. I don't know what to say. She just said it all. I feel how she feels. That's why I ran. I know this is what I should tell her, but honestly, I can't handle another emotional topic tonight. Talking about Kelly will possibly take hours—long, emotionally exhausting hours that neither of us has the energy for tonight.

"Charlotte." I rest my forehead to hers. "I love you, too. You know I do. We still have a lot to discuss, but let's do it tomorrow. I don't think we can walk through another topic tonight. We're both scared. We have so much to gain and so much to lose at the same time. Right now, I can say that not having you in my life is about the scariest it gets for me."

"But ..." She looks up into my eyes.

"I know, Charlotte. I know. Please, not tonight." I palm her face. "Tonight, all you need to know is that I am just where I want to be. Where I intend to stay. Okay?"

"Mitch." She exhales through pursed lips. I can see she's trying to fight off tears.

"I'm sorry. I'm so sorry, Charlotte. I wish I could go back and change what I did. No. Actually, I don't want to change it. If I didn't behave like that, I wouldn't have made it to this point of certainty. I know that none of this makes sense to you now, but it will. I promise it will. I just can't get into it tonight. We've had an exhausting day, baby. We really need to recharge before we pile on more. Trust me. Please?" I plead with my eyes and thumb away the tears she was unsuccessful in keeping at bay.

She finally nods. "Okay."

"Yeah?" I smile and kiss her.

"Yeah."

"C'mon, let's get you into your comfy PJs. We'll have snuggle time instead of sexy time." I pull her with me, leading her up the stairs.

"Snuggle time can be sexy," she says.

"Any time with you is sexy time."

"Well, now you're just pushing it." She shakes her head, then giggles.

Chapter Sixteen

I LOVE LISTENING to her breathe. It's soothing. The way she's sleeping on my chest, I can feel her heart beating against mine. I bring a fistful of her hair up to my nose and inhale deeply. *Mmm, Charlotte ...* my favorite smell. Quickly, I'm realizing, she's becoming my favorite everything.

Scared?

Scared doesn't come close. I feel like I'm in the middle of a free fall. I have no control whatsoever. At the end of the day, though, we don't have much control over anything in life, do we? I thought I did. I thought I could control everything in my life from now on. After losing Kelly, I never wanted to take a chance in obtaining anything I couldn't control, personally or professionally.

Obtain?

I didn't *obtain* my feelings for Charlotte. It's more like they clobbered me over the head. I knew it that first night. I wanted to choose flight over fight. I was scared right then and there.

It's good to be scared. If you're scared—you're alive. If you feel alive—you're living. I wasn't living before. I was existing. Hiding. Coping. Lost. I lost so much damn time. I've pushed away so many people. If Kelly were here, she'd kick my ass for it. I don't know why I handled my grief like that. Why does anybody handle grief the way they do? It's not something that can be expedited. Everyone has to find their own path around the bend and come full circle—some people just get there quicker. Most people, I bet, have gotten there a hell of a lot quicker than me. Maybe my journey was supposed to take this long. Maybe life wasn't supposed to start making sense again until Charlotte was here to help me make sense of it. So ... did I really waste time? She's in my arms, breathing her little breathy noises, her heart beating on top of mine. And she loves me. No. No, I didn't waste time. I was waiting on time. I was waiting for time to bring her to me. To make me scared. To make me feel alive. To bring me full circle.

May 17, 2015
Two Steps Forward Dedication Ceremony

Mitch

CLASPING CHARLOTTE'S HAND, I bring the back of it up to my lips, where I peck it softly and caress my cheek with it. I glance sideways at her and catch her loving smile. I inhale deeply.

"It's unbelievably gorgeous today," I whisper as Kyle steps up to the podium.

"I know," she says with the same happy incredulity. "Look at the turnout, Mitch," she adds.

"I know." I squeeze her hand. "We did good, baby."

I look around at the endless sea of people, then bring my attention to Kyle when he clears his throat. I'm still not sure why PR thought it'd be better for me to sit facing the crowd. Not only do I have to stare at Kyle's ass (uncomfortably, I may add), but I think it would've been more appealing for Charlotte and me to be in the audience. Two Steps Forward was created to help people in situations similar to ours, so we're just a small fraction.

"Thank you!" Kyle bellows out. The crowd quiets down. "On behalf of Colton Technologies and Two Steps Forward, we thank you for showing your support today by being here with us to kick off this fantastic foundation!" Kyle moves his notecards. "As you know, Colton Technologies has always focused on the latest innovations for the cars we drive. But what about the latest innovations for the people who drive the cars?" He looks around, making eye contact with individuals. "What makes you tick?" He points to a random area. "What are you struggling with in your life?" He points to another.

"We all have a story, right? We all struggle with something. Don't we all feel, at some point, that when we take two steps forward, we also take three back?" He looks around again. "Well ... am I right?" he asks, his voice louder. The crowd makes some noise.

"How many of us are so devastated or feel so defeated that we don't even bother to take those first two steps at all?" Kyle asks, raising his own hand. Charlotte and I raise our hands as well.

"Your head's spinning so much, you don't know where to start or what you're even looking for." Kyle takes the mic and starts walking around the stage.

"Well, no more. Whether you've never taken the first two steps or tried to several times, when you walk through these doors behind me, you will be taking two steps forward in the right direction." He holds his arm out, indicating the doors.

"I can tell from the look on some of your faces that you're not quite sure what I mean. Let me give you some basic information. Two Steps Forward is equipped with top-notch people in research, social work, life coaching, and more. Whatever you are going through or need help with, if we don't have the answers in that building already, we have the people who will find them for you—no matter what. See, we don't want you to take two ordinary steps forward. We want two leaps. We want extraordinary." He stretches his arms wide.

"I bet I know your next question." He smiles. I look around at the crowd again. He's got their complete attention. *He's such a politician.* "Why?" he asks into the mic. "Why would Colton Technologies want to do something like this? Why would they care? Why would Mitch and Charlotte Colton care?" He shrugs.

"Well, why don't I let them tell you?" He puts the mic back where it belongs. "I'd like to introduce you all to Mitch Colton, CEO and owner of Colton Technologies, and cofounder of Two Steps Forward." Kyle begins clapping as he looks over his shoulder at me. The crowd joins in as Charlotte and I stand up. We head to the podium.

"Wow, man, you did a phenomenal job!" I shake his hand and pat his back.

"It was nothing, Mitch! I'm so proud to be a part of this." He smirks. Fuckin' smirker—love this guy!

I step up to the mic with Charlotte by my side. After waiting for the cheers to die down, I tell them my story. You could hear a pin drop, it's that silent. The crowd gasps as one when I talk about losing Kelly and Isabella. Charlotte rubs my back. I discuss how the grief changed me. How the guilt took over my personal life.

"Can you survive grief without any help? Sure. I did. It only took me almost twenty years. It shouldn't have. I wore my grief like armor. My heart was caged. Then, out of nowhere, a beautiful woman—in every sense—came along with the key." I look over at Charlotte and wink. She gives me her sexy little smile. *Damn, the things that smile does to me!* "So," I say, turning back to the crowd, "I was cured, right?" I wait until I start seeing some of them nod in agreement, then shake my head. "Wrong. As I chipped away at the grief, the guilt took over—and it terrified me. I almost pushed her away, like I did everyone else. Luckily for me, Charlotte is not the type of woman to give up. She fought, and it helped me realize I didn't want to lose her too." I grab her hand and bring it to my lips again. "I finally did something I should've done a long time ago. I sought out the help I needed. I wanted to make sure, after the trauma of losing my first love, that I fixed my heart and head as much as I could before handing them over to my second one." I take in a deep breath. "Because I did this, I have something I never thought would be mine: an amazing wife and four beautiful children. No, I'm not Superman." I smile. "Three are from Charlotte's previous marriage and, as most of you know, we were blessed with the arrival of Bernadette just six weeks ago." I look back at her sleeping in her car seat.

Yeah, we went with a "B" name. She's named after my mother. Funny coincidence, huh?

I continue to talk about how things could've been different had I gotten the help I needed in the beginning. Not so much my love life, because I couldn't imagine anyone but Charlotte at my side, but my friendships—how I could have saved old ones and gained new ones. I'm lucky to have Kyle as my best friend, especially after once forgetting how nice it is.

Charlotte takes her turn to talk about how Josh abandoned her, and its affect on her life and her children's lives.

"We both suffered from abandonment, though from two different angles. You know, life keeps happening—at a fast pace. It doesn't stand still just because you wake up one day with a life completely different than the one you knew the day before. Your heart ... your mind ... they shut down. Not life, though. It doesn't give you a chance to blink. Life tells you to throw that luggage on your back and carry on. After a while, you stop looking for a place to set that luggage down. You forget there are places to put it, that you can stop the carousel ride that is life. Just for a moment. Stop the spinning. Take a breath. Figure things out. You can do that. Mitch did it. I did it. Two Steps Forward will help you or someone you love do it. Life is a puzzle—sometimes you need a second pair of eyes to see where all of the pieces go. We want to be your second pair of eyes," Charlotte says with such warmth, I swear she verbally hugged everyone in the crowd.

"SHE ASLEEP?" I whisper when I walk into the room. Charlotte's in the rocking chair with Bernadette cradled to her breast. She smiles and nods. I turn the night-light on and the lamp off. Charlotte gets up slowly after Bee unlatches. She carries her over to her crib and lays her down. We both stand here, staring at her. "Have I thanked you today?" I whisper in Charlotte's ear before I nip her lobe.

"For?" She turns her head to look up at me.

"You. Her. Our other three. Our life," I say, pecking her lips after each thing I'm grateful for.

"No, you haven't." She turns to me and slides her arms around my neck. "But I have a wonderful idea of how you can." She smiles against my lips.

"Yeah?" I run my hands along her bottom.

"It's been six weeks, baby." She smiles coyly.

"I know. I can't believe she's been here for six weeks already." I play dumb. I know what my baby wants.

"I'll meet you in our room in a few minutes." She shakes her head at me. Yeah, she's not falling for it.

"Yeah? You sure, baby?" I don't want her to jump back into sexy time if she's not really ready.

"Yes. I am very sure. Besides ... I'm under contract." She bites her smile back.

"Yes, you are, indeed, under contract," I agree as we head out of Bee's nursery. "Tell me, Mrs. Colton, are you still satisfied with the terms of our contract?" As we walk, I wrap my arms around her waist from behind and press her against me.

"Oh, yes! The conditions of this contract are far better than the original version." She squeezes my arms and giggles when I take in a long sniff of her neck.

"Oh, yeah? What are some of your favorite aspects of this contract?" I let go, sit on the bed, and pull her onto my lap.

"Well, let's see. I have an amazing husband who makes me feel special, loved, and cherished every day. He prioritizes me and our kids. He's a fantastic father. We're all proud to have the Colton name." She rests her forehead against mine.

"That was the greatest gift—besides Bee, of course—anyone has ever given me." I close my eyes and squeeze her to me.

"You should send him a card." She laughs lightly.

"Do they make cards that say, *Thanks for being an asshole*?" I ask.

Fuckin' prick. Don't get me wrong, I'm thankful he relinquished his rights to the kids so I could adopt them. I just can't get over the fact that he would give up his kids to avoid tax-evasion penalties. Well, not the penalties, but jail for not paying them. Let's just say Josh hadn't been too honest on his returns the past few years.

Unfortunately, Charlotte got roped into his fraudulent behavior since she was married to him the first two years he started tweaking the returns. That's the only reason things went down the way they did. I would've let him fry for it, but I didn't want Charlotte's name dragged through the mud. So, I made an offer he couldn't refuse. I would pay off all of the penalties if he gave up parental rights so I could adopt the kids. That asshole took all but twenty seconds to think about it.

How did the kids take it? Let's put it this way—Brogan said he felt like he had won the World Series. I love that kid. I love all three of them. They started calling me 'Dad' before Charlotte and I got married. It is the most wonderful sound in the world.

Blessed ... I am fucking blessed!

The adoption took place right before Bee was born. It was perfect. We had a huge barbecue to celebrate. I'm not ashamed to admit that I stopped quite often during that day to take a look around at all the family and friends who were there, sharing in our happiness, and I teared up each time.

Each day, I'm starting to feel more whole—complete. It's not just Charlotte and the B.C.s (my nickname for them). It's the steps we take together as a family to solidify our future. It was building this house together (in the same town, so the O'Briens can linger as much as they like) and syncing the family schedule: trips, dinners, et cetera. Everything in my life now revolves around my family. *My family.* Best phrase in the world. *Family*—best word in the dictionary.

I'm the richest guy in the world, and it has nothing to do with what's in my bank account.

Charlotte

MITCH LOOKS DEEP in thought. He gets like this a lot—reflective.

It's sweet.

"Hey," I say.

He looks into my eyes. A small smile creeps into his, and they crinkle at the corners. His eyes are even kinder these days. I stare into them, feeling a connection—a sense of contentment—that I have never known with another man. He is my one and only. The keeper of my heart, mind, and soul, and the source of my balance. He's the man you dream of when you're a little girl picturing your knight in shining armor.

"Damn it, Charlotte, I could stare at you for hours. So pretty." He caresses my cheek and strums his thumb over my bottom lip.

"Mitch ..." I whisper. My breathing becomes shallow. Two years later and he still has this effect on me.

"What, baby? What do you need?" he asks. *Damn him and that sexy voice.* "Tell me, baby." His lips rub gently against mine—not a kiss, but the slight tease of possibility.

When Mitch talks like this, he wants sexy talk. He wants naughty Charlotte.

Mitch loves him some naughty Charlotte.

"You want to know what I need?" I ask softly and dart my tongue out to lick his lips gently.

"Mmhmm."

I climb off his lap, turn, and straddle him. *Yeah, I guess I'll save the sexy nighty I bought for another night!* I palm his face.

"Open your mouth for me, Mitchy." That's what naughty Charlotte calls him these days. I keep my tone soft and sexy—I know it drives him crazy. He complies and I drop my mouth to his, allowing my lips to taste, my teeth to nip and pull. Mitch releases a low groan. His hands slide back and cup my ass, where he begins rubbing and squeezing. Kitty grinds to the rhythm.

My tongue slides against Mitch's as it enters his mouth. Meticulously, our tongues caress each other. *Fuck ... the way our tongues dance!* Mitch's hand travels up my back until he reaches my neck. He fists my hair and brings my face closer to his as he licks hard into my mouth, showing me his urgency and rendering me breathless. Kitty rubs the boost out of Morale. All hands are on deck. *This could get messy, people—and loud!*

Mitch pulls away to whip my shirt off.

"What do you need, baby?" he asks, his voice breathy as I rip his dress shirt open. *Naughty Charlotte can be aggressive at times.* He tosses me onto my back and yanks my yoga pants off. I immediately part my legs for him.

"Gah—Mitch!" I gasp as he slaps the inside of my thighs, squeezing and pushing them open wider. Mitch and I worked through his manhandling of me a long time ago. I let it go because I do love it, and let's be honest—he's the only man who's ever known how to handle me.

"What do you need, baby? What do you want? Don't make me ask again." His thumbs move around in devilish little circles right beside Kitty. I can hear her purring loudly. I move my hips, thrusting them into the air. Mitch squeezes my inner thighs again—painfully.

"Your tongue," I finally breathe.

"Where do you want my tongue, baby?"

"My pussy," I pant. Sometimes it's still hard for me to talk like this. I think Mitch loves it even more when I feel shy and awkward—kinky bastard!

"I'm sorry, baby, who's pussy?" He hovers over me, hot breath in my face, provoking me. His hand slides between my legs. His fingers pet Kitty, but just barely. "Who does this pussy belong to?" he asks again. I can barely focus on anything but his finger circling my entrance.

"You, Mitch." I tremble.

"Tell me what you want me to do," he murmurs against my lips. *My man is all about the details.*

"I want you to lick me, slide that hot tongue up and down, taste every inch of me." I grind up into his hand. "I want to feel your tongue dart inside me over and over again—teasing me."

"You like it when I fuck you with my tongue, baby?" he asks as he plunges two fingers deep. My hips fly into the air ... craving more ... wanting to be filled.

"Your tongue." I bite at his lips. "Your fingers." I push against them. "Your cock." I reach down between us and rub the bulge in his pants. A low groan escapes his throat. "Your mind." I reach up and lightly touch his temple.

He jerks his head back. "You think I mind-fuck you?"

"I know for a fact, Mr. Colton, that you fuck me in your mind constantly—it's exhausting." I say, straight-faced. Mitch stares at me for a beat, then gives in to the impending laughter. This is how it's always been with us. Sexy and fun ... fun and sexy. I love it. I love him.

Mitch nudges my nose with his and gets serious again. "You want it in that order?" He kisses me.

"I'll take it from you any way I can get it, Mitchy."

"Damn it, Charlotte, the things you say to me." He nibbles his way down my jaw, my neck, my breast ...

Oh, the way he nibbles ...

Mitch arrives at his destination. I gasp as his tongue unleashes all of its wicked talent on me. I fist my pillow, trying to restrain myself. He applies pressure to my clit with his thumb, torturing it with slow circles. I push against it to add more friction, but am greeted by the sensation of Mitch's tongue diving deep inside me, all wet and strong. *Oh, fuck!* I ride it like it's my job. Well ... I guess it sort of is.

Mitch retracts his tongue. "Fuck. I love the way your pussy tastes, baby."

Fuck, I love how he says he loves the way my pussy tastes!

"Mitch, I need you," I beg as my hips fuck the air.

"What do you need, baby?" He climbs up my body—hovering over me. "Tell me." He sucks at my lips, letting me sample my taste.

"You," I breathe.

"You have me. What do you need from me, baby?" *Sexy and smooth.*

"I need your cock stretching my pussy out—making it sore," Naughty Charlotte says. Mitch shifts and I hear a zipper release. Is it weird that I find that to be one of the most enticing, erotic sounds in the world? He drops his pants.

"This cock, baby?" He slides it up and down my center. "Can you feel how hard you make me?" He puts a little more pressure.

"God, Mitch." I whimper from the anticipation.

"I'm going to bury my cock so deep inside you, you won't know where I begin and you end. You know what else, baby?" His breath is hot in my face. His tongue slides across my bottom lip, his cock spreads my wetness around, and my pussy clenches so very fucking hard. I'm about to go out of my mind.

"What?" I push up against him.

He leans down to my ear. "I'm. Going. To. Take. My. Time. Filling. Every. Sweet. Inch. Of. Your. Tight. Little. Pussy."

He keeps his promise. I wrap my arms around him, trying to get to his ass and push him in. He grabs my wrists and holds them above my head before he continues to inch into me slowly.

Oh, the torture ...

"Fuck, baby ... *God*!" He groans once he's completely inside of me. "You okay?" He nudges my nose. All I can do is nod and breathe. I don't think I could find my voice even if I wanted to. It's our first time since I had the baby, and while he feels amazing, I'm not going to lie—things are not quite 100% yet. "Are you sure, baby?" He pecks softly at my lips. I nod again and give in to his kisses. "I'll go easy—okay?"

"Yes," I whisper.

Mitch rolls his hips, keeping his pace slow and steady. Soon enough, I feel completely acclimated to his size and am able to push the discomfort away. My hips get more eager to meet his and he lets out a muffled groan, attacking my mouth with a raw hunger that I'm sure will be visible across my lips hours after our lovemaking is finished.

"Baby," Mitch grunts, "I'm not going to last much longer." He reaches down between us. His fingers find my clit and meticulously rub it while he continues to pump me with his throbbing cock. We've been at it for a while, and I'm having a hard time reaching my climax. I have to admit, a little wave of fear crashes over me. Will I struggle with orgasms again? I've never had a hard time with Mitch. If anything, I come too quickly with him. "Charlotte," he almost begs.

"Go ahead, it's okay." I kiss him. He jerks his head back to look at me.

"Oh hell *no*!" His voice is laced with frustration. He takes in a deep breath. "Baby."

Whispering sexy voice. Fuck, he can make me come with that alone.

"You're going to come really hard for me, and you're going to do it now. I won't fill you with one drop of my come until you do. Your pussy needs to beg for it." He bites my lobe. "You wanna feel your pussy filled with my come? You wanna feel my hand rubbing my come all over your pussy?"

A whimper escapes my throat. *Oh, how I love it when he swirls it around. The wetness. The sliding. The way his fingers dip in to get more.*

"Your pussy's so greedy for my come, isn't it, baby?"

If he wasn't impaling me right now, if his hand wasn't manipulating my clit, he would still be fucking the shit out of me with that voice of his. *Oh, how he fucks me with his voice.*

"Where do you want my come, baby? Do you want it down your throat while your beautiful lips wrap around my cock? Should I flip you and fill you there?"

Oh fuck ... I'm climbing.

"Remember how you whimpered when I took you there for the first time? You were so good, baby." He groans at the memory. "Mmm ... I pulled you up against my chest while we were on our knees and your ass rode my cock. Remember what happened next, baby? What did I do to you?" He licks the shell of my ear.

"You spanked me." I barely get the words out. I feel my whole body tightening. The memory of letting him have something I always thought forbidden is sending me over the edge.

"What did I spank?" He grunts. I can tell he's barely holding on.

"My ... my pussy." I close my eyes tight as the sparks start to ignite the fire deep in my core. My head's about to go for a swim deep in my body's sensation.

"You liked it, didn't you?" He finds some control. "You liked having your pussy spanked while I fucked your ass, didn't you?" he asks sharply.

And ... I'm gone ...

"Gah ... Mitch!" I tighten around him. My hips quicken their pace, hungry for his explosion. He doesn't disappoint. Mitch *never* disappoints!

"Faaaaaaaccccckkk!" he bellows as he empties himself inside me. I may have sung backup. My pussy milks everything he has to offer. Mitch thrusts into me one last time and collapses on top of me. I hold onto him and match his rapid breathing.

"You've got a dirty mouth, Mitch, and I love it." I fight to catch my breath. He chuckles and slowly pulls out. I can feel his come trickling out. Mitch props himself up on my side, and his hand slides between my legs.

And so round two begins ...

"Mmm," I moan as he captures the come and begins painting my pussy with it. *Every time—every fucking time—it drives me wild.* His come covering every velvety inch of my pussy, marking me.

"Feel good, baby?" he asks as he licks at my lips. I moan and open my mouth for him. His fingers dive deep inside me. *I love the sound of his fingers sloshing around in there.* He hooks them, provoking my G-spot into another mind-blowing orgasm. My hips lift off the bed violently, fucking his fingers hard. "That's it, baby. Take it." He slips a third finger in and another orgasm slaps me like I'm its bitch. *Shut up! Stop acting like everything you say during an orgasm is coherent.* It's slapping me like a bitch in heat—I'm not taking the thought back!

"God, I love to watch you come, baby," he whispers as I settle down. He pets Kitty so nicely, like the good pussy she is.

After several minutes, my breathing returns to normal. Mitch and I just lie in each other's arms. No rush for the shower. No checking on the baby. His hand caresses my belly. My still-pudgy belly. It doesn't bother him at all, so it doesn't bother me. That's how it should be. Mitch always makes me feel sexy and beautiful.

I turn my head and stare at him. The moon is full tonight, and shining through our bedroom window. He's staring back. Never in a million years did I think I would ever experience this—my heart swelling, waiting to burst every time I look at him.

I am so thankful I overheard a conversation between two other women. If I didn't pay attention to what they were saying, I wouldn't be in Mitch's arms right now.

"What's going on in that gorgeous mind of yours?" he asks.

"I'm so glad I'm a nosy bitch." I smile.

"Why? What are you talking about?" His eyes crinkle in the corners, as if he's anticipating laughter. I have been known to say a strange thing or two at times.

"You're here with me because I was nosy one day in a restroom at a rest stop." I play with his bottom lip. "I overheard two women talking about a friend becoming a call girl, what to look for, and where to find it. That led me to you," I reveal. It feels like a hundred years ago.

"I always wondered about that," he says. "I never asked because I was just glad I was your first and only."

"Me too." I take in a deep breath. "I was so desperate. I didn't know what else to do. I did a lot of research on a topic that had never before crossed my mind. I was so scared the night I met you. Then I saw your eyes, and I knew ..." I trail off.

"Knew what, baby?" His fingers touch my cheek softly.

"I knew, deep down inside—gut feeling, if you will—that everything was going to be okay. I didn't have to worry anymore." I grab his hand and kiss at the pads of his fingertips.

"Charlotte, baby ... you'll never have to worry again. I'm going to give you the world." He brings his face to mine so we are nose to nose.

"You already have, Mitch. You've given me the world just by loving me. Not only me, though. You love my kids." I shake my head. "Sometimes I feel like the clock is going to strike twelve and I'll wake up. Fairy tale gone."

"It'll never happen, baby." He palms my cheek. "No one fits the glass slipper like you." He kisses me.

"That's good to know, since nobody can fit my heart like you do." I peck his lips.

"Damn," he sighs.

"What?" I pull my head back.

"Your line was way better than mine," he says truthfully.

"Well, to quote Maddie St. Claire, somebody's gotta be the brains behind this operation," I tease.

"I don't think being a smartass is included in that title." He chuckles lightly before kissing me.

"It says so here: 'Smartasses are the brains behind all operations.' See?" I ask.

"I see it. It's right under, 'Charlotte—she who talks out of her ass.'"

"Wow, that's quite a talent." I act astonished.

"Yes. She has many talents." He smiles against my mouth.

I want to ask him what my other talents are, but I can't get a word out with his tongue parading around mine. His hands start roaming my body, making sure to stop by and check in with Kitty.

And you know what?

Kitty wans'more.

The beginning ...

226

Coming Soon

In the Mix

GEG SERIES #2

JACQUELYN AYRES

~ Unedited ~

Chapter One
Secret Packages

EVER HAVE A nosy neighbor? Maybe a family member? Somebody who was always in your shit because they thought it smelt funny like, like—scandal?

I have several of those people in my life, but the most annoying one is my fucking mail lady. *Nosy bitch!*

Here she comes, up my walkway with her fucking frizzed out *please don't dye me again* red hair. I know what she has in her hand. She knows what she has in her hand.

So much for discreet shipping!

I open the door before she can embark on her annoying melody of ring, knock, ring—must be fucking OCD. "Mrs. Magee!" I say cheerfully with a slight hint of stink-eye.

"Carissa Catherine O'Brien?" She looks down at the package asking.

She's known me my entire life.

"Yes, Mrs. Magee, I haven't gotten the sex change yet nor am I in the witness protection program." My pleasantries can only last so long. She's past my ten second mark.

"You have a package here." She darts her suspicious eye up at me.

"You don't say?" I step out and look at it in her hands. "From whom?"

"It has no name of the company." She clears her throat and adds a disapproving look.

Does she really think she's going to embarrass me? *Me?*

Bitch, puhlease!

"Ooh ..." I widen my eyes. "Why, Mrs. Magee, I bet this is from that dildo company I order from!" I tap her hand excitedly.

Mrs. Magee shifts from foot to foot—a bit uncomfortable, I might add.

But no—that's not enough for me!

"I've been waiting on this one!" I take the package. I lower my voice. "This is my new toosh-trainer anal vibrator."

Mrs. Magee gasps.

"It's the intermediate one. I'll only have one more to go before I can finally take some nice cock up my ass. I'm so excited!" I bounce a little for emphasis.

Mrs. Magee places her hand over her heart and stammers over her words. "Hav ... va ... nice ... d-day." Finally comes out before she heads down my stoop. She steps and turns. "Here's the rest of your mail." She hands me the stack. She then races (at an elderly pace) back to her mail van.

Some bitches be crazy yo!

I definitely be one a dos bitches.

No. I'm white.

That was me living the thug life for a sec.

I wave as Mrs. Magee pulls out of the driveway. She shakes her head at me and turns to head to the next house. Well, that was fun ...

I walk back in and glance at the clock on my cable box. I don't have to be back at Bark Avenue for another hour. Hmm ... what to do for an hour? I could clean. *Nope.* I could pay bills. *With what?* I really should just be the smart consumer that I am and test this bad boy out! Get it out of the way ... off the list of things to do! "Yes!" I agree and kick off my sneakers as I head into my bedroom with my new "friend".

I sit on my bed (still not made so like, *hello!*—tell me that's not a sign!) and open the white package. My tongue licks my lips at the anticipation. This is supposed to be the *motha* of all vibrators! I am supposed to see stars and have a permanent smile on my face.

I slide it out of the package. "Now *this* is what I'm talking about!" I stare at it in all its magnificent glory. Purple silicone—soft to the touch. Yeah, I said purple. What? It's my favorite color! Look at all of these settings! I reach into the package and grab the batteries they supply (cuz' there good like that, ya know?) and slip those puppies in. I hit the first button. "Holy shit!" This thing is gyrating in circles. I hit the arrow to up the tempo. My eyes grow wider. I hit it again. It's off! No, I mean like ... ride 'em cowboy! I hit the other button and the rabbit ears spring to life.

I may be a little scared.

All I can think of when I look at this silicone swinging meat is a rodeo. No! A rodeo bar where you get on that fake bull and have to try to stay on. You're holding on with one hand. The other arm is up in the air, swinging around in a circle? That's what my new vibrator is doing. It's an arm, swinging around for balance. I turn it off and stare at it some more. I can feel the heat rising to my cheeks as I think of this one-armed bastard swinging around inside of me like a disco ball at a party.

Ohhh ... imma 'bout to get my groove on ...

I place it gently on the bed then proceed to tear my yoga pants down like there's a gun at my head. I whip my top off and flop onto my back. "Ok, Ceese ... who is the lucky guy today?" Marky Mark? *No. Although I'm sure I'll get some 'good vibrations'!* Kyle ... *Shut up, Ceese!* Henry Cavill. *He is super, but no.*

Damn the way he kissed me the other night!

Kyle it is! I close my eyes and think about the way he pinned me up against my door. He was in my face, all angry and sexy and ... and ... *fuck the way he smells!* I don't even remember half the shit he was telling me. Something about how *when he knows what he wants, he goes after it until it's his.* All I could do was stare at his lips, wondering when the fuck he was going to do something better with them, like kiss me. There was something else on my mind as my eyes took in the scruff on his face. Being the classy lady I am, I told him what was on my mind. *"This,"* I touched the stubble across the right side of his jawline, *"is going to feel so good rubbing against my pussy when you're eating the fuck out of it."* Yeah. I totally fucking said that! I couldn't believe it either. I mean, of course, I have no problem saying shit like that. Just not to guys like Kyle. Good guys that I don't belong with.

What did he do? He smirked. He's a smirker—that one. Then he eskimo kissed me. Yeah, weird, right? He softly kissed my eyelids then leaned in to my ear and said, "I don't do one-night stands, beautiful." He kissed my cheek and lingered there for a moment. Just when I thought he was pulling away, readying himself to leave, he palmed my face and said, "One night could never be enough with you, so I'd like to leave you with something to think about. Something, I hope, will encourage you to consider a chance with me." It was dark but I could still see how crystal blue his eyes are. I just stared into them—cemented to the ground. His palms held my face with a bit more aggression and then ... he laid the mother of all kisses on me.

Slowly, I let my hands travel up to my nipples. I roll and pull on them as I think about the way his tongue swirled around in my mouth. The way he sucked at my bottom lip and dove his tongue back in for more.

I hated it.
I hated every moment that I loved it!
Fuck!

I reach over and grab Purp. What? He's purple and the way he moves around makes him a little suspect. You know what I mean?

I spread my legs and guide Purp down my center. Yup, no lube required this session! I thrust Purp inside quickly, encouraged by the memory of the way Kyle's tongue thrusted into my mouth. *Faaaac-cck!* My overzealous movement now requires a moment of acclimation. Holy crap! *I wonder if Kyle has a big dick. Does it wiggle around like Purp does?*

Shaking my thoughts away, I feel around Purp with my right hand trying to find the magic rodeo buttons. *Finally!* "You got eight seconds, Purp. I'm gonna time this shit!" The rabbit ears are working a good rhythm at my clit. It's time to disco, do the hustle, shake my groove thing—whatever! Let's see what this bad boy can *Holy ... mother ... of ... God!!* "Oh hell fucking yeah!!"

Seven seconds flat.

You know what I'm talking about.

I may be whimpering a little as I come down from this. My toes are still curled almost as if they know just to stay that way cuz' I ain't done! I calm my breathing, gathering energy up for the next round. Everything is finally quiet in my head.

Then ... I hear it.

Brzzzjrrr.

I close my legs a little.

Bbbrrzzzzjerrrrzzz.

And suddenly I feel like Betty Cocker (Yes, I said Cock-er) getting busy mixing a cake in here. Why do they have to make these things so loud? I mean—*oh ... oh, holy fuck of all fuckkkkerrrs! I'm not even holding it! Shhhhit! Yessss!*

Ding!

Cake's done!

I immediately turn Purp off, otherwise, I won't be able to walk today! This thing is lethal! *I love it!*

***

I BARELY WALK through the door of my shop and the phone is already screaming at me! "Bark Avenue, this is CiCi, how can I help you?"

"Did you lose your fucking cell phone again?" Julie asks. Fuck she sounds annoyed!

"No! I just don't have it attached to my ass like some people I know. What's the matter with you?" I glance down at my appointment book then up at the clock. This bitch has fifteen minutes for me to solve her problems.

"What's the matter with me?" She does that sarcastic laugh that makes me want to throat punch her. I'm not really a violent person—just pms-ing. "Let's see!" Oh boy. "My best friend, who tells me *everything*, forgets to mention a certain rich, hot as fuck, CEO-type dude she's met. Same dude who ruffled her feathers so much, I've barely heard from her in three weeks since said event!"

"Dude," I sigh.

"What?"

"I talked to you yesterday."

"So?"

"I have hung out with you just about every other day!" Bitch just lost ten minutes! I'm not in the mood for this shit.

"So?"

"So ... what the fuck are you talking about?" I throw my free hand out before using it to shove the swinging door open to my back room.

"Just because you are here doesn't mean you are fucking present. What is going on with you? What happened?" Her tone dials it up a notch.

"Julie, I can't do this right now. I have a client coming in any minute." I grab the shampoo bottles.

"It's a dog—not a client!" she yells.

"Dogs are my clients and they're people, too. Stop acting like they don't matter." I grab the brushes.

"They are *dogs* you Asswhore—not humans!"

"You know what I mean." Nobody ever understands the way I feel about animals. They don't suck. People suck. Well, except for Buddy, that dog sucks—the life out of me!

"Whatever. We're going for drinks tonight and I want the truth, the whole truth, and nothing but the truth or so help me God ..."

"Ok, Judge Judy. Now will you shut the fuck up and let me get to work?" I head back out to the front as I hear the bell.

"Yeah, yeah. I'm only doing this because I love you." She claims.

"You're only doing this because you're a nosy bitch," I say quietly and wave to my customer. "And I love you, too. Bye, bitch!"

"Bye!" she says in her usual carefree tone. I hang up. She thinks she's won but there is no way in hell that I'm going to talk to her about Kyle. No way!

"Hey, CiCi, I hope you didn't get off the phone on my account." Addie smiles as she brings Pearl up to the counter. Pearl is a two year-old Pug and she's just, well ... a pearl!

"Oh, no, not at all. You actually saved me from my medaling best friend." I say with a sigh of relief. "Hello there, Miss Pearl. Are you all ready to get the royal treatment?" I lift her into my arms. She answers with an assertive licking of my face.

"She loves spa time with CiCi." She gives Pearl's head a little scratch. "How are the numbers coming along for the fundraiser?" she inquires and my heart sinks.

"Slow, but I've added more advertisement. I'm going to see if my sister's boyfriend will help me out. I'm sure he'll be able, too." *Bastard better after the way he fucking treated me!*

"That'll be good. I know I've been driving people nuts about it. They just don't understand how much the shelters need their help. Most people think about people and not these defenseless little dolls." Addie says sadly. She speaks the truth. I'd do anything for these little guys—all animals, really. Even Buddy—that little fucker! That's why I've teamed up with Addie every year to raise money. Sometimes twice a year. I try to do as much as I can. Being a small business owner that curtails to animals does help in reaching the right people to get to our goals. However, with the economy being the way it has been; it's been rough. Not only are people bringing their animals in less to get groomed they are actually giving them up to these very shelters that we are trying to help maintain.

"You look tired today, Addie." I cock my head a bit to the side.

"I am." She nods slightly. "I had to let go of another person and I'm just not getting the volunteers that I used to. I've been working more hours lately." She holds back on her frown a bit. Addie never complains about nothing. She's got the heart of gold, that woman. She's one of the very few people I like. I suppose I could say she's one of the very few people who like me!

"What day could you use me the most?" I ask.

"Oh, Ceese, I couldn't—"

"You didn't. I'm offering. I want to! What day?" I ask again.

"You are an angel. You know that, right?" Her smile hits her bright blue eyes as she grabs my hand and squeezes it. *She really doesn't know me that well.* "Whatever day you find the time, dear." She pats my hand.

"Ok. I'll call you and let you know when I can head over." I pull away slightly. I have a hard time getting compliments. It freaks me out. Maddie calls it Doxophobia. I told her *'Well at least I don't have Dicksaphobia! That would suck!'* She said, *'Seriously, what would you do with your mouth then? You'd have to pick up a nasty habit like smoking or something!'*

"CiCi? You alright?" Addie breaks me out of my thoughts.

"Oh yeah, sorry." I smile. "Well, Miss Pearl should be ready for you by two but you know she can stay here with me till I close up." I hug Pearl to me.

"Good, I'll be back around five." She smiles and scratches Pearl's head again before heading out.

233

I head in to my back room again or *le spa,* if you will, and set Pearl down in the pen. I want to send Mitch a text before I get started on her. Fucking bastard owes me!

Acknowledgments

To the three little amazing people in my life who keep my head spinning and my heart and my mind growing—thank you! It's an honor and privilege to be your mother. I love you.

Thank you to my family and friends who have supported and encouraged me on this crazy ride.

A huge hug and crazy dance for my street team (The G-Team), especially the room's frequent flyers: Wendy C., Heather, Leeann, Tammy, Karen S., Christ, Debbie, Jen, Jamee, Jennifer, Anna, Amy, Nicola, Janet, Natalie, Wendy S and Claire!
Crap, I hope I didn't forget anyone!
I hope you girls always know how much I appreciate your love and support! I cherish you and the friendships we have built! I hope I did you proud with this book!

I have been so blessed to not take this journey alone. Wendy Shatwell and Claire Allmendinger, you both have been my rock. You've helped me wipe away tears of frustration and have caused me many tears of laughter! Little did I know, when I signed you on to do my promotions (almost a year ago), that I would gain two of the dearest friends I could've ever asked for! What a bonus! I love you ladies! ☺

Speaking of friendships, there's a few authors that I would love to thank for theirs!

Olivia Luck and Courtney Cross, since before the beginning, you both have been there, cheering me on and being the best sounding board whether about book life or real life. Thank you! I love you girls!
Fifi Flowers, sometimes the strangest things happen that end up unifying people into a friendship that may never had blossomed without it. Here's to strange things, lady! I cherish you!

And finally ...
T.J. Tims—my soul sister, words can't describe what your friendship means to me. Besides, you're probably already thinking what I want to say (cuz' that's how we roll!). lol. Having you as a friend has been nothing short of a blessing!

Thank you to Jess Huckins, my editor, who has been with me since book one (brave soul). I wouldn't be able to do this without you. Also, our side notes are epic and should have their own book! I love you and am so happy to add "friend" to your title.

Thank you to Robin Harper at Wicked by Designs for another kickass cover!

Stacey Blake is the lady who magically puts all my words in every book format out there. And yes, I do believe it's some sort of magic at play here (I wouldn't have a clue on how to do this!)! Thank you so much for your beautiful work and friendship! I can't wait to see how pretty you make this one!

And last but not least ...

I want to thank all of the fans (new and old) and bloggers! Your constant support and excitement adds so much fuel to my fire! I hope you know how much I appreciate it. A special thanks to Rebecca, Annette, Joely, Kaitlin, Lheanne and Rae for all of the pimping you do for me! It brightens my day to put those three hearts in the comment section!
♥♥♥
I hope that you all will continue on this journey with me!

About the Author

I am a domestic engineer (born and raised in New Jersey) whose sole responsibility is guiding three young, impressionable kids into becoming phenomenal adults. This challenging yet rewarding work requires a lot of love (coffee), patience (wine), and determination (periodic exorcisms). I work all of this magic from the beautiful state of New Hampshire.

Before becoming a domestic goddess (not really), I spent over a decade working in the medical field, where I wore more hats than the queen.

I have loved the written word and the great escape it provides since I was a little girl. When I wasn't reading about people and the places they lived, I created my own characters and adventures.

Having found myself again, through my writing, with The Lost & Found Series, The One, and The GEG Series, has been nothing short of a dream come true. Also, it makes people feel better when I laugh randomly or talk to myself, knowing it's my characters and not "the voices" . . . that would be creepy.

Want to see what I'm up to? You can stalk me here at these spots!

Twitter: @JacquelynAyres
Facebook: https://www.facebook.com/JacquelynAyresAuthor
Pinterest: http://www.pinterest.com/jacquelynayres/
Spotify: Under Contract

OTHER BOOKS BY JACQUELYN AYRES

The Lost & Found Series
Goodbye Caution
Goodbye Secrets
Goodbye Uncertainty

The One